THE Escort's TALE

An MMF Bisexual Romance

M.J. Edwards

A Publication from Snow King Books
An imprint of Robert Winter Books

The Escort's Tale
© 2018 M.J. Edwards

Cover Art
© 2018 Ron Perry Graphic Design

Author Photo
© 2018 Robert Winter

First Publication September 2018 v. 1.0
ISBN: 978-1-948883-06-1
Print Edition
Printed in the United States of America

CHAPTER ONE

MY ARMS TREMBLE as my orgasm begins to ease. "Fuck," I groan with satisfaction.

I lower myself onto Sarah's body to prolong the pleasure, sinking my dick into sweet velvet. She's all juicy and smooth with my come and her own cream. She tugs me into herself even more. I chuckle against her right breast, slowly and languorously tonguing her peaked nipple. She loves that, I can tell.

"Holy shit, that was good," she murmurs. As I start to withdraw, she arches her hips and begs, "No, please stay in me."

I slide out anyway. Rolling onto my side, I face the man who sits in a chair in the corner of the bedroom. He clasps his hands together tightly, and his glasses have fogged over. In the dim glow of the bedside lamp, I see the trace of a tear running down his flushed cheek.

He meets my gaze, and whimpers.

I feel powerful as I stroke my fingers between Sarah's legs. Never breaking eye contact with the man, I adjust my position in bed until I have one arm beneath Sarah. Propping her up, I rest against a pillow. My cock, still half-hard from the Viagra tab I'd taken before I arrived, dangles heavily across my thigh. A last trace of come drips from it onto the bedsheet.

"Sarah," I say as I stroke the soft brown hair over her mound. "Tell Glenn what that was like."

She shudders in my arm. "You're so big, JD. I never had anything that far inside me. I didn't know it could feel like that, to have a man open me up. Go so deep."

Glenn moans. His eyes track my fingers as they stroke lower. They glide over Sarah's wet lips, parsing through the delicate folds to brush against her clit. Glenn shudders and flicks his tongue across his lips.

I smile, making sure he sees a predatory glint in my eye. I love this part of my work.

"You were so warm and wet," I drawl to Sarah. When I dip a finger inside her, Sarah spreads her thighs further. I add a second finger, pressing into her body. Her hips began to jerk as she tries to draw me in further. I smile wickedly at Glenn and pull away my hand, dripping with our combined juices.

His eyes never leave my fingers as I bring them to my mouth to lick clean. Our combined flavors spread across my tongue—tangy, bitter, sweet and salty all at once. So I like the flavor of my spunk. Sue me.

I murmur, "We taste so good together." Glenn's gaze shifts to my eyes. His jaw seems to slacken, his lips open, and his tongue peeks out as he watches. Sarah blushes and turns her head into my shoulder, but spreads her knees even further. She reaches for her breast and begins to tug on a nipple when I return to her sopping folds. I stroke idly, up and down, up and down.

Suddenly I use two fingers to spread the wet, pink lips. "Glenn," I bark. The man stiffens in his chair, alert, alarmed. "I fucked your wife. I came inside her pussy. I made her come on my dick." A moan fills the room. I ask, "Don't you want to taste?"

An exhalation of air gusts from the man in the corner. He glances back and forth between his wife and me. When he nods sharply, it's Sarah's turn to gasp as I plunge three fingers roughly inside. I swirl them, stirring, riling, and say to Glenn, "Take off your glasses and get over here."

He stands shakily. The press of his erection against his khaki trousers tells me everything I need to know. He's hard for this scene, but not well endowed. No wonder his wife was so loud, screaming out once she got my long, fat cock inside her.

Glenn removes his glasses, folds them, and sets them on a small table next to his chair. He kicks off his shoes and climbs slowly onto the bed, approaching us on his hands and knees. He moves tentatively, a puppy seeking affection, unsure if he's to be loved or kicked.

I growl at him. "Come along. We're waiting for you." Glenn moves more quickly then, but hesitates between Sarah's thighs. He looks at me for instruction.

"Use your tongue," I say firmly. "I want you to taste us together. I want you to taste how delicious your wife is when she's been fucked by a man with a big dick."

Glenn shudders, Sarah shifts and sucks in a breath, and I know I've struck the right tone. Glenn needs humiliation, and Sarah needs satisfaction. My job's to make sure everyone leaves with desires met.

I don't have a lot of marketable skills, but what I do have going for me are a big dick and lots of imagination. I love to figure out what my clients really want. Not what they *tell* me they want when they first hire me. If they even know themselves, they're usually too shy or embarrassed to admit it. So I listen carefully, and I ask questions, and I get a sense of what sexual needs are going unmet. I treat my clients like a puzzle, or a mystery novel. I read the clues and try to figure out what's behind the request they actually make. I mean, there has to be *something* going on to hire a man to fuck you and your wife or husband.

Take Glenn. He told me in his email that his wife had a fantasy about being watched while she has sex with another man. I don't like to be explicit on email, so we switched to cell phone after that. I figured out pretty quickly that he had some fantasies of his own. After I'd chatted him up for a half hour or so, we negotiated a simple cuckolding fantasy. That's something of a specialty of mine. Guys who get off on watching their wife or girlfriend take another man's dick, chicks who like their man to watch them get railed… As kinks go, this one's pretty mild. Often the husband or boyfriend just watches, writhing with the shame of a stud making his woman scream in pleasure. But sometimes…

I keep my fingers against Sarah's vulva, spreading the outer lips, as Glenn's head descends slowly. I feel the brush of his curly brown hair against my wrist, his breath on my fingers. He presses his face to his wife's pussy. With a groan, he begins to lick, tentatively at first. When Sarah shudders and cries out, he goes in deeper. She throws her head back as she grasps her other nipple as well and begins to tug on her breasts in alternating pulls.

Once begun, Glenn's ravenous. I move my hand out of the way to let him lick and suck and glory in the fluids that fill his wife. He pushes against the inside of both of her thighs, to spread her so he can get his tongue in deeper. The noises he makes as he worries at her, the scratching of his pants as he rubs his erection against the bed, start to work on me.

Writhing against my body, Sarah squeezes and pinches her tits. I hold her with one arm as my free hand hovers over Glenn's head. He meets my gaze again. A gleam of excitement appears.

This is a delicate moment. I lower my hand. My fingers spread through coarse, wiry hair to grip Glenn's scalp. With a low, contented sigh, he closes his eyes. I press to force his face even deeper into his wife.

My cock stirs again, beginning its slow, heavy rise. Glenn's aware of it, watching it grow even as he tongues the come from that beast out of his wife's body.

"That's right," I order gruffly. "Taste her. Taste me. Taste us together."

His excitement vibrates through my hand. Sarah's whimpers climb until another orgasm begins to ripple through her body. She clenches her muscles and hunches forward as she reaches for her husband's head. Twisting her fingers with mine to hold Glenn in place, she grinds against his mouth. Crying out, Sarah arches her back as she comes again, then drops to the bed in a limp mass. Her eyes close, the hand on her husband's head stills, and a satisfied sigh escapes her lips.

She murmurs, exhausted, "That was so dirty." But she sounds smug.

Glenn levers himself up. One hand still touches the inside of her left knee, but he looks lost, unsure. I wrap a hand around my hard dick and pull on the loose skin so the head's exposed. It glistens red, damp from precome and Sarah's juices.

"Fuck, that feels good," I croon, biting my lower lip as I stroke my cock. I squeeze at its base, forcing a few drops of nectar out of the slit. "You aren't done," I say firmly to Glenn.

The man's eyes widen in shock and fear, and he shoots a panicked look at his wife. She lays in my arm, sated and almost dozing. No relief there for Glenn. I point my dick toward his mouth and stare at him, giving him no further order, but no escape either.

Glenn closes his eyes and drops his head. Leaning over, he hesitates with his mouth an inch away from the gleaming head of my erection. It smells of come and vaginal juices, something he should now be conditioned to, even excited for. Opening his mouth, he stretches out his tongue to touch the tip of my cock. He shudders as he makes contact, but licks the silvery drops. I can see him ponder the taste and...yes, decide he likes it.

He opens his mouth to do more, but I bark, "Wait."

Glenn rocks back in surprise to rest on his heels. He looks like he's been caught stealing from the cookie jar.

I say to him, "Take your clothes off first."

Sarah opens her eyes and looks at her husband. When he hesitates, she murmurs lazily, "Do it. Let us see you. I like your body, you know."

Her husband's expression of shame and fear softens a bit at that. He climbs off the bed and pulls his sweater over his head, then loosens his belt as he kicks away his loafers. Unbuttoning his shirt, he throws it into a corner with his sweater. He has a nice chest, not developed like mine but covered in curly dark hair. He yanks off his socks, but hesitates at the waist of his trousers.

I stare at him, refusing to give him the anonymity to strip unwatched. Glenn swallows audibly, then unbuttons, unzips and pushes down his pants and underwear in one anguished move.

Stepping out of the clothes and kicking them to the side, he stands red-faced in the soft glow of the bedroom.

His dick is indeed on the small side, perhaps five inches long, though his ball sac's nice and full. Glenn's erection drips precome, and it looks red and anguished. That he hasn't shot off already surprises me. With the right words, I could hone his shame—and desire to be shamed further—to make him come even without touching him.

"You run, don't you, Glenn?" I ask with a flirtatious edge in my voice. "Look at your thighs. I bet you can go for miles." I runs fingertips along my shaft, from the head to the root, over my balls, and then back to the slit. His eyes track the movement, jaw slackening. I grasp my dick by the base and again aim it toward Glenn.

"Come here," I order. "Come taste me again."

He makes a low, desperate noise. His hand twitches like he wants to cover his own dick, either from shame at its relative size or from the fact that the scene gets him hard.

I give no quarter. I rise to my knees on the sturdy bed, straddling Sarah's thighs with my ass toward her face. I growl, "I'm losing patience. If you don't get over here and suck my cock, I'm going to fuck your wife again and it will be your fault. Are you enough of a man to want to stop me from fucking her?"

Glenn lurches forward, tripping on his discarded shoes and falling to his knees by the bed. He catches himself with a hand on my thigh. My erect cock arches above his head. He looks at it hungrily, lips apart, eyes intent on the bead of precome ready to drip and fall to the bedspread.

"Stick out your tongue," I coax, and press on the top of my shaft when he complies. I swipe the head of it across his tongue, then thrust my hips so the first inch of meat slides into his mouth. "Suck on that much, like you're a calf finding the tit for the first time. There's a good boy," I praise when he starts to suckle me. I rest a hand on the back of his head, just to encourage him, not forcing him to choke on my length.

Not yet.

Between my spread legs, Sarah slips her manicured fingernails over her clit. Red polish flashes and disappears into her folds as she watches her husband give me head.

"That's good," I praise. "Look what you're willing to do to save your wife from a fuck." I tug on Glenn's head and slide him further down my dick.

He gags and tries to pull away. "It's too much," he moans. From the corner of one eye, a tear slides down his cheek.

I pretend to misunderstand him. "No, it's good that you do this for Sarah. It's never too much, to protect your wife. Is it?"

Glenn shakes his head.

"Tell her what you'll do for her, so she doesn't have to get fucked again."

He flicks a look between my legs at Sarah, then back. His tongue darts over his lower lip. "Anything. I'd do anything."

"Of course you would," I croon. I wrap my hand around the root of my dick and drag it against his lips. "This time you're going to take my big dick all the way, aren't you? For Sarah."

"For Sarah," Glenn says. Maybe he even believes it. He opens his mouth wide, extends his tongue and tilts his head back to make a better entry for me. The move betrays that mine is not his first cock, but we continue the scene as if Glenn really were a reluctant husband, abasing himself to protect his wife.

I slide in relentlessly, the hand in Glenn's hair tightening to keep him from pulling away. He coughs and gags a bit. "Swallow," I command. "That makes it easier, if you swallow while my cock fucks into your throat."

He grabs onto my thighs for balance, his face turns red, but he tries to suck my dick further. I pull his hair hard. He gasps in protest, and I press inward. Lips near my pubes momentarily before he struggles and fights to pull away. Releasing him, I watch my glistening, wet prick reappear as he withdraws his head. Instead of giving up, he reverses direction and plunges onto me again.

The dick slides into his throat. I groan before Glenn backs off. "Oh, that's good. You've been holding out on us, haven't you?" Mouth full of dick, he tries to shake his head. But he doesn't stop trying to deep-throat me.

"Have you been practicing on *other* men?" I ask. "How many men have tried to fuck Sarah but you serviced them instead, to save her aching pussy?"

This time it's Sarah who groans. I look back over my shoulder. Her lacquered nails plunge into her vagina and reappear as she watches her husband avidly. Glenn speeds his motions. His hands flex and grasp my thighs as he bobs his head.

"I think you want your prize, don't you?" I ask him. "You want hot come. You need it fresh from the tap, not lapped out of your wife's used hole."

Glenn sobs and presses his lips to my pelvis, nursing the cock in his mouth as he releases one of my thighs. He grabs his own dick.

"Stop that," I bark and cuff his head. "You don't touch your little boy prick until I tell you."

He obeys but increases the pace, sucking and straining to hold me in his mouth as long as he can. Tears and saliva run over his face. He gulps for air each time he pulls off, only to plunge onto it again.

I moan appreciatively. I'd come this way if I let him continue, but they paid me to take the scene much further.

I grip his ears to hold him steady as I withdraw my cock. Glenn focuses on the purple, glistening head that throbs inches away from his mouth.

"That was good, but look what you did." His eyes meet mine. "No, look at what your wife is doing." Sarah pistons three fingers in and out while she tweaks her nipple with the other hand. "She sees what you're doing to save her and it's got her turned on. Doesn't it, Sarah?" I ask loudly.

In response, she moans and presses her thumb to her clit while her three fingers slide deeply inside her sheath.

"Oh look. She needs something else in there. Don't you think so, Glenn?"

He stares wide-eyed at me again, sensing a trick. But he nods.

"Would you like to fuck her? Would you like to stick your little boy cock inside her and make her come? I bet you could do it, if you try." He nods again, and I bark, "Say it. Tell me what you want to do."

"I want to fuck my wife," he cries out. Then, more softly, submissively, he asks, "Can I fuck her? Please?"

I climb off the bed until I stand facing Glenn, blocking Sarah's writhing body. I tower above him, still on his knees. Running a hand over my chest and to my abs, I draw his eyes along with my fingers. I'm more leanly built than the slightly doughy, middle-aged man before me. My swollen cock juts out and hovers out of his reach.

"Are you going to kiss Sarah when you fuck her?" I ask, and Glenn nods. "Show me." Confused eyes peer at me. "Show me how you're going to kiss her so she knows how much you love her." I coax him to stand, watching confusion fade into shock and then a glimmer of something else.

Something hot.

Grasping Glenn's shoulders so he can't retreat, I bend my head and pause with my mouth inches away. A mumbled noise comes from the shorter man before he thrusts forward to kiss me. It's closed-mouth, desperate, needy and fearful. Just what I want.

I pull Glenn to me roughly and hold our mouths together, gradually opening my lips to coax him into doing the same. When I feel the flick of a tongue, I yield the field. Opening wide, I draw in his tongue and let him explore my mouth. As a reward, I pull him into a tighter hug so that my big cock and his smaller one rub against each other.

Glenn brings a hand to my waist, pulling us together firmly. His hips begin to move, seeking more contact for his prick. I permit it for a few moments, before drifting my fingers from Glenn's waist to the swell of his ass. It's firm from running, belying his soft belly. I cup my palm over one smooth, round globe.

I pull back from the kiss. "That was good. You're going to make Sarah feel good if you kiss her like that while you fuck her." Glenn's eyes turn glassy with the praise. I caress his ass again more firmly, using the stroke to slide my now-hard cock against his belly.

"There's a problem, though." Alarm shows as I shake my head side to side slowly, regretfully. "Between your mouth sucking my dick and the way you kiss, I really need…to fuuuuck." I draw out the word, making it as filthy and suggestive as I can. Stroking his ass again, my fingertips come to rest at the start of the crease between the cheeks.

Glenn shudders under my touch but doesn't pull away. His cock flexes against me.

Leaning down, my lips intimately brush an ear. He shivers at the breath on his face as I say quietly, "You've done such a good job of protecting Sarah, though. I don't think you should have to give up sliding your cock into her. You earned it, don't you think?"

Glenn hesitates, then nods jerkily.

"So do I. But I've got this big cock and it really, really needs to fuck something. Do you have any ideas?"

He licks his lips. "What if…?"

"Yes?" I run my fingertips along the slope of his ass. I'm pretty sure I've won already, but there's nothing sweeter than hearing a man capitulate.

"What if I fuck her first and then…?"

I curve my fingers into the crevice of Glenn's ass. As I drag them against his hole, it pulses under my touch.

He blushes bright red, but doesn't pull away. The hand on my waist clenches. "What if you fuck me while I'm fucking her?"

As soon as the words are out, Glenn nearly begins to hyperventilate. His heartbeat pounds against my chest.

I pretend indecision. "I don't know." I pause but circle against his hole. It flutters under my fingers. "Do you think you're man enough to take my cock? Look—," I back away so he can see it again, "—it's really thick. Sarah loves it because it's so big but a pussy is flexible. She could probably take my fist there, if she wanted."

Glenn moans and quivers at that. Sarah gasps too.

Interesting, I think. *Maybe if they bring me back, we'll go there.*

I press one fingertip firmly against Glenn's asshole until it breaches him. He hisses in surprise and stiffens, but he doesn't try to pull away. "Do you think my cock can fit into your tight ass?"

Turns out it can.

CHAPTER TWO

S ARAH IS A good hostess, at least. She lets me shower after I finish fucking Glenn to an orgasm inside his wife. I leave them slack and satisfied, cuddling each other in sex-stained sheets. I ignore a flash of envy at their closeness and go enjoy their glassed-in shower. My balls ache from two orgasms in such a short time, but the hot water helps.

When I emerge from the bathroom, still wet, I make sure to towel dry slowly and deliberately. I turn my back to show taut ass cheeks. A smooth bend to dry my legs gives them a good look at my heavy ball sac and pendulous dick, just in case they were forgetting.

I admit it. I enjoy their eyes running over my leanly muscled frame. Besides, it's good advertising, either for a repeat call or for a referral to discreet friends.

When I stroll out of Glenn and Sarah's condo building, it's three A.M. The wad of cash in my pocket is going to worry me if I don't deal with it, so I pull out my phone to search for my bank's nearest branch location. It's a few blocks away, and I walk there along the darkened streets.

Downtown Boston is quiet at night. The heels of my boots striking the pavement seem oddly resonant to me. I realize that I'm holding myself loose and ready, alert for the sound of any other footfall near me.

I have this slender build and blond hair that tends to make people think I'm delicate, and therefore soft. The West Texas town I grew up in was Redneck Central, and I discovered early on that I was exactly the type to be targeted by bullies.

It didn't help that I spent all my free time in the library, reading. I hated how worn my Goodwill clothes were, and that I never had money to go to movies or do things with other kids. It was easier to hide in the library, even if I watched the playground through the window. I don't know if I had no friends because we were poor, or if I was so self-conscious about being poor that I didn't try to make any. Either way, I hid out and wished.

Freshman year of high school, solitary as usual, I was jumped by some football goons and dragged into the boys' restroom. One swirly later, I decided I needed a bodyguard. We were reading *Of Mice and Men* in English, so it gave me the idea of looking for my own Lennie Small.

Pretty soon, I buddied up to Wes Cole, who sometimes sat near me on the school bus. Wes was the baddest mofo on the junior varsity football team—six-four, with arms big around as my thighs. Sweet as molasses off the football field, he struggled in remedial English. Well, all his classes, really.

My grades weren't anything special, but English was the one class I regularly aced, so I took a chance. Riding to school one morning, nearly ill with bus fumes and nerves, I cleared my throat to get his attention. Then I offered to tutor him, and cringed as I waited for him to laugh at the idea.

To my surprise, Wes was grateful for the help. We started that afternoon. I never even had to ask—he let everyone on the football team know to back off me. Word spread.

After that I was safe, at least until Wes dropped out of high school at the end of football season his senior year. By then, I was familiar enough to his team that they kind of kept looking out for me. Like a legacy, in honor of Wes, or something.

Sometimes carried along in Wes's wake, I found myself at the occasional after-game party. Wes was the first guy I gave a blowjob. I had a huge crush on him, of course, but I kept it to myself. Or thought I did. We got drunk at a kegger and he actually made the first move. He came in my mouth in about thirty seconds, said I gave better head than his cheerleader girlfriend, and ruffled my hair. We only did it the one time, but it was enough to show me I liked dick.

Shortly after that, I hooked up with this girl at a party Wes threw. That was just as much fun, plus it was a lot easier to date girls than guys, at least in my town, so I stuck to chicks for the most part. The memory of blowing Wes provided jack-off fantasies for years, though.

Once I was in the Army, I occasionally found a guy willing to let me swing on his dick. Besides the opportunity to develop my cocksucking technique, four years in the Army, including tours in Afghanistan and Iraq, left me confident I could protect myself. Hand-to-hand combat training was among the few useful, non-sexual skills I acquired during my service. I'm more likely to use that in the real world than, say, parachuting.

In my case, it means that I feel reasonably safe going into a stranger's house or hotel room. I can handle any fucker who thinks I look like an easy mark. As it is, no one accosts me on my banking mission, and I make the cash deposit without incident. Eight hundred fifty bucks for a few hours of work…not bad. It beats the shit out of Army pay. Besides, fucking strangers is a lot safer than my time in the mountains of Afghanistan.

The couple tonight made for an easy, if long, session. I usually book clients for two hours, but Glenn and Sarah had paid for three. Not that they'd given their real names, any more than I did. They met me as JD Pierce, and didn't probe further. In fact, all of us had blacked out our real names on the health reports we shared via email beforehand. I charge extra for barebacking, and I insist on an STD test result no older than thirty days.

I have a fair number of steady clients. Some save up to hire me for a special occasion like a birthday or anniversary. Others are horny kinksters who can afford my services any time the itch grows. I like the bisexual couples best, where I can get both parties involved. That way, I work the fantasy better. Find ways to push them. Glenn, for example, turned out to be as big a screamer as Sarah. When I worked my dick up Glenn's ass, whispering filthy insults that made him quiver, I figured I'd taught them both something useful. Maybe it'll make their sex life better.

Instinct tells me that they will ask me back within the month.

Banking done, I hail a cab and head to a late-night diner near my apartment. I'm ravenous—I typically don't eat before a job. Even though it's approaching four in the morning, the diner is about half-full when I slide into a booth. My favorite waitress, Essie, meets my eye and nods; she already knows what I'll order. I hope she'll have time tonight to sit and talk. Essie likes to read as much as I do, and we trade book recommendations. Plus, she's wicked funny.

Sad, really, that at twenty-nine, my favorite person to talk to is a waitress I see after fucking for money. Well, her and my personal trainer, Cerise. I hear sometimes from Army buddies, and I check in with this one guy I served with, Owen, when I can get out to the VA. Owen was injured pretty badly while I escaped with nothing more than a bruise.

I've got a few acquaintances in the escort business, too, but no one I consider a friend. I gave up dating early on. It's too hard to schedule dinner and a movie when I reserve so many of my evenings for clients. I don't lack for sex, obvs, so a boyfriend or girlfriend would just confuse my life. The rare times I feel horny, I usually hire a pro rather than bother with a club or bar.

In some ways, it feels like I'm back in high school, pre-Wes, hiding with my books and hoping not to be noticed.

One guy I knew in Iraq told me I'm an introvert and I recharge my energy by being alone. Maybe it's bullshit, but I can kind of see that. When I'm preparing for a session or actually with clients, I'm *on*. With new clients, I invest a lot of time thinking about what they tell me and what they might really want. With repeats, I try to up the ante every time, whether it's pushing a limit or exploring something I pick up on when we're together. I do everything I can to make their fantasies come to life, to put them in the center of their very own porn flick. I'm the scriptwriter, the director and the co-star. Sometimes the wardrobe master too.

One of the guys who got me started escorting tells me that I get too close to my clients, too invested in their fantasies. I figure, for what they're paying me, they deserve my best efforts. When a session is over, I hopefully leave them relaxed and happy while I slink away, my pocket full of cash, to do what I need to get ready for the next one.

Visiting the diner is something of a reward for me, and a way to clear the decks mentally between clients. Tonight, while I wait for my ham and eggs, I scroll quietly through a few personal emails and check my private Twitter feed. Then I check the emails to the account under my professional name, JD Pierce. At a glance, I recognize most of the senders.

There's one email from a new name, though: "A Ballantine". I flag it to read later.

"Mornin', Jasper." Essie slides my plate before me and holds out the glass carafe with its green collar to signify decaf. "Coffee?"

"Yes, please," I say, holding out my cup. "You know me so well."

That brings a smile to Essie's seamed face and crinkles around her rheumy brown eyes. "Well enough, I suppose," she says as she fills my cup. "I finished that mystery you recommended on my break."

"What did you think of it?"

She shrugs. "I figured out who the killer was two chapters in, but the writing was good anyway."

"You're smarter than me. I was gobsmacked when it turned out the kid was faking his injuries."

Essie snorts and shakes her head. "I guess I'm just too suspicious. You got another book for me?"

"Let me think about it while I eat. I'm gonna find one that'll stump even you."

"Bring it." She smirks as she turns away.

Tonight, the diner's too busy for Essie to sit with me. I don't really enjoy eating a restaurant meal solo, so I tear into my food like I'm still in the Army and have only minutes to eat before a patrol. The ham steak's thick and just salty enough for my taste. The scrambled eggs with a little cheese and jalapeño mixed in are much better than anything I cook for myself. The coffee tastes scorched, but that's all right. I only want one cup anyway.

After cleaning my plate, I scroll through a list of books I've marked on Goodreads. During my deployment, between the few moments of terror, I'd often endured days of tedium. Reading hundreds of books on my Kindle was a better use of my time than the poker or video games my squad mates used to amuse themselves.

I spot the name of an old favorite, a mystery with some good plot twists. Jotting the book name on a napkin, I leave it for Essie, along with money for the meal and a nice tip.

I walk the last few blocks to my building. After waving to the night doorman, Lionel, I ride the elevator to the twelfth floor and let myself into my two-bedroom apartment. I flick on a few table lamps; on principle, I avoid the harsh overhead lights that plague so many new buildings. Why do architects insist on cookie-cutter apartments with the same white walls, same lighting fixtures, same granite counter tops and stainless appliances? When I was apartment hunting, I could barely keep the choices straight because they all blurred together.

Eventually, I settled on this one because it's convenient to transportation and has a gym for the residents. I could have afforded a place in a building with character, but who knows how long I'll get away with escorting? As it is, I sock away thousands every month. I don't know much about money, but I know I'll need a nest egg for when I figure out what I want to do with my life. Or for when I get busted for prostitution, or simply age out of the business.

Not that I know what I'll do if I ever stop escorting. When I try to picture the future, I see myself standing alone at a busy intersection. Traffic is going every which way, and I have no idea which road to follow. They all seem frightening and exciting at the same time.

Throwing myself on my IKEA couch, I'm irritated at my self-doubts, and I idly wish I had someone to hang out with. I should have taken up video games with my squad; at least I could log on and play remotely. As it is, I debate whether to start a movie or a new book.

Then I remember I have an email from a new contact, so I haul my phone out of my pocket.

Dear JD, I read, and chuckle at the polite opening in an email to a whore.

> Dear JD,
>
> I learned your name from a friend of mine, Meredith Warwick. She's aware of some personal issues plaguing my husband and me. Recently, she suggested that you might be in a position to aid us. Meredith assured me that you are highly professional and discreet. I've never done anything like this before. Might you be available to meet sometime in the next few days to discuss your services? A consultation, I suppose. My schedule is flexible most afternoons.
>
> I hope to hear from you.
>
> Best regards,
> A Ballantine

I contemplate the email. Meredith Warwick is a good client, one of the few women I see solo rather than as part of a couple. She contacts me once a month or so, and always treats me respectfully. She's sent me several other referrals, most recently a married female couple from out on the Cape with a hankering to share a dick for a novelty. They were cool ladies, and I enjoyed the session.

I'll follow up on the email if for no other reason than to please Meredith. Anyway, the formality of this "A Ballantine" intrigues me. My calendar app shows I've booked a session tomorrow evening, time

with my trainer Cerise the following afternoon… I fire off a reply to
"A" with some possible times to meet.

As a precaution, I need to make sure the referral's legit. I've been
able to avoid arrest so far, and want to keep it that way.

> Hi Meredith,
>
> I had a great time with you last week! Had to sleep in the next day ;). I
> received a note from someone who says you passed along my contact
> info. Is there anything I should know about A Ballantine?
>
> Let's get together again soon!
>
> JD

A reply from Meredith awaits me when I wake around noon.

> What a coincidence. I was just wondering when I'd be able to schedule
> another massage session with you. (I grin at the euphemism. I'm
> not the only cautious one.) I'm glad 'A' reached out to you. She's a
> family friend, completely trustworthy. I have a feeling you might be
> just what the doctor ordered. I'll be in touch soon about an appoint-
> ment for myself as I know how quickly your schedule fills!
>
> M

TWO DAYS LATER, I'm waiting at an outdoor table at a cafe convenient-
ly located a few blocks from my building. As none of my clients know
where I live anyway, the risk is minimal.

"JD? Excuse me. Is your name JD?"

I look up from my cappuccino, sliding my shades to my hair to
assess the speaker. She's slim, in a sleeveless, green dress that reveals
toned arms and long legs. She's pulled her black hair into a ponytail.
Large sunglasses hide her eyes, but reveal a heart-shaped, olive-skinned
face and slightly pointed chin. At a guess, she's my age, or maybe a few
years older.

I rise to my feet and hold the back of the other chair for her. "Ms.
Ballantine, I believe?" I ask, using the low register I affect for JD.

She nods tightly and takes her seat, placing her small purse on the
table. As I sit, she removes her sunglasses. She isn't beautiful in a
conventional sense, but her face is striking. Sharp intelligence shows in
her direct gaze, despite her obvious nerves. Hazel eyes glimmer at me,
green-gray in the afternoon light. She studies me as well, and a slight

flush rises to her cheek.

When her gaze drops to the tabletop, I wonder what she's thinking. Does she like what she sees? I wait. With Meredith's vouching, I seriously doubt this woman's a cop. Still, it's prudent to let her begin whatever conversation she wants to have. I don't necessarily need more clients, so I can afford to make this a casual assessment while we both decide whether to take another step. If she gets too explicit about money or services, I'll deflect the topic.

A waiter appears, and she orders an iced tea. With a glance to me, she asks, "Would you like another, Mr. Pierce?"

"JD, please. And I'm good for now."

When the waiter leaves, she shifts in her seat. "I suppose I should say now, my name is Alethia." Her voice is tight and tremulous, but I hear music in her tones as well. I'm fairly sure she's given her real name. It'd surprise me except that Meredith Warwick also uses her real name. Perhaps they discussed that, when Meredith gave the referral.

"Alethia. What a pretty name. Is it Greek?" I ask.

She nods. "It's something of a family name. My maternal aunt and my grandmother were also Alethias."

"Have you been to Greece?" I ask, trying to ease her nerves. "I went to Mykonos once, on leave. I loved it."

She gives me a small smile. "Mykonos is popular. And yes, I've been many times. I was born in New York but both of my parents are Greek by birth. We went there often when I was growing up. My husband and I—"

She breaks off suddenly, and blushes. I let it go; I'll circle back to the husband. Meredith knows that I tend to prefer taking on couples. That might have been the reason she mentioned my name in the first place.

"How do you know Meredith?" I ask while the waiter sets Alethia's iced tea on a napkin.

"Oh, she and my mother were friends since childhood. She's actually my godmother."

I try to suppress my surprised response. I know Meredith's older than me, of course, but she takes good care of herself. I'd never have believed she's old enough to be friends with this grown woman's mother.

We trade pleasantries for several minutes, commenting on the beautiful weather, how nice it is to sit outside after a brutal winter, and isn't the construction boom in Boston terrible for traffic? The flirtatious tone I adopt comes naturally. Alethia's charming, despite the superficial topics. She shares my delight about the beauty of the first snowfall last December. I confess to an embarrassing fall I took on the ice in front of a crowd as the winter wore on. We share a small, kindly laugh.

As she relaxes, she leans back in her chair, giving me a chance to admire her elegant form. Even amid banalities, she'll throw out a little sharp remark about Boston or whatever that makes me grin. When her fingers trail over the condensation on her glass of tea, I imagine what those fingers would feel like running down my arm. I feel a stir below my waist and have time to wish that we were out on a date.

That surprising notion snaps me back to the reason for our chat. Enough thinking with my dick, I tell myself. It's time to move this along.

"Would you like to tell me how my name came up?" I ask, gauging that Alethia's ready to discuss it.

She sets down her glass and darts glances left and right. Satisfied no one will overhear, she leans closer and speaks in a quiet, private voice. "Meredith is aware that my husband and I are facing some difficulties in our marriage. I mentioned to her recently over lunch that we've been struggling for a solution. She was very, um, detailed about her experiences with you." Alethia blushes prettily. "And complimentary, as well."

I smile at the circumspection. "Meredith has been a good client. I'm happy to hear she says nice things, since I don't exactly ask for Yelp reviews."

She snorts a little laugh, which I find charmingly awkward on such a chic woman. She puts a hand over her mouth to cover a grin. "I understand why, though that makes it tricky for, um…"

"Yes?" I prompt. "For someone in need of my services to find me?" I wink to show I take it lightly.

Alethia bobs her head in agreement. "I'd think in the internet age there'd be some sort of specialized rating service or booking site."

There are a few actually, but I choose to avoid those. I don't like the risk of zealous law enforcement having information about my working name or clientele. Word of mouth has always generated enough business for me anyway.

Since she seems more comfortable now, I dive in. "Why don't you give me a general idea of what you're looking for? We can discuss whether I'd be a good fit."

Alethia inhales sharply and grabs her tea for a quick distraction. I wait her out again as she sips. Eventually, she places the glass back down with a sharp click and takes another glance around. She clasps her hands on the table top, as in prayer. I lean in, close enough to scent a trace of her delicate perfume. The essence of orange blossoms fills the air around her.

"My husband and I have been together for five years, nearly six," she begins. "Nick has always been an avid rock climber. He played rugby, skied, competed in triathlons. Everything active like that you can think of. Eighteen months ago, he—"

She breaks off for a long moment to look at her entwined hands. Her knuckles gleam white, and I find myself reaching out to cover them with one of my own. She gives a shuddering breath at the touch, but doesn't pull away.

"During a climb one afternoon on some cliffs, Nick had a bad fall when a handhold crumbled. The accident left him with a spinal cord injury. My husband uses a wheelchair now. He has paraplegia."

I hear a sympathetic noise come out of me, entirely unplanned. She glances up to meet me eyes so I explain. "I'm sorry. I have a buddy from the Army who suffered an SCI. Rehab helped some, but it's been a hard road for him."

Alethia bites her lip and nods slowly. "It's been…a learning process. Nick is strong-willed, though, and for the most part he's adapted. We have home health aides to address his needs where he won't accept my help. Also, we live in an apartment on a single floor that's been made ready to accommodate his wheelchair." She looks to where my hand still covers hers. "The problem is our sex life," she whispers.

I keep my eyes on her face rather than our joined hands. "Go on."

She flicks a stormy, troubled glance at me, then again looks away. Her cheeks flame but she continues. "Nick can't get or maintain an erection. Or at least, not with the usual, um, stimulation. He can't orgasm. It frustrates him terribly that he can't be a man with me."

She looks quickly at me. "That's what he says. I swear I don't think of it like that. But it's taken a toll on our marriage. Nick frequently gets depressed now. We've been to counselors but the things they suggest about creating intimacy, or finding new ways to please each other…they aren't enough for Nick. He blames himself for throwing away our chance for children and a normal life—again, these are his words—so he could play on the rocks. He feels he holds me back.

"Sometimes…" Alethia trails off. Her voice, when she speaks, holds a trace of tears. "He says sometimes that he wishes I would leave him. He claims it's inevitable and that I'm only staying out of pity. He thinks my physical needs will eventually drive me away so I should get it over with."

She shakes her head forcefully. "I don't want to leave. I love Nick and I plan to spend my life with him, even if it doesn't look like what we used to picture. But the issue of our sex life has become such a focal point that we can't seem to move on."

I try to imagine myself in this Nick's situation. An athlete, denied the full use of a body that he'd probably taken for granted. A lovely, desirable wife who he can no longer please, at least in the way he's likely been pleasing girls since high school.

Sex isn't everything, but it's important. Sometimes I think all I'm good for is sex. It's literally my livelihood. What would I do if some injury took it away? I don't have any other commercial skills. The things I learned in the Army are fine for warfare, but not much use in the real world.

I clear my head to focus. "Tell me what you think I could do for you."

"Nick thinks that if I have sex with another man, he'll know my needs are met. Then perhaps we can find a way to make all the rest of it work too." Resolve grows quickly in her hazel eyes, surprising me. "I said I would only consider it if we find a way to keep Nick a part of the, um, situation."

Ah. "I take it you discussed this with Meredith, and she said—?"

"That you have something of a specialty clientele. A niche."

I nod slowly. All right. Time to see if she wants to discuss this frankly.

"I do have a niche. I'm bisexual, and I usually take on couples. Sometimes it's to explore a kink or fantasy. Other times it's just fucking. But once in a while, I've been with clients who struggle with intimacy issues. A couple I saw a few times suffered because the husband thought he might be gay. He was too conflicted to find out by cheating on his wife, even with her permission. Happily, after our first sessions, he decided he was bi. They found ways to make their sexuality work by practicing with me."

Alethia barely blushes, but her eyes glimmer. "That's similar to what I have in mind. Nick isn't bisexual, but if we do this, if we have someone who's comfortable with another man being present, who can help make Nick feel like he's a *part* of things—"

"Then you won't feel like you're abandoning him or cheating on him," I finish.

"Exactly. To be honest, I have no idea how Nick will actually react in the moment. He's the one pushing me to have sex with another man, but I know he really doesn't want that. He *hates* the idea, but he hates more the fear that I've got unfulfilled needs. Maybe he'll be able to accept it, if he's there to see that it's just sex. Maybe he'll realize it's a mistake to push me onto another man. Or maybe—" She trails off, biting her lip nervously.

"Maybe he'll enjoy it?" I guess.

She nods. "I thought about another woman to make love with me. Perhaps that would make it easier for Nick than seeing me with a man, you know? But it really doesn't address his fear. He projects all his anxiety onto the idea that I'm not getting what I need. If I brought in a woman, I think it would just magnify his insecurities. There'd be two women he felt he couldn't satisfy. But if I bring in a man who's open to finding ways to involve Nick, perhaps there's a chance."

I lean back in my chair and think quickly. Part of me screams to turn Alethia down. I'm not a qualified sex therapist, and it sounds like that's what this couple needs. I'm not even a trained surrogate. I'm just a guy with a big dick who realized he could make better money with it than by driving an Uber or working in a restaurant.

I remember my buddy, Owen, sipping beer in his wheelchair the last time I visited him.

"It's fuckin' lonely, bro," Owen had said. "I used to get all the pussy I could handle. You remember? I didn't even have to buy dinner before I'd be balls deep in some chick. Now—" he scoffed and took a pull of his Amstel "—I literally can't pay someone to fuck me. I got so horny last week I called one a them services you see advertised. An escort service. This lady answered the phone, sounded like my grandma. I told her I was in a chair. The lady said how sorry she was to hear it but she didn't have any girls who were 'into that'."

Owen's voice was bitter and harsh. "Jesus fuckin' Christ. I'm not 'into that' either, but it's my goddam life now."

I'm aware of Alethia watching me with hopeful eyes. "Tell me more about what Nick thinks of your suggestion," I say, to buy time.

She inhales deeply. "He's...nervous. He understands why I want to approach it this way, but he wishes I'd just leave him out of it. I can't do that. I can't shut the door in Nick's face as I take another man into my bed, no matter how much he says he wants me to."

The love in her voice pushes at me. Alethia's willing to take a pretty extreme measure to help her husband resolve his guilt at not being able to provide sex the conventional way. I have no illusions about myself or what I have to offer. I'm a sex worker. I provide comfort and pleasure. Maybe that'll be enough, and I'll leave the relationship dynamics to them.

"All right," I say. "When would you like to meet?"

Alethia flashes me a look of trepidation mixed with eagerness. "Really? Well, what about tomorrow evening?"

It'd be crass to pull out my calendar and look, but I'm pretty sure I'm free. "I can make that. How about nine o'clock?"

"Yes, that's fine. I'll email you the address. About your fee—"

I hold up my hand to stop her. "Not here. I'm going to guess Meredith gave you some idea of our usual arrangement?" I charge five hundred for a basic two-hour session. Meredith can afford it easily, but I keep my eyes on Alethia's face to gauge whether she balks. She just nods confidently, so I let the unspoken price stand. I'm probably overcautious, but the people who'd helped me start in the business warned not to discuss a fee in public. "Fine. I'll see you tomorrow." I reach for my wallet but Alethia stops me.

"Please. Let me cover this, for meeting with me."

I tip my head to say thanks, and have almost turned away when a thought strikes me. "Would Nick feel more comfortable if we had some kind of communication beforehand?"

Alethia frowns thoughtfully. "Well, I don't know." She holds a finger against her lips, then nods slowly. "Actually, he might."

"Then give him my email address. If he wants to ask me any questions, or lay down any ground rules in advance, he can tell me that way. Otherwise, we can talk about that stuff tomorrow evening when I arrive."

CHAPTER THREE

L OUNGING ON MY sofa with a vodka tonic and *Guardians of the Galaxy* playing for the fifth time on Netflix, I snag my phone when it buzzes. It shows an incoming email for JD Pierce. I swipe open the app and nod at the name of the sender. Nick Ballantine.

> *My wife explained that you're coming over tomorrow. I don't know what I'm allowed to say in an email so I don't know what to write. This situation is pretty out there, but I'd do anything for Alethia. I'll try to be as unobtrusive as possible. Please, just make my wife happy.*

I tap a finger on the edge of my phone. Nick's right; I'd rather not have a record of any discussion of specifics. I think about Owen's situation, and how desperate he is for human contact. Hell, if Owen were open to it, I'd have tried taking him to bed. He doesn't face the same marital issue that drives Nick. The fear in my friend's face, though, that he'll never again have a woman make love to him… It haunts me. Nick must be desperate, to consent to another man bedding his wife, and being in the room when it happens.

Desperate enough that things might turn sour?

I narrow my eyes as I think. A distraught, jealous man could conceivably turn violent if pushed the wrong way. I doubt Meredith would have sent these clients to me if she had the slightest concern. Still, I'd feel better if I speak to Nick myself before arriving at their house.

I contemplate the email. *Fuck it*, I think, and type, "Let's talk about this," adding my cell phone number.

A few seconds later, the phone rings in my hand. The caller ID flashes a number with a Boston area code. "Hello," I answer.

"Is this JD?" The voice on the other end is deep, almost a bass. It asks the question softly, nervously, but not with obvious anger or concern.

"Hi Nick. Thanks for calling. You're right that I'd rather not exchange a bunch of messages. I think tomorrow might be easier if you and I talk a little in advance though. Are you okay with that?"

"Yes," Nick answers slowly. "As okay as I can be with this situation. Alethia explained why we've come to you? And what to expect—I mean, about me?"

"I know that you've had an accident and are in a wheelchair. Other than that, she didn't share many details."

Nick laughs bitterly. "That's about it. My injury was complete at T10, if that means anything to you."

"Sorry, it doesn't. I have a friend from the Army who suffered a spinal cord injury. I don't talk to him about the medical details though."

"No worries. I didn't know anything about this shit either, eighteen months ago. My upper body is fine, but I can't move my legs at all. I'm a lot bigger than Alethia so I'm tough to move around. We have home health aides in daily to help me." Nick pauses, then said, "I'd prefer it if we all met in a hotel. You know? To keep this separate from our home life? But there are a lot of logistical issues involved for me to be away from home for any length of time."

I know Owen needs help getting in and out of a shower, wears a catheter to piss, and vague details like that. It makes sense that some kind of extended trip would require planning and preparation.

Plus, Nick wouldn't want to explain to his home health aides why he needs a hotel room set up for him and Alethia.

"Okay. Let me ask, Nick. Do you have a guest room? Somewhere we can meet but keep it separate from the room you share with Alethia?"

Nick mutters, "We do. That's a good idea."

I debate my next question for a moment. "So, can you tell me, what is it you want to happen here?"

"What do you mean? You know why we're hiring you—"

"I understand why I'm coming over, yes. What I mean is, what is it you want to accomplish?"

"I want Alethia to be able to have sex again. To enjoy a man." Nick swallows audibly. When he speaks, his voice sounds rough. "We had a great sex life together, before. Very active, almost every day. She loves sex, always told me her drive was high. It isn't right, that she shouldn't be able to still have that, just because I fucked up our lives.

"I mean, I fucked everything, but for the most part we've been able to figure this shit out. Sex, though, we can't make work. I want to know Alethia is satisfied. I *need* that. If it can't be me, I'm not going to stop her from finding as much normality as she can in our life."

I hear so much guilt and self-loathing creeping in to Nick's words that I almost cancel the appointment right then. The sense that the situation could get too big and complicated pulses in my head like a warning light.

I think again of Owen, though, and his desperation. My buddy's problems are big, but sex shouldn't be on the list of things he has to suffer without. What Nick and Alethia are hiring me to do is unusual, sure. But if I can find a way to help them connect, is it that different from the cuckolding scenes I run? Or the simple threesomes where a couple wants to add some spice?

Maybe the situation calls for honesty on my part. "Nick, I'll be frank. I'm kind of nervous to step into this, but I want to help you both if I can. This is a business transaction, right? Can we be upfront about what that means, and what you want me to do?"

Nick gives a shuddering exhalation, then—strangely—a chuckle. "You're nervous too, huh? Not your usual gig, I guess. Okay, what do you want to know?"

"How about some Do's and Do Not's? Kissing, for example. Should I kiss Alethia when we're together?"

"I—I hadn't thought of that." More shuddering breaths, then a surprisingly firm answer. "Yes. Alethia loves to kiss when we have sex. You should kiss her."

"Good to know. How about touching? Stroking?"

"You, or her?"

"Well, let's agree it's up to her how much she wants to touch me. But how will you feel if I stroke her body?"

"Oh Jesus." Nick sounds like he's on edge, but not as distraught as I'd feared. "She likes to be touched. Breasts, obviously. The back of her neck gets her hot. Like, gripping her at the base of her skull while I'm, uh—"

"I understand," I assure him. "Thank you for sharing that. And oral?"

Nick pauses for a long time. When he answers, his voice sounds steady, but deeper. Richer.

"She loves it. Giving and receiving. I want her to have that."

Something in the way Nick answered pings inside me. I take a huge risk. "Nick, are you picturing these things happening to your wife?"

Another pause, and then a curt, "Yes."

"Do you...like what you're picturing?"

That gets me a hoarse chuckle. "Maybe like is the wrong word."

"But you want this for her, right? You want Alethia to enjoy herself?"

"God, yes. I need to know she's happy. That you'll take care of her."

"I will, Nick. I promise." The slight breathlessness in Nick's voice clues me in to something I hadn't realized earlier. Nick worries for his wife's pleasure and needs, but what about his own? I have only the most vague idea what impact the spinal cord injury could have on Nick's equipment. Is their problem just that he can't move his legs?

I take another leap. I give a throaty laugh and say, "I've got to tell you, Nick. Talking about this is getting me hard."

Nick answers in a near whisper. "Me too." I let the silence hang, until Nick volunteers. "I have what're called psychogenic erections. That means sexy images and thoughts work on me. But I don't feel anything on my junk. I can't get off."

Maybe it's because of my profession, but I think of five or six positions I wonder if Alethia and Nick had tried. *No, not the time. Remember, you aren't a sex therapist. Do the job you're qualified to do.*

But in the back of my mind, I'm already beginning to think of ways to handle the appointment. Alethia said she wants Nick to be part of things. Maybe I can indeed have Nick feel involved. I decide to test the waters further. "Can you tell me anything else that you'd want Alethia to experience tomorrow?"

"Wh—what do you mean?"

"Well, are there other places she likes to be touched? Are there things she likes to do to you that you think she's missed?"

Hesitation, then Nick says slowly, "She, uh, she likes me to use my thumb on her. On her clit, I mean, while I'm inside. Just...round and round."

"I can do that for her."

I wait, but Nick volunteers no more suggestions. As the silence draws out, I decide that we've spoken long enough. Hopefully, the talk has helped Nick find the right frame of mind for tomorrow evening. I also have a few things I want to think through, and maybe even research on the internet. "Tell you what, Nick. I'm glad we talked, but I need to get some dinner. So I'll see you both tomorrow, at nine. Right?"

"Yeah, okay." If Nick sounds disappointed to end the call, I think that's good. Leave him in a state of anticipation, and hope that it's enough to balance his shame or fears.

THE NEXT EVENING, I climb out of my Uber in front of a very stylish, very new apartment building in downtown Boston. The neighborhood is vibrant and, at this hour of the evening, bustling. Restaurants and bars line the streets for several directions. A marquee for a theater that features touring Broadway shows glitters above it all. A few blocks away is Boston Commons.

I whistle to myself. It's an expensive neighborhood. If the Ballantines can afford to live here, no wonder Alethia hadn't batted an eye at my fee.

When I stop at the concierge desk, I'm glad I've worn a sport coat over a polo shirt. I do my best with my clothes and appearance anyway, to make sure clients feel they're with someone special and not a street hustler. Sometimes I adopt an overtly sexual look if I sense clients are into the thrill of hiring a whore. With clients such as Meredith, I go the other way. I dress so she feels she's out with a real beau on her arm.

Tonight, I took my cues from the way Alethia had dressed, with casual elegance. My dark blue, tight jeans are nonetheless neat, hemmed a half-inch to show a surprising streak of red. My sky-blue polo brings out my eyes and lets me show my trim body and muscled arms when I remove my jacket.

The very pretty young man seated at the desk looks alert at my approach. He scans me, flashing a sexy smile. If I weren't there in a professional capacity, I might have flirted. Instead, I smile back winningly and say, "JD Pierce to see the Ballantines."

"Of course, sir. Please wait one moment." The twink-concierge picks up a house phone and presses a few buttons. After a pause, he says, "Mr. Ballantine? It's Tommy at the front desk. I have a Mr. Pierce here to see you." He nods and disconnects. To me, he says, "Please go on up. It's apartment 1019, on the top floor."

I wink at him—in case I'm left horny by this session—and head for the elevators.

The mahogany and mirror-lined elevator slides open to reveal a hallway. Subdued lighting creates pools of illumination on a thick, forest-green carpet. Unusual pieces of modern art grace the walls. I follow the numbers on the doors, until I spot an open one at the last unit on the right.

Alethia steps into the hall and lifts a delicate hand in greeting. She looks lovely but tense in a simple blue sleeveless dress. When I get close, I see that the color of the dress brings out silver in her hazel eyes. They shimmer like twilight on a lake.

"Welcome," Alethia says, reaching out to take my hand and draw me into the apartment. Her hand is cool and steady, belied by the slight tremble of her lips.

"It's nice to see you again," I say in my low register. "You look beautiful this evening."

"Thank you," she says with a slight smile, running her eyes over my body appreciatively. "So do you."

I relax. I sense no self-doubting here, even though I had kind of expected it after her hesitations yesterday. Plus, she seems to like the way I look. Sessions are easier all the way around when clients feel attracted to me, and see a person rather than a commodity.

I step into the apartment and feel my eyes go round. The large unit features an open plan, hardwood floors and minimalist furniture. From the front door I face a wall of floor-to-ceiling windows that look out across the Boston skyline. A three-quarter moon sits framed perfectly in an upper pane.

Pinpoint spotlights cast a soft glow over the kitchen island and counters, which appear to be a pale marble. The appliances, faced in wood and steel, coordinate with the cabinets. A crystal bowl filled with oranges glows, shockingly vivid, in the center of a long dining table of some dark wood.

A few photographs in silver frames appear here and there; at a glance, none shows people. The living area features two facing, low-slung upholstered sofas and a pair of coordinating chairs with their backs to the windows. No coffee table but a few end tables, I notice. The seating arrangement is open and fully accessible from one side.

The reason for that rolls into sight, and I feel my mouth go dry.

Nick's handsome, disturbingly so. I'm not sure what I'd expected, but it isn't the man with dark hair, beard, full lips and penetrating gaze who faces me. Nick wears a collared short-sleeve shirt much like mine, but in black. Heavily muscled arms, dusted thickly with hair across the forearms, grip the wheels on either side of his chair. A well-developed chest and broad shoulders confirm how much of an athlete Nick still is.

The lower half of his body is encased in blue jeans and penny loafers. From the loose material of the pants legs, it's obvious that Nick's limbs have atrophied to some extent. It doesn't matter to me. This is exactly the type of guy I'd often gone for when I used to prowl for myself rather than working with a client. Even in the Army, it was the big, muscled men like Nick who drew me to take risks. I used to drop hints I was willing if such a stud seemed to need some relief before he could get leave.

Alethia strides over to her husband and rests a hand on his shoulder. They're a stunning couple together. I can't tell how tall Nick would be standing, but I'd bet well over my own six feet. Why had I first thought Alethia other than beautiful? Seeing her glow as she looks at her husband takes my breath away.

I imagine Alethia and Nick standing side by side, dressed like glittering stars, ready for a night of expensive restaurants and fashionable clubs. My hunger for them both surprises me. In a different circumstance, if this couple had picked me up at a bar, I'd gladly have gone home with them. I'd have tried to rock their world.

Nick offers a hand. "Hello, JD. I'm Nick Ballantine." That bass voice thrills me as it had on the phone last night.

Dropping my surprising line of thought, I step forward and take the hand. "Hi Nick. I'm glad to meet you." Am I imagining the spark of surprise and maybe approval in Nick's eyes? This close, I can tell they're a warm brown.

Nick drops his hand and looks at his wife. "You were right, babe. He's good looking."

My heart beats a tattoo. Alethia said Nick isn't bisexual, so I'm not sure how to take the compliment.

"Have a seat, JD," Alethia says, gesturing to one of the sofas. "Can I fix you a drink?"

Excellent, I think as I lower myself to the thick cushions. *That's what we all need—a drink to relax them and get past the awkwardness.*

"What are you having?" I ask.

Nick answers, "Bourbon on the rocks for me, and Alethia will probably have a glass of this really good Greek white wine she likes." Alethia laughs softly as she heads toward the kitchen.

"A bourbon for me too, please. Though I don't know much about them. A friend turned me on to Woodford Reserve, but I'm not sure I could tell the difference between that and, I don't know, Four Roses."

"Blasphemy," Nick says with a chuckle, then seems surprised at himself. He looks as if he wants to say more, but nerves catch his tongue.

"Amazing view," I say, inanely, as I gesture to the windows. "I've never seen Boston like this."

"We've lived here a little more than a year," Alethia says, returning with our drinks on a small tray. I take my tumbler with murmured thanks. "We used to live outside Boston, but the commute wasn't worth it."

I want to ask what they do professionally to afford such a gracious and obviously expensive place, but that was one of the first rules I'd learned. Never ask personal questions that might make a client feel you're prying or overstepping. But be a good listener, and talk about what the client wants to discuss.

Bourbon seems like a safe topic, so I sip my drink.

"Ah, that's good," I say, nodding. "Very smooth and rich."

"It's a 17-year-old, 90 proof Eagle Rare," Nick comments. "A Christmas gift from my father-in-law."

"Nick and Bampás bond over their whiskeys at the holidays," Alethia says fondly.

"Bampás means her dad," Nick offers.

Alethia strokes her hand across Nick's cheek before she seats herself. Folding her legs elegantly to the side, she leans into the corner of the sofa opposite mine. Nick rolls near to her, close enough that she can reach his knee.

We chat some as we drink, slowly relaxing and opening up to one another. The conversation isn't deep, but it's funny and kind of flirty. For the most part, anyway. Nick makes a few self-deprecating remarks about his chair as we talk—"If the building catches fire, just push me toward the stairs. This thing would probably let me bounce to the bottom." And "I'd pour the next round but we didn't spring for the butler's tray attachment."

The comments make Alethia flinch slightly, and I put that away to think about. I steer the conversation back to the neighborhood. Nick's a native Bostonian, it turns out, and I visited my mother's family in a nearby suburb a few times when I was younger. We have a few recollections in common of the city before the most recent waves of gentrification.

"You know, this building is smack in the heart of what used to be the Combat Zone," Nick observes.

"Wow. I would have liked to have seen that, before it all changed," I say, then take a sip of my bourbon.

"What's the Combat Zone?" Alethia asks.

"New Yorkers," Nick scoffs gently. "If it didn't happen there, they don't know about it."

Alethia cuffs his knee but she laughs. "MIT. Harvard. The Charles River. These things I know about. Not this Combat Zone."

"Well, you should know Harvard since you got your PhD there," Nick says.

Wow. Alethia is a doctor. I wonder, what of? But my trained caution again kicks in. Instead, I go with the racier topic of the Combat Zone as a way to move the evening along. It's too bad, really, because I'm having the best time talking with the Ballantines. Still, I'm not here just for drinks.

"From what I've heard, the Combat Zone was a lot like Times Square before it was all cleaned up," I explain to Alethia. "Adult movie theaters, rough dives, gay bars and drag shows that were notorious and raunchy. Organized crime." I pause and sip my drink. "Prostitution."

The two of them regard me with similar expressions. I see surprise there, probably that I bring the topic up so bluntly. Some curiosity, and also—I imagine—appreciation. The word's enough to put us all back into the mindset of what the evening is for. I'm not a friend they're getting to know, or a colleague.

I'm here to work, and it involves my body.

The drinks have done their job in loosening everyone a little. I notice Nick shifting from side to side in his chair—is that about his injury, or me? In Alethia's eyes, I fancy I see some heat begin to grow as she recalls what I'm about to do for her. Maybe Meredith told her about my dick? I lean back and let my knees fall open naturally. Her eyes flick to the bulge between my legs, and the tip of her pink tongue licks her lower lip.

Oh yeah. Classy, smart, lovely, but horny as hell. That's Alethia.

I curl one side of my mouth into an inviting smile. Then I notice Nick's eyes. It isn't anger that shows, though his expression's dark and his thick eyebrows draw down. His ears turn red. If I had to guess, Nick is…ashamed. Ashamed at the reminder of why I'm there, what role I'm to perform. A role that Nick can't fulfill any longer for Alethia.

I set my glass on a side table. The ice shifts and clinks. Alethia glances at her husband, fraught again, and then looks into her wine, drawing into herself. Slowly, I stand and cross to where Alethia sits, inches away from her husband. I sink to my heels, resting one hand on Alethia's exposed knee.

Nick grips the wheels of his chair, his gaze burning into the back of my hand. I can feel the weight of his stare. Again, instinct takes told. I reach out with my other hand and grip Nick's right wrist, linking the three of us.

Nick huffs in surprise and darts a look at my face. But he doesn't pull away.

"I know this is new to you," I say softly, looking between the two of them. "And what's new can be a little frightening. But I'm here for you." I focus on Alethia. "For both of you. You've talked about this, and you've decided this is an experience you need to try. Together. Right?" Alethia nods, and I look again into Nick's burning eyes. "Right?" I prompt.

Nick swallows hard, but nods.

"Good. I want to make something clear. I have no expectations. I'm here for the two of you. We go as far as you are comfortable, and no further. Maybe we do nothing but kiss." I look at Alethia's lips. I hope we do more than kiss, to be honest. She's sexy, graceful, and funny. I sense that Nick's on to something, about her having needs that are going unmet. The tension I feel in Alethia's leg tells me that she wants this to happen, and would feel disappointed if we stop at kissing.

Disappointed, but she'll do what Nick wants. She'll stop if Nick grows uncomfortable, and I respect that. I'm not here to please Nick physically, which is too bad because I'd really be into that. Yet I agreed to conduct matters so that Nick feels fully involved. I've thought about it after his phone call, and all through the day. Some ideas occurred that I'm very interested in trying out.

Nick and Alethia share a look, one of those silent, couple-y exchanges that exclude me. I continue to crouch quietly, connected to them both by my touch, and wait. After a moment, Nick gives his wife the slightest nod. His grip on his chair relaxes marginally.

I rise smoothly to my feet again. "Why don't we go into the bedroom, and see what happens?"

CHAPTER FOUR

A LETHIA RISES AS I do. A tremble in her full lips betrays nerves at what's about to happen. She waits for Nick to reposition his chair, and leads the two of us along an unusually wide hall to a bedroom.

The room's a generous size, with a queen bed covered in a thick duvet. A few simple pieces of art hang on the walls. Low lamps burn on either side of the bed. An anonymous quality to the room makes clear that it's a space for guests, which relieves me. I'd bet the Ballantines never sleep in this room. That'll make it easier for them to set aside their nerves.

Nick rolls into the room and positions his chair so he faces the bed but at a distance of a few feet. Alethia slips off her heels, nudging them into a neat pair with her bare foot. I glance at them both for permission before I close the door.

The room feels intimate now, and it takes on an air of heavy expectation. I move closer, as Nick swallows hard and flushes. Alethia reaches slowly to release her hair from its ponytail. The mass slides free, framing her face and brushing her shoulders. I run my fingers through the black mane, letting my fingernails graze her scalp. Alethia inhales raggedly as she tilts her head against my touch. Nick makes a faint noise, but whether in frustration or pleasure, I can't say.

Slipping off my jacket, I look for a place to store it. Alethia takes it from my hands to hang in the closet. I kick off my shoes and hold out a hand. Alethia steps into my arms, positioned so Nick can see us both. Drawing her close, I tilt my head down but wait for her to make the contact. Her hazel eyes fixed to mine, she stretches her neck to meet me in a kiss.

It's my turn to make a surprised noise. Her lips are lush and soft. They remain closed so I don't use my tongue, but I let the heat build slowly. She shifts in my arms, sliding her hands around my back. Silky hair brushing against my face makes me cup her chin, then slide my fingers slowly along her cheek and again into the mass of raven locks. I press my nails against her scalp as I push the hair back, making sure Nick has a clear view of his wife's face. Alethia gives a shudder at the stroke.

In my arms, she feels sleek. The hand on my back slides lower to my waist, then to the top of my ass. A fire kindles in my belly, and my erection grows quickly. I brought along a few tabs of Viagra just in case the situation got too tense, but apparently that isn't going to be a problem. Alethia might have begun reluctantly, but from the way she holds and kisses me, she clearly wants this to happen.

I break the kiss to meet her eyes, and smile. She returns it tentatively, before she darts a nervous glance to Nick and stiffens in my arms.

"It's fine, honey," Nick says throatily. "I'm good."

I decide it's time to put my notion to the test. I step away from Alethia for a moment and draw my shirt over my head. Her gaze drops to my wide and nearly hairless chest. I look down at my flat, reddish nipples and the planes of my torso. My hard-won abs ripple below. A light treasure trail begins at my navel before disappearing into the waist of my jeans.

I toss my shirt to the corner, and run fingers slowly, provocatively, down my front. Alethia's eyes track my movement. I rest my hands on the top of my jeans for a moment, before flicking open the top button.

Eyes locked with Alethia's, I say, clearly and distinctly, one word. "Nick."

I hear a shift against the leather of the wheelchair. After a moment, Nick replies, "Yes, JD?"

I turn to look at him. I see the fear, the shame from earlier…but also anticipation. *Excellent.* I crouch by the chair, dropping one hand lightly on Nick's forearm and the other on his knee.

"Nick, I'm going to be your hands tonight. Your lips and tongue." I pause and say breathily, "Your cock."

Nick's eyes widen and he gives a little huff of air.

I nod to show I'm serious. "Use me. I want you to tell me how to undress Alethia. How to kiss her and touch. Let her know how desirable she is." I look at Alethia. "She is beautiful, isn't she?"

Nick says reverently, "Yes, she is."

Alethia smiles at both of us, then reaches behind to unzip her dress.

She slips it off her shoulders and steps out of the material. Like me, she throws the discarded dress to the corner of the room and returns to stillness.

As I'd expected, Alethia's body is toned and slim. A black bra covers luscious breasts, not big but high and firm. Smooth, olive skin gleams in the light of the room. Through the lace of her panties, I can see the dark shadow of hair at her mound. Her flared hips taper back to long, graceful legs.

"You're stunning," I breathe out, and Nick murmurs agreement beside me. I squeeze his forearm. "Where shall I start?"

Nick licks his lips, then says, "Take off her bra, and play with her nipples. Use your tongue."

I grin and rise to my feet. I'm relieved that Nick seems willing to play along with this. I step closer and Alethia turns her back to me. Unhooking her bra, I slide my fingers up her back and under the straps. I then carry it forward along her arms, removing the confection with my fingertips. Alethia faces me and Nick again, breasts pointing firmly with their nipples pebbled and erect. She has no tan lines, which both surprises and delights me.

I drop the bra at our feet and bend to kiss each nipple lightly, darting my tongue against the firm peaks and swirling around the rose-colored areolae. Cupping her left breast gently, I stroke along the side of it while my thumb teases the nipple. At the same time, I love on the right breast with lips and tongue and breath.

Alethia moans and arches toward me, pressing her tits more firmly into my mouth and hand. She grasps my hair, tugging gently to the side until I reverse my actions, tonguing her left breast while stroking the right. Her fingers clutch tighter as she presses against my mouth.

"Bite it," Nick says roughly. "Not too hard, just enough."

I do as instructed. The cry Alethia gives back is full of passion and want. I switch breasts again and bite at the other nipple sharply, then soothe it with gentle swipes of my tongue.

"Perfect," Alethia sighs. I sense the praise is for Nick, not me. I don't mind.

"Use your thumbs to slide her panties down," Nick tells me. I go to my knees, with her fingers still tangled in my hair. Running my nose and then cheek against Alethia's smooth, flat belly, I discover the lightest down of hair. When I ghost with my lips over the warm skin, the firm muscle beneath, I can smell her arousal.

As instructed, I slide my thumbs into the sides of her panties and lower them to the ground. Alethia steps out of them delicately. Turning with a wink, I toss the panties so they land on Nick's lap. He growls and brings the garment to his nose.

I turn back to Alethia's body. The black hair covering her mound is natural, which I prefer to trimmed or shaved. I press lips to her flesh, enjoying the scent of her body, the silky hair. Dipping my head, I dart out my tongue to tease the edges of concealed folds that I can reach. Alethia inhales sharply and shifts her stance to give me access.

I want to dive in, but instead I look again at Nick. "What next?"

Clenching the panties in his hand, he spears a burning look at his wife and me, her hired lover. "Use your tongue. Rough, then soft. That's what she likes." He meets Alethia's eyes. "You taste so good, baby. Will you let him taste you?"

She smiles and nods, moving to the edge of the bed. With a swift gesture, she pulls the duvet to the floor, then climbs up the bed on hands and knees. Her smooth ass waves in our faces as she positions herself in the middle before rolling over onto her back.

"Come closer," I whisper to Nick, before crawling after Alethia. I nibble and lick at her ankles, then her calves. I raise one leg and swipe with my tongue against the back of her knee, drawing a gasp and moan. Repeat it on the other leg.

I sense Nick roll closer and position his chair. Alethia reaches out and takes his hand. He watches me lick my way along his wife's legs and to the glistening lips at their juncture.

Nick meets my eyes and he nods. I extend my tongue, sampling the nectar dampening Alethia's hair. When she spreads her legs wider, I grow more aggressive. I tongue my way deeper, using my thumbs to spread her private flesh. Around and around the little nub of her clit, I drive in circles.

She begins to squirm and I step it up again. With only my lips, I play with her bud as if it were a small cock, drawing and sucking on it. Then I use my teeth, lightly scraping until I hear a gasp, before reverting to strokes of my tongue. I delve deep, exploring and licking and savoring. Alethia's taste is exotic and delicious. I snuffle like a pig, grunting as I root in deeper.

"Yes, like that," I hear Nick growl. "I love eating you out, sweetheart. I love when you clench around my tongue, and drive your pussy against my mouth."

Alethia does just that, arching and writhing her hips to grind her mound against me. Her body begins to ripple and undulate as her breaths turn to pants.

Oh my fuck, I think. *So sexy.*

The sounds she makes are incredible. She grabs my hair again to hold my head steady as she uses me. She brings herself to climax against my oh-so-willing mouth and lips and tongue. Alethia's nails drive needlepoints of perfect pain into my scalp. She suddenly convulses, her upper body rising, her thighs clenching on either side of my head as she pulses against me. The sweet juices all but pour out of her body. I lap them with wide swipes as her cries go on and on.

Finally her orgasm eases, and she melts onto the bed, panting. I'm painfully aware of my erection—trapped behind my jeans—pressing into the sheets beneath me. I think, *Just a little rubbing and I could shoot.*

At a small sigh, I suddenly recall Nick. I raise my head to him cautiously, unsure of what reaction to expect. To my relief, Nick smiles at his wife gently and meets my gaze. Tears shimmer in the dark depths, but he also has a smile for me.

Nick mouths the words, "Thank you."

Pride and relief suffuse my body. I didn't fuck up after all, with my amateur psychologist routine. Nick and Alethia both enjoyed what happened, apparently.

So did I, for that matter.

I've always liked giving head, whether to a man or woman, and I'm confident in my skill. Having someone as responsive and delicious as Alethia proved, though, is special. A bonus.

Indecision strikes me now. I've been here less than an hour, and they're paying me for two. Have we gone far enough and I should dress? Or will there be a Round Two?

Perhaps Nick sees my hesitation, and understands it. Holding my gaze, he lifts Alethia's limp hand to his lips and kisses her fingertips. She opens her hazel eyes languidly and watches her husband. Flipping her hand, Nick lowers to kiss her palm. She croons at the touch and curls her fingers to cup his chin.

They both turn to me. The look holds an invitation and a challenge.

I smirk right back at them. *Game on.*

Rising from the bed, I make a show of unzipping and stepping out of my tight jeans. My cock tents my boxer briefs obscenely, and I smile with satisfaction at the look of lust in Alethia's eyes. Nick's expression is harder to read, but he seems engaged.

I turn around and bend to pull some condoms from the pocket of my jeans, showing my ass. I spend a lot of time in the gym working on squats and other exercises to make my butt firm and shapely. From Alethia's low noise of delight, the effort pays off.

Facing them again, I stand straight, hook my thumbs in my shorts, and push them down. My cock springs back to my belly with a satisfying slap. The sound coming from Alethia as she gazes at me can only be called a purr. Nick also looks at me, intent though still unreadable.

I knee-walk up the bed until my hard cock bobs inches away from Alethia's grasp. A hand job, a blowjob, or straight fucking...I don't care. I'm horny as hell right now, into the scene, and I'll make damn sure the Ballantines get their money's worth out of me.

"What should I do next, Nick?" I ask sultrily. "What do you want to see Alethia do?"

Nick makes a strangled sound as Alethia glances at him. He clears his throat before saying huskily, "Take him in your hand, Ali. Feel that thing."

I roll onto my back as she wraps her slim fingers around my thick shaft. I'm used to compliments for it, which I enjoy but don't take too seriously. After all, my eight-inch dick is a genetic stroke of luck, not something I earned or worked for. It pays the bills, though, and I'm grateful for what nature put between my legs. I wait for Alethia's praise.

"It's nice," she says, giving me a smile, "and almost as big as Nick's."

Surprised, I look over at Nick to see an odd combination of smug, regret and that ever-present shame. He uses his arms to shift in his chair, and I realize that he has an erection. A very long, very thick erection that visibly stretches down the leg of his loose blue jeans.

Desire pools in my stomach. Even if he can feel nothing there, he's responding to the eroticism of what he's watching. I almost want the chance to put to the test whether Nick truly is incapable of sex.

Stop it, you selfish bastard, I hiss at myself. *This isn't about you, and they've tried everything already.*

I gift myself a small flirtatious comment anyway. Raising my eyebrows and tilting my head at Nick's lap, I say, "Good thing this isn't a competition. My ego might never recover, based on what I'm seeing."

He blushes and looks away, but I think he also seems a little pleased. Every man enjoys hearing his cock's big.

Alethia chooses one of the condoms, opens the packet, and skillfully rolls the sheath over my dick. "Unlubricated. Good," she says. "I hate the taste." Then she guides me into her mouth.

It's my turn to gasp, because Alethia is good at this. She pulls off just long enough to get me flat on my back. Sliding down my body, she holds her hair out of the way with one hand as she swallows me again. I cry out in pleasure.

That she knows what to do with a big dick is obvious, as she takes me deep with no obvious effort. The heat of her mouth and the pressure she uses are perfect. One hand around the root of my cock, she sucks and licks me like she'd been starving.

Then she shocks the hell out of me. She removes her hand and takes me even deeper, into the back of her throat. No woman, and few men, have ever been able to do that to me. She swallows around the head of my cock, making me gasp.

"Christ, that's good," I gasp, one hand flying out to clench a hank of her hair. I'm careful not to force her down or pull, but I need an anchor. My other hand flops open to the bed, palm flexing rhythmically in time with Alethia's sucking technique.

A warm, heavy hand covers my palm, and I look over in surprise. Nick has reached out for me, in a sort of bro-clasp so our fingers aren't intertwined.

Amusement and heat fills Nick's face as he stares at our joined hands. "She's something else, isn't she?"

I nod, then groan as she licks the crown of my cock.

"So good. If you keep that up, I'm going to come. Do you want that, or…?" I let the question trail off.

Alethia raises her head from my glistening rubber-sheathed shaft, taking it in her hand again. She notices my palm joined to Nick's, and indecision crosses her face. I have a feeling I know what she wants, but she isn't sure Nick can truly handle crossing that major line. Yet the fact he's willing to touch me while she gives me head…

Nick smiles lovingly at her. "Go ahead, sweetheart. I'm fine. I want you to have this. Let him give you what I can't." I hear no bitterness in Nick's words, just honesty.

Alethia must hear it too. She climbs off the bed and bends to kiss her husband. Hands on his cheeks, she says, "Thank you. I do want this, and I love you for being with me."

The connection between the two as their eyes lock brings a lump to my throat. They're so right together, despite the shitty hand they've been dealt. It takes me a moment to identify what makes my stomach churn.

Jealousy.

Not for either of them, but for *both* of them together. For what they share.

From a night table, Alethia pulls out a small bottle of lube. I see a box of condoms in the drawer as well, obviously in case I didn't bring any. I move out of the way as she rejoins me on the bed. Popping open the bottle, she drizzles liquid over the rubber that covers my aching erection. She throws aside the bottle and lays back. Her knees bend, one hand traces around a nipple and the other strokes through her pubic hair.

I spear Nick with a look, waiting. He blinks in surprise, then says, "Oh. Right. Uh, start slow. Use your fingers to make sure she's wet."

I position myself over Alethia, and between her knees. Angling my body so Nick can watch, I slide a finger inside her juicy depths. Using my thumb, I tease her jewel at the same time.

Impatiently, she bucks her hips. "More."

"Two," Nick croaks. "Give her two."

I do as I'm told. I press harder with my thumb and crook my fingers so they slide along the roof of her warm cave. "Like this?" I ask Nick in a deliberately sultry voice.

Nick nods. His tongue darts over his lips as he stares at my fingers disappearing inside his wife. Unbidden, I add a third. Alethia clenches herself around the intrusion, desperate for more.

"Nick," she pleads, rolling her head toward him.

"Now, JD. Fuck her now," Nick orders, the heat in his voice sparking a blaze in me. "Kiss her as you slide in."

I reposition myself so the head of my cock brushes against her labia. Resting on one elbow, I cup her breast and lean in for a kiss. Unlike the first time, Alethia opens for my tongue, drawing me into her mouth. Our heads slant together as the desire between us grows and catches. When her hand comes around my back to deepen the kiss, I know she's ready.

I press with my hips, splitting her folds, sliding slowly and carefully into her body. She's tight. Lord, is she tight. Even if she'd been used to Nick's envy-inducing cock, it's been a long time. The fingers helped ready her, but still I slow my pace.

I barely move for long, agonizing moments as she adjusts, pressing in by half-inches as I feel her passion grow. The wait is excruciating. Maddening. All I want to do is drive into Alethia's luscious body.

"That's right," Nick croons. "Oh, take it, baby. I know how much you miss this. Your cunt split open by a big, hard cock. It makes you go all creamy inside."

I shiver at Nick's filthy words, and Alethia clenches around me. She cradles me with her hips, pulls me all the way in with hands on my ass. Giving a sharp cry, she arches into me so her tits mash against my chest as she throws back her head and groans. I run a tongue from her clavicle up her neck to her ear. She shudders and tightens around me again, the hot core of her body pulsing around my cock. It takes all my years of practice to keep from coming.

Barely holding on, I kiss her hard as I shift my hips, just barely withdrawing and then ploughing in again. She spreads her knees wider and tilts her hips as she draws my tongue with her own. Taking that as permission, I give her a fuller stroke, withdrawing half of my length before plunging in again. She rewards me with a guttural groan. Her eyes flutter.

"More," she hisses.

"More," Nick says in his deep, strangled tones.

I look over to see his eyes fixed firmly on his wife's face. The hunger I read is raw. Primal. Nick burns to fuck his wife until she's mindless with pleasure. Since he can't, I'll do my best.

I unleash all of my skill on Alethia. I swivel my hips in circles. Pull out until my cock nearly slips free, before plunging back in a single thrust. Alternate short, powerful jabs with deep-dicking until Alethia begins to sob and moan beneath me.

"Rub her clit," Nick says hoarsely. "With your thumb."

I obey, reaching between our joined bodies to her mound, stroking the nub as I mine out her cunt with my dick. Remembering what Nick told me, I make steady circles with my thumb, in counterpoint to my violent thrusts.

Alethia convulses along my length, her black hair shimmering like a storm cloud against the white sheets. I take a hard nipple into my mouth, biting at it before soothing with soft strokes of my tongue. At the same time, with my other hand I grip the back of her neck.

She comes apart on my dick, and under my thumb, panting and crying out as her entire body ripples.

"Don't stop," Nick commands. "Keep fucking. She can climax again when you do."

Alethia looks at him with shimmering eyes as her hand on my ass pulls me into her. "You're so good to me," she whispers to Nick. "You always know what I need."

My thrusts had slowed as her orgasm waned, but I take Nick at his word. If she needs more, then I'll give it to her. I'm so hot myself I could explode at any minute, but I fight off my orgasm. Ramming into Alethia with deep, steady strokes, I mentally review the months of the year. Math tables. The heat and dust of Afghanistan.

That thought takes me to memories of the communal showers. Big guys parading around, wet, naked, flicking each other with towels. Guys built like Nick—

"Aaaah," I scream, my gaze flashing between the woman I'm buried in and man I also hunger for. I begin to come, filling the condom with shot after shot of jizz. As promised, Alethia erupts again, wailing to match my cries as she squeezes my length and rakes nails across my back.

Nick pants nearby, wide eyes burning into Alethia's, his cheeks red as with exertion. He squirms in his chair, a look of confusion and ecstasy mingling in his face. His eyes fly to mine, and I instinctively reach out and grasp Nick's wrist. I stroke over the bone there, loving the feel of silken hair against my thumb, and Nick's head flies back. He cries out and shakes once. Twice. Then freezes, panting.

His wide eyes meet Alethia's, then mine.

"Nick?" Alethia asks, squirming to get free. I withdraw carefully, letting her go to crouch naked by her husband. "Are you all right?"

Nick blinks slowly a few times. His color returns to normal, but then he flushes again. "I, uh…I think I, um, had an orgasm."

CHAPTER FIVE

A LETHIA LOOKS SHOCKED. "What? I thought—"
"I know. Me too. Can you, um—" he shoots a sheepish glance at me, then back to his wife "—check?" He tilts his head toward his pants.

I turn away to give them some semblance of privacy, stripping off the condom and tying it in a knot. I hear a zip and a rustle of cloth. Then Alethia says, "There's no semen."

When I look, Nick's large cock lays in her delicate hand, seeming almost monstrous by contrast. It is indeed bigger than mine, uncut, and thick as my wrist. But it's undeniably dry. Not even precome glistens on the purple head that peeks from its cowl of flesh.

Alethia tucks it away and rezips Nick's pants. Unmindful of her nudity or mine, she stands slowly and rests a hand on Nick's neck. "The doctor told us you likely ejaculate into your bladder," she says thoughtfully. "But maybe—"

"I can still feel like I'm coming?" The trepidation and hopefulness in Nick's voice stir something in me. Something warm, but new. A desire to help Nick any way that I can.

"Did it feel like the same kind of orgasm?" I ask, then regret it when two pair of eyes turn to me. They'd almost forgotten I'm here. "Sorry. It's not my business."

Well, actually, it is. In a way.

As if I hadn't apologized, Nick says thoughtfully, "It did feel different. It wasn't centered in my dick. More like...my whole body exploded with sensation."

"It felt good, though?" Alethia asks. "Like before?"

"I… It felt maybe less intense, but still good."

"That's wonderful," Alethia says, her hazel eyes flashing. "I don't even know what it means, but it has to be positive."

Nick gives her a more cautious smile. "Maybe, hon. Let's see." He appears to notice her nudity then, and his eyes jerk back to me, also standing nude. My cock hangs thickly, still partly hard and red from my fantastic orgasm. Nick flushes and I suddenly feel embarrassed.

I quickly begin to find my clothes around the room and put them on. That triggers a similar response in Alethia, who pulls on her panties, bra and dress. She turns her back to Nick and holds her hair as he pulls up her zipper.

The two of them face me, united in their awkwardness. "I should get going," I say, and Alethia nods.

"I'll see you out," Nick offers.

Alethia holds out a hand to me. "Thank you. That whole experience was remarkable."

I resist the easy joke that springs to mind about it being my pleasure. What happened between the couple moved me deeply, and I don't want to ruin it. I simply take her hand, kiss the back of it, then turn away regretfully to return to the hall.

Nick follows behind. I hear Alethia say, "I'm going to draw a bath. Will you—?"

"Yes, I've got it covered," he replies.

"Good night, JD," she calls softly. I turn back, realizing I've forgotten my jacket, only to see it lies across the arm of Nick's chair.

We pause at the front door, and he reaches into his jeans pocket. Pulling out a cream-colored envelope, he meets my gaze and says, "I believe this is what was agreed."

I don't look inside. Not only would it be crass, but instinct tells me I have no need to doubt these people. I simply nod and tuck the envelope into my jacket's inner pocket. I'm confident I've given the Ballantines a good night, and I'm curious where they'll be able to go from this beginning.

Maybe it will encourage them to get more adventurous together. A couple so in love should find a lot of ways to connect sexually, even if it doesn't involve a penis in a vagina.

A slight sadness creeps in. I'll probably never know how it turns out, whether I've helped them see they have alternatives to explore beyond celibacy or hiring an escort. For a couple I've just met, I'm surprisingly invested in their situation. I suppose I could ask Meredith, but that would be unbelievably unethical—

"Thank you," Nick says intently, jarring my maudlin thoughts. "Tonight could have gone wrong in so many ways. You made it into something really special for us. I feel more connected to Alethia than I have in a year and a half."

I feel my cheeks warm. "I'm really glad I could help. And believe me, I enjoyed it too."

Nick glances away and says nervously, "Do you think we could schedule another session?"

My brows fly up. Somehow I've convinced myself this will be a one-and-done. Only professionalism stays me from babbling eagerly that I'd very much want to do it again. Cautiously, I say, "That's no problem for me. But, maybe you and Alethia want to discuss it first?"

Nick nods thoughtfully. "You're right. I'm probably surfing on endorphins or whatever. We need to talk."

I add quickly, "If you decide you want to bring me back, just name the date and time."

Nick smirks and looks at me from under his eyebrows. "Alethia's hot, isn't she?"

I smile back. "She is. And so are you." I turn and leave before Nick's surprised expression leaves his face.

A WEEK PASSES, of my usual routine. Daily workouts at the gym keep my body fit and marketable. I make a trip to my tailor to get fitted for a new dinner jacket—an unexpected present from Meredith. I don't ask why, and she doesn't volunteer, but I suspect I know.

Sessions with Cerise, my personal trainer, every three days push me with new techniques or challenges. On Wednesday, under her watchful eye, I work through a set of pull-ups. She's tall and wiry, with neat, black dreads hanging to her shoulders. Sprinkles of freckles dot her nose and each cheek. Her medium-brown skin with its reddish-orange undertones has helped her get a few gigs as a fitness model.

During one of our sessions, though, Cerise had confessed to me that she really doesn't like modeling. "You have to watch everything you eat leading to a shoot. I'm always hungry and by the time the day arrives I can't stand the sight of chicken."

I'd grunted. "I know the feeling." I watch my diet religiously. The only indulgence I allow myself is breakfast with Essie at the diner, usually after a client session and only if I've burned enough calories to justify it.

When I was fresh out of the Army and going on my first client calls, keeping my twenty-nine inch waist had been easy. Now that I'm nearing thirty years old, though, I can already feel my metabolism slowing. The look I've long cultivated—sort of a "tennis pro" leanness—has started to feel unsustainable. My body is maturing naturally, becoming thicker and broader. Some of my clients definitely appreciate the man I'm becoming, but others prefer the fantasy of a youngish rogue who they can corrupt.

I see one of my regular couples on Thursday for a kinky little date that involves some rope play and candle wax. Harmless fun for them, but nothing I get off on personally. I leave the husband and wife cuddled together, murmuring softly, and show myself out.

My Friday session gets a little rough. The woman—who calls herself Alice—likes to taunt her husband Miles while I fuck her. It worked fine the first two times I saw them. Something's different tonight though. I sense it in Miles as soon as I arrive at their hotel room, a coiled tightness in the man.

Discreetly, I swallow a Viagra. I have a feeling I'm going to need it.

The session begins much as the previous two. Miles sits in a chair in the corner, a beer in his hand. Alice pretends I'm a man she's picked up in the hotel bar and brought to their room.

"Don't mind him," she coos, then sticks her tongue in my ear. "He's not a real man. Not like you." She presses her hand to my crotch, squeezing a little too hard. I need to give the Viagra time to work, so I pull Alice close and dance her around the room sexily. She grinds against me, telling me again and again to ignore Miles. I glance over anyway, to see Miles getting red in the face.

Alice pushes me onto the bed and fumbles my belt open. Luckily, the Viagra has kicked in enough that I begin to stiffen. She pulls my boxers partway down my thigh and begins to suck me off. She blows me messily and loudly while she waves her ass in Miles' direction. Her technique's nothing special. Nothing like Alethia's…

Stop it.

I play along, grasping her hair, pretending to force her. "Yeah, baby. Suck my big dick. Choke on that fucker."

"You little whore," Miles growls, and launches himself from his chair. I think at first Miles is talking to me, but then the man grabs his wife by the hips. She jerks in surprise, nicking me with her teeth. I yelp and grab my dick to get it out of the way. Miles tears Alice's panties off. Still bent over and trapping me, she cries out as Miles apparently shoves himself inside her.

"You cunt. You won't suck my cock but you'll do it for a stranger," Miles rants as he fucks her hard. Only the light in Alice's eyes clues me in that she likes the change of direction.

"That floppy, smelly thing you've got?" she taunts. "I can barely feel it inside me, let alone stand it in my mouth. Aaaah," she cries, dropping her head as Miles smacks her bare ass cheek.

"I'll *make* you feel it. You, from the bar," Miles bellows. It takes me a moment to realize I'm the one meant. "You came here for some cunt, right? Well, get ready." He tosses something; I catch it and realize it's a condom package. As Alice gets pumped above me, I fumble open the wrapper and roll the rubber onto my cock. Even with the Viagra, I'm sort of rubbery myself. This scene isn't going the way I like.

"Get on that dick," Miles orders, pulling out and spanking Alice again. Hard. She moans and shakes as she crawls higher to straddle me. Wrapping a hand around my shaft, she guides it into her and sinks down.

"Fuckin' whore," Miles growls again. "Can't get enough dick, can you? Let's see how much you can take."

I hear the sound of spitting, then Miles steps close to Alice. He grabs her hips, stilling her on my cock. She howls, Miles grunts, and I realize he's taken her anally. Tears spring to Alice's eyes. She begins to sob as Miles starts to fuck her brutally from behind.

I'd stop the scene, except that Alice cries out suddenly. She begins to shake in the unmistakable signs of an impending orgasm. I can feel Miles' dick through the thin wall of her body, pounding harder and harder. I couldn't move in Alice if I wanted to because the weight of the two of them holds me trapped. Alice squeezes around my flagging cock, hopefully unaware of my situation. If Miles knows at all, he doesn't care. He roars and plunges deeply into Alice's ass, holding her still as he comes. Alice erupts in orgasm when he does, her sobs an odd mixture of pain and excitement.

I get out of there as quickly as I can, resolving never to accept another booking from the couple.

A NEW POTENTIAL client contacts me on Sunday, hoping for a date Wednesday or Thursday. Still shaken by my session with Alice and Miles, I stare at the message for a long time, debating.

Maybe it's time for a break.

I rarely schedule blocks of time off for myself. From the beginning of my escort adventures, I assumed it couldn't last long. I figured that I'd get busted sooner or later, and I'd better make as much money as possible.

When months turned into years, I still resisted the idea of taking a true vacation. Of course there are ebbs and flows in my work. Since I don't do street corners or same-day appointments, frequently evenings arise where I have nothing scheduled. Still, I always try to keep my hand in. I regularly check JD's email account, respond to inquiries, send little flirts to my regulars so they'll keep me in mind.

The idea of a break is still percolating when my phone chimes with the tone for a JD Pierce incoming email. I glance at it, surprised when my heart beats faster at the sender's name.

Nick Ballantine.

I open the email right away.

Hi JD. I know you don't want to chat in depth by email. Is it all right if I call you? I don't want to presume.

Nick

I write back immediately.

Of course. Please feel free to call. I'm not doing anything important today as it is and it would be nice to catch up.

A few minutes later, my phone rings with the same Boston area code and number I recognize. Even knowing who's calling, I answer, "This is JD."

A throaty, bass chuckle on the other end sends a curl of pleasure through my body. "It's Nick, but I think you knew that."

"I didn't want to presume," I tease, happy when I hear an answering laugh. "So, how are you? How's Alethia?"

"We're, uh, good. Really good."

"I'm glad to hear it. By the way, you overpaid me." I'd been shocked to open the envelope at my bank and find ten one-hundred dollar bills. "By a lot."

"Oh." Nick sounds embarrassed. "I figured since the situation was so unusual and we'd made you nervous, you were entitled to hazard pay."

I bark out a laugh. "I got combat pay when I was in Afghanistan, but I earned it there. Believe me, the other night was far from a hardship for me."

"Well, that's good," Nick says, a smile in his voice. "Then let's just say it's a bonus for exemplary service." He drops his tone. "We paid you to make Alethia come. My orgasm or whatever wasn't part of the deal."

Okay, we're going talk about it, I think gleefully. "May it be the first of many."

"Yeah, about that…" Nick falls silent, self-consciousness appearing to defeat him for a moment. I wait, eyebrow raised. "So, uh, Alethia and I have tried since. We tried a lot of things, went back through materials we got from the sex therapist, all that shit. We couldn't, uh, replicate it."

"Oh. Well, have you—?"

Nick cuts me off. "Look, I talked with Alethia and we agreed. That night was so important to us. We'd like to see you again. Maybe, if it happens the same way, we'll be able to understand how to build on it."

"Wow, that's a lot of pressure," I say on a gust of breath.

"I don't mean it that way," Nick says reassuringly. "Maybe it was lightning in a bottle. Maybe the stars aligned and that's the last one I get. I don't know. If it is, that's okay. You gave me one more orgasm with my wife and I can live with that."

"I hope that isn't the case," I murmur sincerely.

"Me too, buddy," Nick says with a chuckle.

I crook my head. *Buddy?*

"The thing is," Nick continues, "Ali really enjoyed it too. You took good care of her, and that makes me happier than I can explain. I know it sounds fucked up. I mean, I'm saying I'm grateful to another man for screwing my wife. But it doesn't really seem like that. You made me feel like *I* was the one loving her. That was as important to Alethia as it was to me."

I swallow hard. Nick's words bring a surge of emotion that I can't explain, except that I feel honored and proud to have helped them. Not just given them a few hours' pleasures, but maybe actually made a *difference.* That's something I've lacked since I got out of the Army. Even though another tour wasn't in the cards for me, I felt a part of something bigger in those days.

"Thank you for saying so," I mumble, hearing the hitch in my own voice. "I'm grateful, that you let me be a part of that. What's between you and Alethia is palpable. I know you can work through any issues together, because of the way you look at each other."

A pause, and then Nick quietly asks, "Will you come over tonight, JD? Or, whenever you're free? Maybe you're right, but for now, we need you."

I inhale raggedly. Here I'd just been thinking about taking some time away. But I touched something powerful, with Alethia and Nick. I feel like I have a purpose, and I like it.

"Okay," I say finally. "What time?"

CHAPTER SIX

A T NINE O'CLOCK, once again I stride to the front desk for the Ballantines' condo building. I've gone more provocative for my outfit this evening—a tight black Henley, black jeans and motorcycle boots. A wide leather cuff wraps around my left wrist.

I don't know why I've decided to change it up, since everything worked so well last week. I just sense that, if I really have something to offer Alethia and Nick, it's in pushing them to explore new ways to be together. Part of that might well be in changing their routine, and getting them into a different perspective on each other.

Tommy the twink-concierge, at least, appreciates the new outfit. His eyes widen as I approach the desk. "Nice to see you again, Mr., uh—"

"Pierce," I say. "JD Pierce. Here to see the Ballantines." I lean an elbow on the desk as Tommy calls upstairs, fully aware of the desire in the kid's eyes.

When Tommy sends me along, he gives a small sigh and says hopefully, "Maybe I'll see you later."

I can feel eyes on my ass as I walk to the elevator bank.

This time Nick waits at the door. He rolls back and away to let me in, scanning my outfit with a raised eyebrow and smirk. "You hitting a club afterwards?" he asks cheekily.

I chuckle. "I just felt like being someone a little different for you tonight." I raise an eyebrow. "Is that all right?"

Nick nods slowly, his grin spreading. He glances at his own polo and jeans, nearly identical to the previous visit. "It's fine. Maybe I need to be someone different too."

Alethia joins us, saying, "You're perfect already, Nick." She looks over my outfit appraisingly, and shares Nick's smile. "I admit, though, that I like this look. Darling, didn't you have a shirt like that one? I seem to recall you drunk in a bar in Ireland, conducting the crowd through a chorus of 'Danny Boy'."

"Couldn't have been me," Nick says, a twinkle in his eye. "I can't sing."

"Too true," Alethia agrees ruefully. She steps over and kisses me on the cheek. A scent of orange accompanies the brush of her lips. "Thank you for coming. It's nice to see you again."

Unexpectedly, she takes my hand and leads me to the seating area, Nick rolling along behind us. "Will you have a bourbon with Nick, or would you like something different?"

"I enjoyed the bourbon. If Nick is having it again…?"

Nick nods, so Alethia scoots off to the kitchen. I hear ice tumbling into glasses. To Nick, I say, "You know, I stopped by a liquor store near my apartment to see about a bottle of your small-batch Eagle Rare. I thought it would be nice to have on hand."

"Did they have any?" Nick asks. "Like the name says, it's rare. A very limited production."

"So I was informed, along with a guess at the cost. I nearly had a heart attack. You're ruining me for something ordinary like Woodford now."

"I like Woodford, too, especially in a manhattan. Believe me, I don't treat myself to the Eagle Rare either."

Alethia hands us each our tumblers, but pauses by where I sit. She offers me her glass of white wine. "Would you like a taste, JD? This is a special wine from Greece, so you may not have had it before."

"Well, thanks." I take the glass from her fingers, enjoying a slight frisson as our fingers meet, and sip the wine. "Ah, that's good," I say appreciatively as I return the glass to Alethia.

"Isn't it? Luckily I know the producer." I see her smile warmly at Nick. "I don't know where in Boston I'd find it otherwise."

"Snob," Nick chuckles. He angles his head for a kiss. She obliges before seating herself, once again opposite me and in reach of Nick. It occurs to me that the three of us form a perfect triangle as we sit. The atmosphere is markedly different from last week. Far more relaxed, with the bantering and teasing. Nick seems calm and certain of himself. Almost…flirtatious.

We chat lightly as we enjoy our drinks, revealing minor likes and dislikes without delving into anything too personal. I still have no idea what either of them does for work. I'd been tempted to do a google search, but I resisted. They're my clients and entitled to privacy. Whatever they want to share is fine.

After all, it isn't like I volunteer details of my life, or even my real name.

Nick and Alethia both turn out to be voracious readers, apparently devouring books like some people eat candy. I get into talking about books with them, since Essie is the only other person I know who shares my passion.

Time seems to fly as we chat. Despite Nick's teasing, Alethia really isn't a snob. She knows the recent popular novels, though her tastes run more toward literary fiction. Nick, however, favors thrillers, action stories, and—to my delight—mysteries. They also both love to binge-watch on Netflix, and Nick tells me animatedly about some of the series they follow.

"*The Crown.* I fuckin' love Clare Foy," he enthuses, moving his body to lean on the right arm of his chair instead of the left. "You watch. She'll be one of those actresses people talk about for years."

"I haven't seen that show," I admit. "I'm a big re-watcher for movies I loved."

"Oh?" Alethia asks as she sips her wine. "What are some of your favorites?"

I flush and chuckle. "I'm embarrassed to admit it in this classy home. I love the superhero flicks. Well, the Marvel stuff anyway. DC movies usually suck."

Nick holds up his hand in a high-five gesture, and I smack it. "My man!" Nick enthuses. "I love those. *Deadpool* was the *shit*."

Alethia gives an exaggerated roll of her eyes. "Oh no. I can't listen again to a lecture on how the superhero movies are a modern update on ancient Greek and Norse myths."

"But it's so clear," Nick says excitedly. "JD, back me here."

"Nuh uh. I'm not getting involved in this. It's bad for business."

Silence falls, and I nearly bite my tongue off. *Shit. What a stupid thing to say.* We'd been having such a nice, relaxed time, and I ruined it.

Nick swallows, glancing suddenly at Alethia. Their eyes meet and I wait for a reaction. Perhaps they'll decide the evening is a bad idea and cancel.

To my relief, Alethia smiles. "You're quite right to remind us, JD.

We asked you here for a reason, and I, for one, am looking forward to it. Nick?"

He nods, and looks again at me. "I'm, uh, sorry if we got off-track. That was my fault."

"Not at all," I say quickly. "I really enjoy talking with the two of you. What I said was graceless and dumb. I apologize."

"Let's move this into the other room," Alethia says, setting her wine glass aside and rising. She holds out one hand for me, and rests the other on Nick's shoulder. He rolls his chair down the hall to the same guest room, Alethia and me in his wake.

Nick's words from earlier in the day echo in my mind. I ponder whether to ask about what they've tried since my visit. Realizing that would more than likely be a mood killer, though, I begin in the same vein as last week.

Though I have a variation in mind I'll bring up, if it feels right.

Alethia removes her dress and loosens her hair, then turns to face Nick and me. She swivels to the left and right teasingly, posing in a scarlet set of panties and bra for our admiration. Nick's shining gaze seems to make her stand taller, and she throws a burning look at me as well.

Noticing again the lack of tan lines, I suddenly guess that Alethia has a slight exhibitionist streak. Perhaps that's an aspect of the prior scene she got off on—having her husband watch her in the throes of sex.

I drop to my heels next to Nick's chair and daringly rest a hand on his forearm. Nick grins uncertainly at me. "You're so sexy, Alethia," I say. "Turn around for us. Give us a show."

With a Mona Lisa smile on her lips, Alethia raises her hands to hold back her hair. She begins to sway slowly to a musical beat only she hears. Her eyes drifts shut as she turns, moving her hips and arching her back.

Lost in her own world, moving sinuously, I find her enchanting. Maybe there's a stripper fantasy buried inside the head of this smart, feline woman I'm growing to admire?

A wild idea pops into my head. It's risky, could throw us out of the mood, but I had good instincts last week. Why not?

I reach into my pocket and pull out some money, a couple of tens and twenties shoved in loosely. I put a few bills in Nick's hand and wink.

"Hey, sexy lady," I call out softly, making my voice rougher. Gruff. "Take off your top. Show me and my buddy here what you got."

Her eyes fly open and she tilts her head curiously. When I'm sure I have her attention, I wave a twenty in the air. "Come on, pretty thing. My buddy and me only got this one night before we hit the road again. It's his birthday, hon. Give him a show."

Nick picks up on it. "Yeah, baby. It's my birthday. If I get to make a wish, I wanna see your tits."

After the slightest pause, Alethia smiles more broadly, then drops her arms and her gaze. Her hair falls around her face as she curls her body and juts out her hip to us. Her eyes gleam through the curtain of her black hair and she again raises her arms to pull it to one side.

Wordlessly, she rotates so her ass is to us. Sweeping her hair over the shoulder, she raises her hands to the clasp of her bra. She pops it open and stays facing away as she lets it drop to the ground before rotating to face us again. Her hands rise to cover her breasts just as they're coming into view, and she smiles at us from under lowered lids.

"You're killin' me," I say gruffly. "So sexy. Show us."

"Show us, sweet thing," Nick says, raising one of the bills I gave him. "Come here and give me my birthday wish."

Alethia dances closer, sleekly crossing the room to us with hands still covering her breasts. When she's less than a foot away, she uncovers them slowly, gliding her hands over her ribs to her taut stomach and then to her hips. Her nipples stand erect as she bends at the waist to pluck the money from Nick's hand and then from mine. She raises her arms and undulates, giving us an eyeful of her tits, as we begged, before slipping the bills into the leg of her panties.

"You just want to watch, boys?" she asks in a sultry voice. "Or did you have something more in mind?"

"I wanna see you blow out a candle," Nick says, surprising me. His voice sounds different, both more confident and more rough. He gives Alethia a lewd look up and down. "My bud here," Nick continues, tilting his head toward me. "His girlfriend dumped him while we was on the road. He needs some cheering."

"Well, that's a shame," Alethia says, vamping in my direction. "A good looking man like you? She's a fool. C'mere, honey." She gestures and I rise to my feet, feeling the scene slide delightfully beyond my control. All I can do is enjoy the ride.

Alethia draws me into her arms and gives me a filthy, wonderful kiss, full of fire and tongue and certainty. I close my eyes and go with it, loving the press of her breasts against my chest and her hands on either side of my head. She takes my earlobes between her fingers and rubs them.

"Aaaah," I gasp, shocked as the pressure goes straight to my cock. I'll have to remember that move.

"This what you had in mind, honey?" Alethia asks Nick.

He nods and says hoarsely, "That's good. That's helping him, I can tell. Will you suck his dick, sweetheart? He's got a nice unit. I've seen it when we take a shower on the road. I think you'll like it."

"Is that right?" Alethia smirks. "I do like blowing on a big…candle. Okay, honey, just for you."

She shoves me until I fall, willingly, onto the edge of the bed. My knees drop open as Alethia crouches between them, her scarlet-covered ass aimed at Nick. She opens my belt and then shimmies my pants and briefs over my butt and to my ankles, where my shoes trap them.

A flash of the scene with Alice and Miles runs through my head, but I chase it away. This is honest and fun, nothing like the buried rage of that couple. My cock juts thick and wet at the head where I've been leaking precome since Alethia's bra came off. These clients of mine have me ridiculously turned on, with their willingness to play the scenes I dream up.

I push against the shaft of my dick, making it stand tall and proud. Maybe I'm not as big as Nick, but I'm still impressive.

"You're right, honey," Alethia coos, looking back over her shoulder at Nick. "That's a pretty candle. I think I want to give it a taste." Then she grasps me at the root and aims my dick at her mouth. She laps at the head, moaning prettily as she licks it clean of the leaking fluid.

"Does it taste good?" Nick asks in a husky voice. "Do you like it?"

"I love it, honey," Alethia purrs, and proves it by swallowing me down. Jesus, I'm not wearing a condom. I'm confident I'm disease-free, but still. Should I break the scene?

Before I can decide, Alethia pulls back her head with a gasp. "Oooh, that's nice, honey. But you know what? For your buddy with a broken heart, I think I need to do more."

"Is that right?" Nick growls. "What ya got in mind?" He leans forward intently, his eyes flicking between Alethia's lips and my cock in her grasp. I can see that he's hard again, that monster dick snaking along the leg of his jeans.

"The best cure for an ungrateful woman is to fuck a willing one," Alethia says. She slides her hand along my dick with a twisting motion that makes me gasp. "You wanna see your friend fuck me, honey?" she asks Nick.

He nods eagerly. "Yeah, he needs it. On the road, all he can talk about is getting a piece of ass. I'm sick of hearin' about it. Give it to him, baby. I'll make it worth your while."

Alethia rises smoothly to her feet and resumes her swaying as she pushes her panties off and steps free. Following the cue from last week, she dangles them before Nick. When he reaches for them she laughs and holds them away before swooping in to steal a kiss. A filthy kiss, every bit the match for the one she gave me. Nick's hands rise to her breasts as they kiss. I love watching them together. It's just beautiful, to see the way they fit. Again, a hunger for both of them rises in my belly.

Alethia straightens until Nick can reach her breasts with his tongue. As I watch, he practically chews at each nipple, alternating with soothing swipes of his tongue.

Suddenly Nick opens his eyes and catches my gaze. He continues to love on his wife's tits even as he seems to be conveying something. Some need.

Alethia's moans reach a fever pitch. She needs attention, the kind I can give. But I have some ideas, too. A way to take back control of the scene and push us all forward.

"That's hot, baby," I call out to Alethia. "My buddy's mouth on your tits. You ready to get this party going?" I grab my dick and shake it at her, playing my crude role for all it's worth.

Alethia looks at me, lazily at first, then with a sharper gaze on my cock. I stand to whip off my shirt, then deal with my shoes and remaining clothes. Fully naked, I move closer to Alethia and work a hand through her black hair. Pulling her face to mine, I plunge my tongue into her mouth, imagining that I can taste Nick on her lips. Her breasts press against my body, the nipples wet and hard from Nick's loving.

Pulling back, I hold Alethia's burning gaze and call, "Hey buddy?"

"Yeah?" Nick answers.

"Don't seem right that me and this hot chick are the only ones in our birthday suits. It being your birthday and all."

Alethia nods to me, getting it. "You're right." Turning back to Nick, she brushes her hand over his polo. "Why don't you take this thing off, honey? Get more comfortable."

Nick hesitates for a moment, but then he shifts and pulls his shirt over his head. His chest is massive and covered in soft-looking dark hair. Freckles scatter lightly across his broad shoulders. I hear a slight groan in the quiet room, and then realize, embarrassingly, it came from me.

Alethia gives me an amused but heated glance. "Your buddy is built."

I nod shakily and extemporize. "I know. Every damn day we have to find a gym in whatever shit town we're passing through so he can work those guns."

Nick blushes at the comments, but he doesn't seem to mind them. He almost preens, squaring his frame, flexing his arms subtly by gripping the wheels of his chair more tightly.

Alethia moves to the bed and lays back. "All this skin has me really worked up. I need some attention, boys."

"What should I do, buddy?" I ask. "I want to get my dick wet in the worst way, but it's your birthday. Your call."

Nick swallows. "Fuck her for me," he says in a low voice. "Show her how we do it."

The quaver in his voice makes me perk my ears. Nick's eyes glint as he watches his wife slide delicate fingers down her mound, through her folds, and then dip inside her pussy. He gives a low moan and leans forward, intent on that hand.

"Oh yeah. That's what I need. Come on, honey. Fill me up." Alethia puts her heels on the bed and raises her knees, spreading her lower lips with her fingers. My cock throbs in anticipation; I know already how good she feels and I'm ready to get back inside.

But first... I crawl forward and, with hands around her thighs, lower my head until I can lick her out. Smacking and rubbing my face against her wetness, I'm rough and crude. She loves it, bucking against my tongue, grabbing a fistful of my hair to control my movements.

"Oooh, like that. Eat my pussy," she moans.

"Yeah, do it," Nick says. "She loves it, you can tell."

I oblige willingly, working every trick I know until Alethia's body begins the ripples I'm already starting to recognize. The shivers build and build until she sobs. She writhes under my tongue, panting and bucking, and then it breaks like a wave all over her body.

When the orgasm releases her, she sags, momentarily exhausted. "That was only Round One, baby," I say with a leer. "We're just getting started." I look back at Nick. "Right, buddy?"

Nick's red in the face again, and his eyes shine as he nods slowly. A trace of sweat glistens on his bare torso, and he clenches Alethia's scarlet panties in one hand.

"You ready to help me out?" I ask. Nick's eyes shoot from Alethia's naked body and to my face. I sense Alethia freeze on the bed as well. "C'mon, buddy, like in Detroit. Remember? I was rocking that chick so hard. I needed you there, holding her so I could really go to town."

"What—?" Nick clears his throat, trying to stay in the moment. "What did I do?" he croaks.

"Remember, you was there on the bed with us. It was so hot. That girl lay against you in your arms while I tore her pussy up."

Come on, Nick. Go along with this. You get it.

Alethia speaks. "That sounds really sexy. Your big arm around me, keeping me still while your friend does what he wants to me. You'd keep me safe if he tried to get too rough, wouldn't you?"

Nick swallows and nods. "Yeah, my bud here gets carried away sometimes. But I can keep him in line for you."

"No shit," I say. "Tough motherfucker like you? I wouldn't dare get outta line. Soon as I sink into that sweet cunt I'm liable to lose control. But with you there? You'll beat my ass if I go too far."

Nerves show on Nick's face as his gaze drops to his denim-covered legs. I already thought about that aspect; I'm not going to push Nick to get naked.

I studied some internet videos after Nick's call earlier today, with a scenario like this in mind. I figure if I ask permission, it'll ruin the mood. Nick's certainly able to transfer himself in and out of his chair but it'll take time. His embarrassment in front of me will kill his boner for sure.

Before I can doubt myself too much or lose Nick's focus, I stand and move to the side of the chair. In a low voice, I ask, "Can you trust me?"

Nick blinks at me, but nods. I slide an arm under his legs, and another around his naked back. I scoop Nick up and pivot him to the bed. Nick only has time to give a shout before I complete the move.

Nick opens his mouth, probably to complain or squawk. Before he can, I jump in. "Shit, buddy. You've put on some weight since Detroit. Next time you can get your own damn self in bed."

Alethia gives a startled laugh, then puts a hand over her mouth. Nick looks back and forth between us, indignantly at first, but then he laughs too. He drops back onto the bed with a chuckle. "That isn't how... Never mind."

"Exactly," I say, grinning. "All that matters is you and me got this hot chick in bed with us. Let's show her how we do it."

Alethia drapes herself across Nick's torso, her bare leg nestling between his still, splayed legs. Discreetly, I adjust them so they lay straight and more naturally. I run my hand up Alethia's thigh and along the side of her smooth ass. Nick's arms curl around Alethia as they kiss, and she grinds her pelvis against his hip.

Nick can't feel it, I know, but he's still hard. That thick cock makes a log along his leg.

In fact, it looks like the angle would be painful, if Nick had sensation. I clear my throat to get Alethia's attention, then tilt my head at his erection. She gets it right away, opening his pants without a word and reaching in to reposition it. Nick gives me an embarrassed grin.

"That's the pride of Seattle in your hands, babe," I say. "Take good care of it or women across the country will weep."

She adjusts herself so her back's to Nick's chest. He brushes his fingers lightly along her arms. The smile he gives me might be out of character, but it's beatific.

Alethia's ready to move the scene forward, though. She spreads her legs again, flashing me with peeks of her coral-colored folds. "Yours is nothing to be shy of, sugar. All that big talk... Are you going to rock me out now?"

"You couldn't keep me away from your sweet pussy," I growl. I retrieve a foil packet from my discarded jeans, tear it open, and roll the condom the length of my cock. Alethia spears her gaze at my erection.

"That's what I want. Come here, sugar." She spreads her arms and legs for me. "Come on and slide into me."

She's just as tight and wet as I remember. I cry out when I'm balls deep as she squeezes with her inner muscles, milking me. I claim her mouth fiercely, brushing her hair back out of her face as I plunge in with my tongue and with my cock. She arches into me, hands on my ass.

I'm completely aware of Nick just inches away. The masculine smell of his skin, of his sweat, blends with Alethia's scent to create the most enticing perfume I've ever experienced. I lift my gaze to find Nick smiling at me from over her shoulder. The heat and excitement in his eyes fires my blood.

I groan into her mouth, deepening the kiss as I thrust and grind my hips into her. I'm intentionally raw and rough in my fuck, staying in character, and it seems to draw out the passion in Alethia as well. She huffs and bucks under me, pulling me deeper with her hands on my ass.

I raise a hand to her tit and find Nick's already there, pinching her nipple fiercely. When I start to withdraw and cede the field, Nick grasps my wrist to stop me. He draws my fingers back to her breast. We work it together, me kneading her flesh as Nick toys with her nipple. Alethia moans and shakes, eyes rolling back into her head as an orgasm rockets through her.

Nick presses his lips to her hair. I can feel his arms tighten around Alethia. He pants and quivers. Calls out his wife's name. Then his jaw clenches, his eyes close, and he shakes through an orgasm of his own. I'm so turned on by feeling them both come that I can't take it anymore. I speed my movements, ploughing into her and filling the condom before Nick's orgasm ends.

Exhausted, I collapse against Alethia's body, my eyes closed as I rest my cheek on her soft breast and try to catch my breath. Her hands on my hips and ass stroke lightly, soothingly, and she croons in my ear. Then a heavier hand settles on my back and begins to move in gentle circles. *Nick.*

I could stay here a long time. Her body is lush and warm, and his touch grounds me in unexpected ways. It's peaceful. I nearly fall asleep that way.

Which of course would be a huge mistake for an escort being paid by the hour.

"I, uh, need to deal with the condom," I say, shifting out of the couple's combined warmth.

When I return from the bathroom, Alethia's eyes have closed. She lays curled into her husband, between his legs, still naked and absolutely lovely. Nick seems to be asleep, a hand woven into her hair, a satisfied curve on his full lips.

Quietly, I dress. I have to assume he can maneuver back into his wheelchair, and I hate to disturb them. They look so peaceful together. So right. Again that feeling of envy makes my heart clench. I want what they have.

Or…do I want to be a *part* of what they have?

Oh no. Surely not.

Blood rushing in alarm, temples suddenly throbbing, I turn away and slip out of the apartment as quietly as I can. Tommy is at the front desk still and looks my direction hopefully, but I just wave and hurry to find a cab.

Only when I'm nearly home do I realize I left without getting paid.

CHAPTER SEVEN

*Good morning. You rock, man. I just wanted you to know that. I hope
we can meet up again.*

Nick

Dear JD,

*Thank you for last night. You left something behind when you slipped
off, though. Can we have coffee at the same café tomorrow afternoon
and I'll bring it to you?*

Truly yours,
Alethia

I STARE AT the emails to JD Pierce on my phone for long moments.
I'm not missing any items of clothing, and I never wear jewelry or a
watch to a client visit. She can only be referring to my payment.

Part of me wants to respond that they overpaid me the first time so
we're even. That isn't exactly discreet, though.

Part of me wants to see Alethia and Nick in the light of day.

Oh, what could it hurt, I reason. *Just a cup of coffee. I shouldn't blow
off five hundred bucks, or potential repeat clients.*

Yeah but... My more rational side tries to warn me away. In the
seven years I've been escorting, I've never identified this way with any
of my clients. I never found myself thinking about them afterward,
unless it was for something practical like planning a session or keeping
in touch with my network of contacts.

*Screw it. I'm a big boy. I'm perfectly capable of dealing with an attrac-
tion to my clients. Or even a little crush.* Before I can argue myself out of
it, I tell Alethia I'll be there tomorrow at three o'clock. Then I send a
short message back to Nick:

Detroit FTW!

The rest of the morning, my resolve wavers. One of the reasons that I've been successful for so long is that I keep the lines between myself and my clients firmly drawn.

I'm also pretty good about easing into conversations, participating in what those around me want to discuss without drawing attention to myself. Particularly when I'm on the arm of a businesswoman like Meredith, that talent ingratiates me. People accept me as a charming friend and don't overtly speculate about what Meredith is doing with a man so much younger than herself.

The fact that no client knows my real name, my background or goals, likes or wishes, is a plus. I can be a blank slate for them, fitting into the fantasy of a dream date or whatever it is they're after for a night.

Realizing that I like Alethia and Nick as people, that I wonder about their real lives, that I'm looking forward to having coffee in the middle of an afternoon—that concerns me. Not enough that I seriously consider cancelling on Alethia, but still, I feel uneasy.

At the gym that day, I drive myself hard as I try to work through my confusion. My trainer Cerise normally gives me shit about slacking. In the middle of a set of kettle bell swings, though, she says, "Whoa, Jasper. Slow down. You're throwing that thing so hard I'm afraid it's going to slip and bean someone."

Panting, I slow my pace for the remaining reps before lowering the bell back to the ground. I swipe at my face with a towel provided by the gym, and then sip at the water Cerise hands to me. "What's with you today?" she asks.

"Aw, nothing," I say. "Just some personal shit that's got me a little on edge."

"Well, I like the fire, don't get me wrong. It's nice to have to hold you back for once instead of kicking your butt into gear. Do you want to talk about it?"

I only grunt. I know I'm on edge, I suspect the reason, but I'm certainly not ready to say any of it out loud. Particularly not to my personal trainer who knows nothing about how I earn my living.

Cerise crooks her head at me until I glance away awkwardly. "Okay. It's none of my business. Now get your ass onto that mat and give me ten physioball passes. You won't hurt anyone if you send the fitness ball flying across the floor."

I MOVE THROUGH my afternoon in a slight fog, reliving the scene from last night. No doubt about it, Alethia likes to be watched. And I like to look at her. I think she let herself go wild that little bit extra because Nick was in bed with us, making it all right for her to take pleasure in what we were doing.

Nick, though. I don't quite know what to think about the look on his face, his hand on my back.

Then I get stern with myself. Nick was just comforting me, letting me know it was all right that I'd fucked his wife. He got off, sure, but he wasn't responding to *me*. It was what happened to the woman lying on top of him that made him come. Like being up close on the set of a porno, I guess. It isn't that Nick wants me; I'm just an actor in the flick. If anything, I probably pissed him off.

I flush as I recall scooping him up like a bag of cement. That was very rude, and I'll owe him an apology the next time we get together.

Next time, I repeat to myself, savoring the words. I wonder what other things I can try to bring them both pleasure. What if…?

A FEW HOURS later, it's time to get ready for this evening's appointment. It's a married couple I've been with a handful of times, allegedly named Will and Cindy Smith. They live in Springfield, Massachusetts, and sometimes come to Boston for one of Will's conventions. I think he's in recycling, or waste management. Whatever, they can afford to hire me.

They have detailed and explicit fantasies, which is great for me because I don't have to put so much effort into planning our sessions. They also pay in advance by Venmo, so commerce doesn't ruin the mood when we meet.

I'm particularly glad tonight, since I'm so distracted. I'm supposed to show up at their hotel suite at ten, dressed in clothes that make me look like a teenager. When I spoke to Will by phone a few days earlier, he teased me that he wasn't going to spell out the scenario because he wants it to feel natural. I'm just supposed to knock on their door and ask for Marcy.

I go commando, and pull on some skinny jeans with rips at one knee. I pick a tight retro T-shirt with the image of a box of Fruit Loops cereal, a ball cap, and dirty vans. I check myself in the mirror—with my slight build, I think I can pass for eighteen or so.

I breeze through the lobby of their usual hotel like I belong there, avoiding eye contact with the security desk people. I spend the elevator ride to their floor trying to get the Ballantines out of my head and into the character of a surly teenager. By the time I knock, I've created a character for myself—who I name Charlie Sorenson, for some reason—and a sort of back-story. Charlie takes Shop, I've decided, and deals a little weed on the side.

At my knock, Will answers the door dressed in a fluffy white hotel bathrobe. He's a big guy, probably about fifty, with the build of a weightlifter who's let himself go a little soft. Thick neck, wide shoulders, and a slight beer belly. It works on him.

"Yes?" Will says, pretending not to know me.

"Hiya. I'm, uh, here to see Marcy," I say, mumbling a bit and looking down at Will's feet in white hotel slippers.

Behind him, I can see Cindy sitting on the sofa in the living room portion of their suite, similarly wrapped in a bathrobe. Cindy's hair is gathered up in a scrunchy, its artificial streaks obvious despite the soft lighting. She has an oval face and a lush, mature body. She also knows some terrifically dirty jokes. I get a real kick out of her.

"Marcy's still in her room, getting ready," Will says, stepping back to let me into the room. "She didn't tell us your name."

"Oh. I'm Charlie. Charlie Sorenson."

Will extends his hand and I take it, shaking limply. "It's nice to meet you, Charlie. Where are you taking our daughter on your date tonight?"

Oh, I get it. Will and Cindy are the naughty parents, planning to seduce their daughter's boyfriend. It's a slightly kinky, borderline-taboo fantasy.

I'm almost relieved; I've had some clients with full-on incest fantasies who wanted me to be a nephew or a son. One couple wanted me to be their baby, and they fed me a bottle and diapered me. No actual sex that time, thank God, though they fucked while I lay there in my oversized bassinet.

"We're gonna hit a movie and then meet up with some friends at the Waffle House," I say, nodding hello to Cindy. "Is Marcy almost ready?"

Cindy pats the couch beside her. "Oh, you know teenage girls. She's probably on the phone with her girlfriends, getting advice about her outfit."

I shift nervously on my feet, in character, then sink to the sofa with a good foot of space between Cindy and me. "Yeah, why do girls do that shit?" I say. "It's just a movie, you know?"

Will pulls a beer from a bucket dripping with condensation and offers it to me. As I take it, Cindy shifts closer.

"Well, you know Marcy. She wants to make sure she's pretty enough for a cute boy like you." She puts a hand on my thigh then, and squeezes lightly.

"Gee, Mrs. Smith. She's the hottest girl in school." I take a swallow of my beer, then add, "I guess she's lucky she looks like her mom."

Cindy coos appreciatively. "Aren't you sweet? My days of turning boys' heads are over, I'm afraid."

"Bullshit," Will chimes in, sitting on the arm of the sofa near me. "You're the hottest mom around, I bet. What do you think, Charlie?"

I mumble, "It's true, Mrs. Smith. A lot of us have noticed you when you pick up Marcy after school. You're really sexy." Cindy demurs prettily. "I mean it. Joe—he's in Shop with me—he's got these really crude fantasies about you. I mean, the things he says he wants to do…"

I pretend to be stricken. "Oh, jeez, I hope that's okay to say. I don't want Mr. Smith to get mad at him or anything."

Will chuckles. "Why would I get mad, that some good-looking boys think my wife's hot."

"How about you, Charlie?" Cindy asks. "Do you ever fantasize about me?"

I take a quick pull of my beer and manage to blush. "Well, yeah. Sorry."

Will drinks from his own beer, then sets it on the table. "Don't stop there, kid. Tell us one."

"Aw, that's really embarrassing. What if I bone up or something?"

Will slides from the sofa arm down to the seat next to me, sandwiching me with his wife. He puts an arm around my shoulders. "Humor an old man. Marcy won't be ready for a long time, I bet. Tell me what you kids think about when you look at my sexy Cindy."

I lean slightly into him, and he squeezes my shoulder. Both of us face Cindy as I say, "You've got a great rack, Mrs. Smith. I think about how much I'd like to have my mouth on your tits."

Cindy pulls her robe open to expose herself. "These tits, Charlie?" she asks innocently. "Are these what you think about?"

I nod, and shift my elbow to brush against Will's cock. He's already starting to get hard. "Yeah. They're just great. I'd like to know what Mr. Smith does with them when you're having sex."

"Oh, he loves to play with my breasts," Cindy purrs. "Don't you, honey?"

Will nods. "Sometimes…," he says to me in a low voice, "I like to slide my dick between them. Feel her squeeze those tits together for me."

"Wow," I gulp, and quickly drink the last of my beer. "I'd sure like to see something like that."

"You would?" Cindy asks. "You'd want to see an old married couple make love?"

"No, I want to have a hot-ass couple like you teach me how to really fuck."

"What do you think, babe?" Will asks. "Should we show this sex maniac how to please a woman?"

Cindy giggles. "He'll just use what we show him on our daughter."

"That's so hot," I moan. "If I could see you two fuck, and then do some of the same things to Marcy… It'd be kind of like you fucking her."

Will's hard as a rock now, totally into the fantasy. I really hope they don't have a daughter named Marcy, but I'm not going to break the scene.

"Come on, honey," Cindy says to Will. "We can give him a little peek, can't we?" She slips off her robe and drops it to the floor beside the sofa. To me, she says, "Come sit here, Charlie. You can see better what Mr. Smith does to me."

Will stands when I do, his cock jutting out of his bathrobe. I glance at it, wide-eyed. "Jeez, you're huge, sir." Okay, he's really just average, but whatever. "I see lots of guys in the showers after gym class, but none of them are hung like you."

I sink to my knees on the floor next to Cindy and she puts an arm around me to draw me in. Will braces one foot on the floor and scoots up until his dick is resting between Cindy's breasts. He takes one in each hand, flicking his thumb over her nipples until she moans and writhes, clutching my shoulder more tightly. When she rolls her head away, he presses them together, making a tunnel that he starts to fuck.

The sight of the head of his cock emerging from between Cindy's tits is hot, actually, and I shift to get my own growing erection positioned better. Will thrusts faster, swiveling his hips, throwing back his head as he mauls her. I almost want to slow him down, help him make it better for both of them, but that's not my role tonight.

"Aw, fuck, that's so sexy," I say breathily, cupping my groin. "I've never done that."

Will grunts and slows. His eyes burning, he asks me, "Would you like to?"

"You mean...do Mrs. Smith like you are?" I ask.

"Cindy won't mind. Will you, hon?"

She pulls me closer. "Of course I wouldn't mind. You say you've fantasized about me. Let's see if I can give you some new things to fantasize about."

Will rises and tugs me to my feet. "Let's get that shirt off," he says brusquely. I raise my arms and he pulls my T-shirt up and off, then tosses it aside. "Nice," he says, staring at my chest.

I kick off my shoes, and hesitate with one hand on my belt. "Should I...?"

"Oh yeah," Will says, then sinks to his knees in front of me. "Here, let me help." Nudging aside my hands, he unbuckles my belt, opens my pants and pulls down my zipper slowly. My erection swings free as Will chuckles. "No underwear. I like it. You weren't going to waste any time getting into Marcy's pants, were you?"

"She won't see us, will she?" I ask, trying to seem nervous, but then flex my dick so it waves hello at Will's face. He gulps audibly, and narrows his gaze to the head of my dick. He licks his lips.

I know everything that's about to happen, from the moment he'll wrap his mouth around me, to the moment I'm inside his wife and he'll sink his cock into my ass.

And then it happens. Suddenly...

I don't want to have sex with the Smiths.

I mean, I like them. We've had a good relationship, respectful scenes, and they're genuinely nice people. Will and Cindy love each other, and they understand they have a common need to bring in the occasional third. They're cool with that. *I've* been cool with that.

Fuck me if I don't feel like I'm cheating on Alethia and Nick.

What. The. *Fuck.*

Will must register the flag in my commitment to the scene as my dick falters before him. *Get your head out of your ass,* I yell at myself. *You can't piss away the money, and they need tonight to work.*

I throw myself to my knees. "Mr. Smith. I can't believe I'm here like this with you," I toss out, trying to save the evening. "I remember when you came to my freshman assembly, talking about your work. You were so fucking hot in your tight black pants and your shirt with the sleeves rolled up. I jerked off twice that night thinking about you."

It's over the top, I know, but I'm desperate to save the mood. I turn to look at Cindy. "What's it like, when he slides his big dick into you? God, I've always wanted to see that. I want to see him eat you out and make you come."

Cindy's hand goes to her mound and begins to rub in circles around her clit. "You'd like to see that, Charlie? You want to see my stud of a husband make me crazy?"

"God, I do," I cry out. "When I fuck your daughter, I pretend we're you guys. I wish I were this big sexy monster like Will, fucking Marcy into a puddle of goo and come and sweat."

Will surges to his feet, rapt in the image I've conjured. "Yeah, boy?" he says, panting. "You want to see what it looks like when a real man fucks his wife until she screams?"

"Sir yessir," I try. "Show me, please. Show me how I should be fucking Marcy so she knows how much I love her and want her."

Will all but throws himself onto Cindy, shoving her knees open with his big hands before he plunges into her. Cindy wails, grabbing her tits and squeezing them as Will begins to pound.

"Oh my God, sir," I pant. "I never knew what it was supposed to be like. You fuck so good. Mrs. Smith, is that nice? The way his cock shoves up into you?"

She cries out, head back. I slide a hand between the rutting couple, find her nub and stroke it with my finger. I'm almost brutal, with the way I rub and pinch her clit, but it only eggs her on. With a sob, Cindy arches her back and convulses.

My knuckles are against Will's belly so I feel him tighten and clench his muscles. "Kiss me," he roars at me, and I do. I rise to my knees, wrap my other hand around his head, and suck in his tongue as he pumps relentlessly and desperately into his wife. He's close, so close, but not quite falling over the edge.

Moving my hand between their bodies, I make a ring of my thumb and forefinger so he's fucking that as well as his wife. I squeeze, Will grunts, but he still isn't coming yet.

I lean forward, swipe my tongue along Will's neck, and then whisper to him, "Marcy will be so happy when I tell her that I'm fucking her like her daddy fucks her mom."

That does it. Will curses and shudders, his rhythm falling apart as he comes inside Cindy. He hunches and jerks, shaking his head violently until sweat flies from his brow. I free my hand and grasp his ass, squeezing and pushing him into her again, until he finally sags in exhaustion.

"Oh, wow," I say, gently, kindly. "You're the coolest fucking parents of all time. I wish you were my dad and mom."

Will collapses on top of Cindy, breathing hard. Cindy rolls her head in my direction, and strokes my hair, her eyes glistening. "What a good son," she mouths, soundlessly.

I have no real idea what their story is, and maybe it's better that way. All I know is, when I usher them into the bedroom of their suite, get them situated under the high thread count sheets, stroke their hair and kiss their foreheads, they both seem content.

CHAPTER EIGHT

I SLEEP BADLY, worried about the effect Nick and Alethia seem to be having on my career. I'm halfway through an episode of *The Crown* on Netflix when I realize I'm watching it so I'll have something to talk about with them. Oh shit, this could be bad.

The next afternoon, carefully dressed in jeans and a casual button-down shirt designed to be worn loose instead of tucked in, I take a seat next to Alethia at an outdoor table. I've lectured myself sternly to keep up the professional walls.

"JD, hello," she says, looking at me with a warm smile that makes my resolve waver. Those hazel eyes shine vividly green today against the emerald top she wears. It's open at the throat. A lovely gold necklace draws attention to the lines of her neck and to the beginning of the valley between her breasts.

"You look lovely," I remark, "but then you're always dressed beautifully."

She smiles a little. "I probably spend too much time on clothes, I know. It's so girly, but my mother used to love to shop and I think it was catching."

"Nothing to apologize for," I say, grinning back despite my unease. I gesture at my own clothes. "I think way too much about it too. There I was, looking at a rack of about fifty shirts in my closet today, and I realized, I may have a problem."

"Whereas Nick finds one shirt he likes and buys ten so he doesn't have to shop with me for another year."

"That explains the constant man-in-black routine then," I say. "He talks like a bro but he dresses like a bouncer at a bar."

Alethia throws back her head and gives a genuine laugh, topped by a snort. She promptly blushes and puts a hand over her mouth. "Oh God. That's so embarrassing."

"Not in the slightest," I reply. "I think it's charming."

She shakes her head, but her eyes dance anyway. A waitress arrives with a pot of hot tea and a cup for Alethia, and I order myself a latte.

"Before I forget," Alethia said. She reaches into her handbag and pulls out a cream-colored envelope. "You left this behind the other night."

I take the envelope but don't open it. Even without looking, I can tell it likely contains ten more hundred-dollar bills. "This is too much," I murmur. "You gave me double the first time as it is."

Alethia leans closer as she pours herself some tea. Quietly, she says, "What you charge doesn't reflect the value of what you've done for us. Please don't fuss."

Reluctantly, I tuck the envelope in the back pocket of my jeans. "All right. Thank you for your generosity."

"No, thank *you*," Alethia says seriously. She opens her mouth to say more but pauses as the waitress returns with my order and a small plate of cookies. We wait until we're alone again, and then Alethia continues.

"What you bring out in Nick seems like a small miracle to me. You can't imagine what it's been like these past few months, watching him grow more depressed and even angry at himself. Of course I hoped when I came to you that such a drastic move would change things. To be honest, though, I didn't expect it to work. If nothing else, I hoped that Nick would realize he didn't want me to enjoy another man's attention."

I nod, unoffended. It had been a solid plan by Alethia. Either this escort referred by Meredith would somehow succeed where professionals had failed with Nick, or she'd put an end to his obsession with seeing her take a lover. "I get all that."

"You've given Nick a shot of confidence that he's been lacking. His health aides, his doctors, his friends…everyone remarks on it. Nick just glows and explains nothing to them." She raises her teacup with both hands, and glances at me over the lip. "And there's what you've done for me. I didn't want to admit to myself how much I missed…well, you know."

I sip at my latte, feeling my ears burn at the praise. My clients are often complimentary in the moment, satiated by an orgasm. I haven't heard such words in the light of day, far from a bedroom.

My voice sounds thick to me when I say, "Believe me, Alethia. It's been a privilege to be there for you. And that isn't something I've ever said to my clients."

"Then you feel it too," she murmurs, making my heart rate ratchet higher.

"Feel it?" I ask.

"There's something special about the three of us together. Nick and I have talked about it quite a bit. Sunday night, after you slipped away, we woke around midnight. We ended up talking for hours more about the role-playing you began, how you guessed things we hadn't even admitted to each other, why it got us excited…" She trails off, then sets her cup on its saucer with a clink. "Other things we might like to try. With your help."

What do I do? I demand of myself as butterflies tickle my stomach unmercifully. Lord knows the gig is good and easy work. But I've already become aware of the strange things I'm thinking about Alethia and Nick, blurring the lines between *client* and…*friend?*

What Alethia said just blurs it further. Every bit of my instinct for self-preservation warns me not to get any more involved. I should thank her but refer the Ballantines to any one of a half-dozen other escorts I know who might work out for them.

That thought produces an immediate feeling of unease. Who do I know who would take the time with Nick to keep him involved? No one. My colleagues would take the money gladly, probably even enjoy banging Alethia, but leave them frustrated as a couple.

Alethia's hazel eyes on mine quietly plead for a response. Self-preservation can go fuck itself, apparently, because I say, "Just tell me when."

She smiles warmly, gratefully. "Wonderful. What about Friday night?"

I consider it. I have an appointment booked, but I can handle that. "Same time?"

Alethia nods but begins toying with the handle of her teacup. She darts a glance at me, then again looks away.

I lean closer, getting her delicate orange perfume again. "Is there something else you want to ask? Maybe a fantasy you'd like me to work with?"

She blushes at the suggestion, but shakes her head. "It isn't that. Besides, you seem to do marvelously on your own. We're happy to follow your lead."

I wait her out, finishing my latte and helping myself to one of the cookies. Finally, Alethia bursts out with what she wants to say.

"Would you be willing to meet with Nick before the three of us get together again? We think, that is, we discussed that, if Nick talks to you about what we've tried, it might occur to you where we're going wrong. Your instincts seem remarkable. Perhaps you can help us see why it doesn't work when it's just the two of us."

She apparently sees the alarm on my face and misreads it. "Of course we'd pay you for your time."

"It isn't that," I say, shaken. "Alethia, it sounds like you need a professional therapist. I'm not qualified in anything like that."

Alethia huffs impatiently. "We've been to therapists. Psychologists. Counselors. None of those so-called professionals had the impact that you've had already. There's a kindness in you I could sense from the first time we met. You treat Nick as a person, not a victim or a project. And that helps me see him too."

Her eyes glisten and she dabs delicately at the corner of one lid. "You can't imagine how different Nick is to before the accident. We've been together almost six years, as I said. We travelled all over the world, in one extreme sport or exotic adventure after another. Nick was huge and wild and magnificent."

She chokes back a sob. "Sometimes...I miss that man. I loved our life together. I still love our life, overall. We're very lucky people, other than his condition. Financial security, professional success, and we really do think of each other as our best friend. I can't help it, though. I grieve for how it used to be."

Tears spill over and she quickly blots her eyes with her napkin. "Oh my God, I'm sorry. What you must think."

I cover her hand with mine. "I don't think anything but the best of you. And of Nick. I see the way you two connect. I know you love him. And you're human. You're allowed to have regrets or doubts or moments where you just want to scream. I told you about my buddy Owen, from the Army. His girlfriend left him because she couldn't deal. But you're still there for Nick, despite everything. And he's there for you."

Alethia sniffles and wipes her cheeks dry. She gives me a tremulous smile. "And you say you're not qualified to help."

I squeeze her hand, then let go and lean away as the waitress approaches uncertainly with our check. She looks wide-eyed at Alethia's face, blotched from crying. "Can I, um, get you anything else?"

I reach for the check. "No, thank you. We're done." I glance at the bill and throw some money into the folio.

"I should get this," Alethia protests.

"You bought last time," I say with a shrug. "Besides, you insist on overpaying me so the least I can do is buy you some tea."

"Will you go talk with Nick?" she asks uncertainly.

I sigh. Already I can't say no to these people.

"Of course. Have Nick reach out and suggest a time."

CHAPTER NINE

T HE NEXT AFTERNOON is a Thursday. At one o'clock, as Nick suggested, I present myself at the concierge desk of the Ballantines' building. Tommy isn't on duty, so the young woman there clears me to go up. My stomach is slightly upset with nerves, and my heart seems to be too loud as I ride the elevator and walk down the hallway.

Nick waits for me at the open door to the apartment again, a grin splitting his face. My heart thumps oddly when I look at that handsome face, dark tousled hair, and broad chest. God, I'm pathetic.

"Hi JD. Thanks for coming over like this," he says enthusiastically.

My unease begins to fade away because I apparently find it impossible to be uncomfortable around this open, engaging man. I rest a hand on his shoulder and squeeze. "Of course. Alethia is a hard woman to say 'no' to."

"Don't I know it," Nick says with a chuckle. "I figured out early on that she had my number, so I stopped resisting. What was the point? Ten minutes after I met her, I would have brought her the moon if I could."

He rolls his way into the kitchen, with me following behind. Platters with grilled chicken breasts, salad and a pasta dish spread across the marble surface, next to white china and silverware. "Chloe just delivered this so everything should still be hot," Nick says. "She's our cook."

"You didn't have to go to this trouble," I protest. "I usually just eat a sandwich for lunch."

Nick eyes my tight shirt and jeans. Okay, so I dressed sexily for him. Sue me.

"Come on," he says. "You obviously work out a lot and watch your diet."

I return the frank appraisal. It'd be awkward, if we hadn't already seen each other naked. Well, partially naked in Nick's case.

"How about you?" I ask, taking advantage of the opening. "You don't get a body like that without serious time lifting."

Nick grins shyly. "I hit the gym in the building almost every day. There's this physical therapist we hired who used to be a competitive body builder but now specializes in paras. He beats me to shit every day but I love it. I've put on two inches on each arm and four on my chest since he started."

"That's amazing. I'm a hard gainer when it comes to muscle." I gesture at my body. "I can maintain as long as I watch what I eat. But I don't have a frame like yours. I'm not sure I could add much bulk."

"Maybe some time you'd like to come work out with me and Billy," Nick suggests. "He'd take one look at you and tell you exactly where you could go with your body if you wanted to."

I'm hit all over again with the strangeness of the situation. Not only am I having lunch with a client, but the client is inviting me to work out.

The bitch of it is, I want to do it.

"Maybe," I answer neutrally and pick up a plate. "Well, thank you for the lunch. This looks great, though I think there's enough to feed a small army." Only when I bend to get a grilled chicken breast do I realize the counter is a little lower than usual. Glancing around, I now see that all the kitchen surfaces are slightly low, which is why I didn't register it before.

"Oh," I say before I can think about it. "Sorry," I stammer to Nick. "I just didn't notice earlier."

"It's cool, right? Alethia found a designer to redo the apartment while the building was still under construction. He specializes in people in chairs like me. He made lots of changes, like the extra-wide hallways, space to turn my chair, all the bullshit that goes with this. The coolest mods were so I can use the kitchen. Watch this shit."

Beaming, Nick presses a button under the lip of the kitchen island. The entire unit sinks several more inches into the floor, until Nick can easily reach for a plate and food. He loads his with three chicken breasts, a huge mound of pasta, and a generous salad.

I'm thunderstruck. "That's amazing." I can't even guess how expensive something like that must have been to design, engineer and install.

"All the cabinets and counters can raise and lower like this," Nick says. "Bathroom too. We've had a bunch of shit adapted for me, like a tub where I can latch my chair in and swing myself easily into and out of the water."

"Hey, I want to apologize for the other night," I say suddenly. "The way I picked you up. That probably wasn't all right with you, but I didn't want to break the scene."

Nick blushes and looks at his plate. "No worries. I can do it myself, but it does take some time to get my legs situated." He glances shyly at me. "Actually, it was kind of hot to be thrown around like that. A big guy like me? That's never happened before. But you asked me to trust you, and so I did."

I feel I'm blushing too. "Good. I'm glad it's not a problem. Next time I'll ask in advance."

"Next time," Nick grins broadly at me. "I can't wait to see what you come up with."

"Lord, you and Alethia like to put the pressure on me, don't you?" I huff in pretend annoyance.

"Nah, just keep those creative juices flowing and it's all good. That was…" Nick breaks off and swallows hard. He puts his plate on his lap and rolls to the dining room table, parking at a space with no chair.

I have no idea what that's about, but all my doubts and insecurities begin a parade through my stomach. *He wants to tell me to back off, to refer them to someone else, to stop ogling him…* The brass band of my nerves accompanies me as I bring my plate and sit at Nick's elbow.

Two glasses await us, which he fills from a pitcher of ice water. He starts to eat, then puts down his knife and fork decisively, like he's resolved something during the short pause. I clench involuntarily.

"No, you know what?" Nick bursts out. "I refuse to be embarrassed or shy about what we're doing." He stares into my face. "The way you got me into bed with the two of you and made me a part of it. That was fucking hot. Ali loved it, and I was so turned on watching you pound into her that I could barely see straight. The role-play helped too, because I could forget for a little while that she was my wife. I really let myself believe she was a hot stripper, you were my buddy on a road trip with me, and we did that shit together all the time."

I look down at my plate, shaken. Inspired to honesty by Nick's frankness, I mumble, "I really enjoyed it too." I cover my confession by taking a bite of chicken and pushing around my salad.

We eat quietly for a while. I finish while Nick is still on his second chicken breast, watching in amusement as he consumes the entire plate of food. "I can't believe you scarfed every bit of that."

He wipes his mouth with a linen napkin, and takes a sip of water. "You don't want to mess with Billy. When he tells you to eat two hundred grams of protein a day, you better believe he's going to make sure you did."

"Fuck, that's a lot of food," I say, amazed.

He gestures at himself. "Hey, you like the results, right? It takes fuel to keep this carcass going."

It's the first time Nick has acknowledged that he's aware of my attraction to him. Well, the man says he isn't going to be embarrassed so I take the bull by its metaphoric horns.

"Does it bother you? That I'm turned on by you?" I ask.

He sucks in a breath and his cheeks redden. "That's direct. But it's a fair enough question. Honestly? No. I get off a little on that." He nervously sips some more water.

"Actually, I think it's part of why this works," he continues, waving a hand vaguely in space between us. "You're a stranger, or you were, and you find me attractive despite—" He gestures at his legs. "You didn't know me before everything. My family, my old friends, even Alethia…I can tell they still see the man I was. They think about Cannon—that's what my friends started calling me in college when I got up to some crazy shit. I'd do a cannon ball off a roof into a pool, stupid crap like that."

"Yeah, that's why they called you Cannon," I scoff. "I've seen your junk, remember."

Nick blushes and shakes his head ruefully. "Anyway, they remember Cannon. When they see me now, they can't help comparing the two. And then *I* can't forget what I looked like. *I* remember what it was like to throw myself off a bridge with a bungee cord, or spin out in an ATV or whatever."

Bitterness creeps into his voice. "I had every-fucking-thing on a platter, JD, and I threw it away. Rock climbing. Is that some stupid-ass shit or what? Rich, beautiful wife, great job and friends, travel whenever and wherever we wanted to go… Wasted, because I thought I could handle this one cliff."

For the first time, I see the version of Nick that Alethia told me about, the depressed one. I suddenly guess that the reason none of the photos in the room show people is probably that Nick can't stand reminders of himself in prior days.

"Hey, buddy," I interject softly. "Look at me." I wait until Nick lifts his gaze. The pain I see in those brown eyes breaks my heart. I have no way to talk him out of his depths, don't have the training or background about his life to change his mind. All I can do is embrace the role I serve in the life of the Ballantines. "You're one hot-ass motherfucker. I swear to God, I wish you were bisexual because I'd be all over you like honey on bread."

Nick blinks at me, probably surprised at the declaration. It does seem to help though. His troubled expression clears, and some of his cockiness tries to resurface. "Yeah? You want a piece of this?" he mugs wryly, flexing a bicep.

"In a New York minute," I say firmly. Nick regards me steadily, and the slight smirk on his face dies away again. He lowers his arm, but never lowers his eyes from mine.

"You really mean it, don't you?" he asks solemnly. "It's not an act, for a paying client."

"Yes, I mean it. You and Alethia, both. You're two of the sexiest people I've ever been with, hooking or otherwise." He reddens, but I'm going to take him at his word about not being embarrassed. "It's what I am, Nick—a hooker. I've been with a lot of clients, in a lot of scenes. I've made good money because I listen to people and I hear what they *aren't* saying they want, and that's what I give to them."

Danger, Will Robinson, my brain screams at me. *Stop it now. Get out of here.* Nick says nothing, just keeps his eyes fixed firmly on my face.

I continue, heedless of the alarm bells in my head. "It's what I do with the two of you as well, but it's different. I get so into it, so into *both* of you, that it doesn't feel like a job. It feels like we're friends, making each other feel good."

"Feel *great*," Nick whispers, so softly that I barely hear him. He clears his throat and says more normally, "I'm glad. We've talked about it too, Ali and me. There's energy when you're with us. I think that's why I get off when it's all of us, and I can't manage when you're not here."

I take a deep breath. What Nick brings up is why I'm supposed to be there, not to flirt. Shakily, I say, "Alethia mentioned that you'd like to talk about the situation between you, to see if I have any insight."

He blinks and nods. "Yeah, okay. Let's go sit in the living area. Don't worry about the plates and stuff. The housekeeper will take care of that when he arrives in an hour or so."

I follow Nick and take what's becoming my usual place on the sofa. He stays close to me, as close as he usually sits to Alethia, his knee in arm's reach. His hands dangle in his lap.

He glances at me, shy despite his earlier declarations. "I guess it's too early in the day for a shot of whiskey," he observes with a small, crooked smile. "But I could use one."

"I don't mind. Want me to pour?"

Nick directs me to a liquor cabinet, then to the tumblers. I find ice and make us each a small drink. I figure having something in his hands might help with his nerves.

Plus the bourbon really is hella good.

Back in my seat, I sip my drink. Nick tosses his down, and then toys with the glass between his hands. "So, uh…" he begins, "I'd like to talk about what we've tried. Usually we go through this stuff with a therapist of some kind or another. I feel like I have to say 'penis' and 'vagina' and whatever. Can I…can I just talk to you like a buddy?"

I say firmly, "I hope I'm your friend now, whatever else is going on. Role-play if it helps. We're two guys sitting in a bar, strangers if you want. In fact, I'm the bartender."

I get up unasked and pour another small measure of bourbon into Nick's glass. Resuming my place, I husk my voice with a thick Southie accent and ask, "You here for the convention?"

Nick quirks a small grin, but he goes along with it. "Something like that. Plus I needed a little break from my girlfriend."

"Ah, woman trouble. Keeps the liquor flowing and guys like me employed. Wanna bounce it off me? Is she cheating on you?"

"God, no," he huffs. "The problem is me. I can't satisfy her."

"You ain't the first man to feel he ain't givin' his woman what she needs. What does she want you to do? Some kinky shit?"

"She likes handcuffs sometimes. We never really talked about more."

I'm surprised, and I file the information away for future use. Alethia in cuffs…that could be very hot.

Hmm. Or maybe it's Alethia who likes to use the cuffs on Nick.

The embarrassed look on his face reminds me that's something to explore at a better time. In my accented voice, I say, "So tell me about it. What's your playbook?"

"Well, I eat her out. No problem. I love doing that for her, and it really gets her hot."

"Good start. Not enough men like to go downtown. What else."

"Fingers."

"A' course. You can get a lot done with a thumb and index finger."

"It gets old, though, when she's used to the real thing."

"And that's a problem?"

Nick swallows hard. "Can we stop this game, JD? I get it, but I'm ready to just talk."

"Sure." I revert to my normal voice. "I've seen you though, Nick. I know you get hard."

"I do, but I don't feel anything there. We've tried having Alethia ride me anyway, but it gets frustrating for both of us. I can't respond, or move my hips. She feels like she's using a dildo, or that she's just using me." Nick flushes and looks away.

"Do you feel like she's using you?" I ask softly when the silence grows.

"Not exactly. It's more…" He breaks off again and chews his lip. I wait him out as his face grows red.

Finally, he bursts out, "I'm dead below the waist. You know? To me, it's all dead. She puts this appendage inside her but I hate her to touch it that way. It sullies her."

Dead? Oh God. I freeze at the dark image Nick presents. Once again I've blundered into a topic I'm not qualified to handle. *Think, asshole. Say something,* I order myself.

The silence builds painfully. Nick sips his drink, then mutters, "Anyway, that's what I think about, and that's a boner killer right there."

Tentatively, I lay a hand on his knee. "But you aren't dead. Your blood is flowing. Your legs are warm. I can feel it right now. I've seen you get hard. There's this vibrancy that flows out of you from everywhere. Just because you can't feel your cock doesn't mean it isn't there and full of life."

Nick just stares at me, his mask of control crumpling to reveal his sadness and desperation. "I wish you'd known me before the accident," he says, so softly I almost miss the words. "As soon as I fell that day, I think I knew what had happened to my legs. I woke up after surgery, and Alethia was leaning over me, crying and trying to smile. I felt so bad for doing something that stupid, because I knew what it meant for Ali's life after that. I wished for a while that I had died in the accident because she could grieve and then move on. Now she has to see this reminder all the time.

"What we had before? That was life. This—" he gestures at his chair "—is some kind of purgatory for both of us."

I give a sound of protest, but I don't know the right thing to say. All I know is that I hate to see the strongest man I've met swamped by his fears. I reach to find something—anything—to distract Nick from his morbid turn.

"I'm really glad you didn't die, and I got the chance to know you. Alethia loves you, man. There's no way she'd be better off without you."

Nick tries for a grin, but it falters. "She tells me that too. I couldn't have gotten through those first weeks without her. Every day, in the hospital with me, refusing to let me give up. She helped me hang on until I—" He drops his head and chuckles wryly. "I was going to say, until I found my feet. Shit, that's a cliché that doesn't even apply anymore."

"Until you found your strength," I supply, and he nods. "I don't pretend to know what you've gone through, but you give off such positive energy. I could feel it even when we talked on the phone that first time."

Nick shifts his arms restlessly. I figure I've said the wrong thing, and take his gesture as a cue to withdraw my hand. He surprises me by seizing it in his big, rough grip and keeping it on his knee.

I go for a change in topic. "Have you tried toys?" I ask. "Some people completely get off on those."

Nick clears his throat and admits in a rasp, "We've tried a bunch of different things. Dildos, vibrators, Ben Wa balls. It's not bad, and sometimes she can come with those."

He meets my eyes with his own brown ones swimming in tears. Desperation shades his words. "I *know* her, JD. At a gut level. I can tell Ali's not getting what she needs from me. It's crass but she needs a big, live, warm dick thrusting away at her." He looks away, shame and misery wracking his body. We sit in silence for long moments, while Nick gets himself under control.

Still connected by the hand holding mine on his knee, I have a thought. Softly, I say, "It sounds like you've put all your emphasis on Alethia's orgasms, and her needs. What about yours?"

Nick flushes and looks at our joined hands. "I don't know. The therapists talked about 'finding new pleasure centers' for me or some horseshit like that. Stroking my earlobe. Pinching my tits. Whatever." He falls silent again, but my instincts ping.

Cautiously, I say, "Nick, I'm an ex-grunt, and a current whore. I may just be talking out of my ass here. You get that, right? Could it be that the reason the three of us work is I take the pressure off you to please Alethia, and that gives you freedom to connect with your body? With these other pleasure centers the pros are talking about?"

Nick's expression morphs slowly from anguish to puzzlement and then to consternation. "You think? I don't know. Somehow, it sounds all new age-y. Like, if I get my chakras stroked the right way, I'll have a tantric orgasm."

I huff a laugh. "Fuck if I know. I'm just trying to talk it out with you."

He squeezes my hand. "I know. And it really is helping." He falls silent again, but I watch his eyes shift and narrow as he thinks about what I put out there.

Gradually he begins to nod a little. "You know, I can almost see that. When you're inside Ali, I'm remembering what she feels like around *my* dick. How tight she is. How wet. I hear the moans you bring out and I'm thinking, 'That's right, you like that'."

He looks up, his alert expression pinning me. "That first time, when you had me tell you what to do. I could imagine it was my hand, my tongue. I could *see* it, and you did just what was in my head, like you were in here with me." He crooks his head, "Or like I was in her with you. We were sharing her body and that got me so fucking turned on I almost couldn't stand it. And you're right. I wasn't worried about her because I knew you had it covered. I just let myself imagine and feel."

"What was it like?" I ask gently. "The orgasm. You said it was different, but can you tell me more?" I cross my leg, trying to hide the erection that's grown at Nick's words. It is *so* not the time for me to get a hard-on.

Rapt in his own memories, Nick seems not to notice. "It sounds dumb but…it came from my heart. I mean, when I felt the orgasm, I was just so fucking *happy* that Alethia was getting what she needed. It just built and built in my heart. It felt too big for my body. I wanted to yell or scream or kiss or jump off a rooftop. I couldn't contain it, and then when you popped off…" He freezes, suddenly embarrassed. He shifts and tries to withdraw his hand but I'm too quick.

I flip my palm over and twine Nick's fingers in mine. "Don't stop now," I encourage. "When I popped off…"

"Jesus, you were beautiful. Both of you. I could see the muscles of your back and your ass rippling while you went at her. I knew she was doing that thing where she squeezes her pussy around your cock and I was so glad you got to feel that. And the look on her face. I know that look and how good she felt at that moment. I was just…"

He looks down, as scarlet as Alethia's panties. In a near whisper, he says, "I was so in awe of both of you at that moment. Then you took my wrist, connecting us. It was only my wrist but I'd never been touched like that by a man. Your fingers kind of twitched, and electricity from them shot somewhere deep inside me. You came, and you made me come."

I lean away, stunned. My hand slides off Nick's knee and dangles uselessly. I have absolutely no idea what to say, or what any of it means. Is he saying that he liked my touch sexually? Or just that it helped him feel closer to his wife? The confusion threatens to make me back away, even if just long enough to go to the bathroom and splash water on my face.

Nick probably feels my turmoil. He can't look at me anyway. "It's dumb. I know that. I'm just telling you what it felt like."

"It isn't dumb," I say quickly, then fall silent. Is this what Alethia meant when she spoke of the special feeling among us? Has Nick told her what he's said to me, and was she gauging my reaction? Does it even mean anything, or is it just endorphins and release confusing Nick? I need to say something, but find myself speechless.

When the silence has stretched uncomfortably long, he begins to roll his chair away, muttering, "The housekeeper will be here soon."

My blood throbs in my temples. I rise to follow to the kitchen island, where he goes through the motions of straightening out our lunch platters. He avoids my gaze, though, and his ears are still red.

"Nick," I hear myself say. I crouch next to the chair. He looks at me, then away again. "What about the second time, when you were in bed with us?"

The long pause makes me wonder if he'll answer. Finally he admits, "It was even more intense. Ali was laying on me, and I could feel your rhythm through her body. When you got close, when it changed, it just magnified everything for me. I was so fucking *proud* of you, for being such a good man to my wife. I was so proud of her for taking her pleasure. That huge feeling just had to go somewhere, and it pulsed through me like I came. Even better than the first time. My heart was full and I felt this...well..."

He can't finish, but I'm terrified I've guessed what Nick is trying to say. *Love?*

My brain screams at me to get out, to get away, before I fuck this couple's life beyond repair. Something is happening that's completely beyond my experience or ability to process. I don't have the first clue at how to translate what I'm hearing into any kind of advice or guidance.

Nor am I prepared to think about my own feelings. I'm a paid employee. Anything more is...out of the question.

What will happen, if I refuse to see the Ballantines anymore? Will Nick and Alethia figure out how to use what they've experienced with the help of some other man? Someone more qualified to help them?

A hot burst of jealousy flares at the thought of anyone taking my place.

For fuck's sake, I've only been with them twice. This is...transference or some shit like that. Nick's confused. Hell, *I'm* confused.

He still hasn't turned to look at me. He murmurs in a low voice, "I guess this was a mistake. I shouldn't have said anything." The sadness and desolation I hear in his tone make my heart ache. "I'll tell Alethia that you won't be joining us tomorrow. It's okay, JD. I know I unloaded more than you were prepared to hear."

"Jasper," I say, before I plan it.

Nick rolls around to face me, head crooked. "What?"

"My name," I say hoarsely. "I go by JD Pierce with my clients. My real name is Jasper Dylan."

Nick and I look at each other for a long moment, neither of us saying another word. Nick nods slowly. Hope edging his tone, he asks cautiously, "Will we see you tomorrow evening, Jasper?"

Against all reason, I agree.

CHAPTER TEN

I MOVE THROUGH the rest of the day and evening in a sort of daze. The intensity of Nick's experience terrifies me. The *responsibility* it places on my shoulders… I don't know how to deal with that. I should probably cancel, and never see the Ballantines again.

At least, not until I have time to go to college, get a degree in psychology, and understand what the *fuck* is happening.

Because it clearly isn't just happening to Nick. Alethia, in her own restrained but passionate way, made a point of letting me know that they both think something special has occurred. Maybe for her it's just knowing her husband is finally moving forward sexually, and wanting to continue that as long as possible.

The way she'd opened to me, though. Her guilt and her shame. I'd lay money that isn't something she does often.

None of my clients have such a personal reaction to me. They enjoy my services, maybe even share a drink with me before hitting the bedroom, but in the end, it's always a business transaction. I gave my attention, my imagination and my cock in exchange for cash. The morality of my career choice has never bothered me for a moment. It's my body, I'm going to fuck anyway, and the fee is always something my clients can spare. And when I leave after an evening's fun, everyone goes on with their lives.

What Nick and Alethia want from me seems to be more than orgasms. It's connection, healing, growth. Perhaps even emotion. Now *that* revelation makes me begin to question my morality for the first time. I don't know how to feel about putting a price on those things, especially because I think I've been *lucky* rather than *good* for them. I just guessed what Nick might enjoy, and at how to amp the eroticism of what we do together. The immediate results appear to be very positive, given what Alethia says about Nick's confidence. For fuck's sake, I can see it for myself. The openness with which Nick talks to me about things that shake him soul-deep reveals his bravery and his trust.

But couldn't it just as easily go FUBAR the next time? What if I guess wrong, and steer them into a scene that devastates Nick, or Alethia? I can't bear the thought of hurting them accidentally. The smart thing to do would be to quit the relationship while I'm ahead. Nick is on an upward swing. Alethia is learning again to see her husband as he is now—as a sexually vital partner—rather than through her memories of a fundamentally different man.

With the best will in the world, I don't know how I can do more for them. All I can do is damage or set them back.

A reminder chimes on my phone, prompting me about the appointment I've already scheduled for tomorrow evening with another client. In my fog, I forgot to cancel. It's the perfect excuse, really. I can email Alethia and Nick, tell them I've overlooked a previous commitment so I can't come to their place. When they ask to reschedule, I'll put them off until they get bored of waiting and move on.

Yes. That's *exactly* what I should do.

I begin tapping out the email to them, polite as I would be to any client. *So sorry, already promised, too late to find a substitute…*

Then I flash on Nick's reaction when he opens the email. I can see that expressive face, those big brown eyes, crumpling in disappointment. He'll see it as rejection, I'm sure, and beat himself up for saying too much at lunch. Alethia will cover her own regret by tending to Nick, but she too will be hurt.

I hit the back arrow key, wiping out my escape route one letter at a time. Instead, I contact a colleague, Cliff, who has a similar style to mine, and ask him about swapping in for the new client. It's a couple I've never worked with before, in Boston for an anniversary weekend and thrill-ride. The husband had contacted me based on a referral. Cliff will do as much for them as I could. Fortunately, he's available.

I text the husband then, claiming an emergency has arisen, and explaining my solution. I vouch profusely for Cliff's looks, skill and honesty—all true. Then I suggest obliquely that I'm willing to pay half the agreed-upon fee to Cliff to apologize for the inconvenience. The client replies shortly, indicating no objection.

Well, that solves one problem. The looming matter of what to do with the Ballantines, though, remains a worry through a restless evening. It drives me out of my apartment eventually, and I wander the streets, thinking. Passing my diner, I spot Essie through the window, pouring coffee. I go in and grab a booth.

"Well, stranger," Essie says when she shuffles over. "Ain't seen you for a week, and now you're here at the wrong time of day. Next thing you'll ask me for a menu."

"No menu. Just coffee and maybe—" I look over at the counter, "—a slice of that apple pie."

"Is it the end days?" Essie asks, laughing. "I ain't never seen you take a bite of dessert."

I chuckle along with her, and look around. Most of the booths are empty. "Can you join me for a cup?"

"Why not? Boss complains, I'll tell him it's the end of the world so I'm takin' five minutes to get my soul right." Chortling quietly to herself, she retrieves my pie and comes back with two mugs as well. She sinks into the booth opposite me with a groan. "Lord, it feels good to rest my feet."

"Have you worked here long, Essie?" I ask as I stick my fork into the pie. I moan at the taste of apples, cinnamon and sugar. "Oh, that's good. I'd almost forgotten."

"I been here goin' on thirty years," she says. "Never planned it. I just kept comin' in day after day. Next thing you know, I'm gettin' notices from the Social Security Administration, and thinkin' about retirement."

"Yeah? Where would you go?"

"I got me a daughter in Miami. She and her husband bought a nice place a few years back. They have two girls, ten and twelve, so I don't think I could stand to live with them. The texting alone is like to make me lose my mind. No, I'll probably get me a little place close enough to visit but far enough that they can't ask me to babysit every day."

"You're a smart one," I say. The idea of waking in twenty or thirty years, finding that I've spent my life doing one thing, never seeing what else I might be able to accomplish, suddenly makes me restless. "Actually, Essie, you're really smart. Did you never want to do something else? I don't mean to knock waitressing. I just wondered."

"Oh sure," Essie replies, taking a sip of her coffee. "A chance for something would come my way, though, and I never seemed to recognize it in time." She watches me scrape the last of my pie from my plate as she thinks. I can almost see regrets swim in her face. Essie shakes her head to herself, and asks, "You thinkin' you want to try some other line?"

I chew and swallow as I think about it. Finally I say, "What I do now can't go on forever. Maybe I should leave it while I'm ahead. The thing is, I have no idea what else I might be able to do with my life. I never did know."

"Well, you like to read. You're good with people. That's at least a place to start."

THE PROBLEM WORRIES at me all night. My concerns over the Ballantines get muddled with my growing sense that time's running out on my luck as an escort. I've had it good for a lot of years, but bad scenes like the one with Alice and Miles gnaw at me. Even what Will and Cindy wanted squicked me out, apart from the fucked-up feeling that I was cheating on Nick and Alethia. I don't know how much longer I can—or should—keep doing this. Holding those sessions against what I've shared with Alethia and Nick just makes me more confused and keeps me from sleeping.

Cerise pushes me hard at the gym on Friday, ignoring the circles under my eyes. "Best thing for a hangover," she crows as I grumble.

"I'm not hung over."

"Well, whatever's got you wimping out here needs to stop. You pay me to push your limits, and I can tell you're just going easy on yourself today. That shit wouldn't have flown when you were in the Army, would it? 'Sarge, I'm a little moody today. I think I'll just hump my pack a mile or two, call it a day. Okay?'"

I laugh despite my crappy mood. "Yeah, I'd get latrine duty for that, if I was lucky."

"Then let's try a carrot-and-stick approach. If you give me ten *real* barbell curls with a weight I know you can handle, I'll give you a pass on crunches today. But if you give up before ten, you're cleaning the toilet in the staff locker room."

I groan but nod. "Load me up then." Cerise bustles around the weight rack, setting the curl bar to ninety pounds. "Holy shit. I can't lift that twice, let alone ten times."

She smirks at me. "I say you can. Who are you gonna believe? Your awesome trainer or your wimpy, piteous self?"

"Fine," I sigh. "When the vessels burst in my biceps and you have to call an ambulance, my blood type is B-positive."

I heft the bar, elbows tight at my waist, knees slightly bent and core locked. Curling the weighted bar, I'm surprised when it moves in a smooth arc. By five reps, I'm groaning but I'm not done. I pause at the top of my eighth rep, arms burning, sure I can't finish.

"The toilet looked especially nasty this morning," Cerise says thoughtfully. "I think one of the trainers must have had the runs, because it was literally everywhere…"

"You bitch," I moan, completing the rep and starting the ninth. "I hate you."

"Naw, you think I'm awesome. You wish you were as strong as me." I couldn't eke out a laugh at this point to save my life, but I finish the tenth rep.

"Fuck," I spit out as I return the bar to its rack. Shaking out my arms, I complain, "That was just cruel."

"Got you out of your head, didn't it?" Cerise asks with one eyebrow raised. "See? I'm all that and then some."

"You're a marvel of a trainer," I say sarcastically. A thought strikes me. "Hey, you get close to a lot of clients, right? Did you ever have anyone start to feel *too* close?"

"Are you about to ask me out? Or go stalker on me? Because I swear—"

"I don't mean *me*, Ego-tina. I just wanted to know how you'd handle something like that."

She regards me thoughtfully as I sip at my water bottle. "Yeah, once or twice. You get to talking to a client while you're pushing him, sometimes it can get confusing. He might think your interest in him is more personal, and he might mistake a touch to adjust his stance as an invitation to touch back. Easiest thing is to just say you can't work with him anymore, and get a new trainer assigned."

I wince. That isn't what I want to hear, even though I know already it's what I should do with the Ballantines.

"Does it ever go the other way?" I ask. "Have you ever been the one who got confused about a client? Felt too much?"

Cerise chuckles at me. "You could say that."

"Well, what happened?" I prompt eagerly. "How did you deal with it?"

"I married her."

ADDING TO MY consternation, Tommy frowns slightly as I approach the reception desk that evening at nine. "Hello, Mr. Pierce. Back again?" the twink asks with a quick glance at his watch.

Uh-oh. I make a mental note to mention to the Ballantines that I'm being too consistent in my arrival time, and their nosy concierge is aware of it.

Perhaps I can deflect the suspicion. Resting an elbow on the desk, I smile. "Maybe I just know that you'll be on duty."

The flirt seems to hit home because Tommy smirks slyly. "I only work Tuesday to Saturday, afternoons and nights." His eyes run over my chest, this time covered in a fitted, long-sleeved silk shirt, tucked into a pair of trousers that hint at my package.

As I'd dressed for the evening, I worked out a story about all of us being in Las Vegas for my bachelor party. Nick would be my best man, and Alethia the girl he'd hired to give me a proper send-off. She really seemed to get behind the exhibitionist fantasy…

Tommy still stares at me expectantly. I raise a brow and say, "Good to know. Sundays are a nice day to be off, aren't they? Lazy afternoons…"

I trace a finger across the desk surface and watch Tommy swallow. "Can you buzz them for me?" I ask in my lower register.

That makes Tommy widen his eyes. Without breaking my gaze, he reaches for the house phone and gets Alethia's permission to send me along.

I give Tommy what I intend as a look of promise before patting the desk surface and sauntering away. I wonder idly if I should give Tommy a quick lay, but reject the idea almost as soon as I think it. It would just lead to different problems. Besides, I have no real interest in sleeping with Tommy anyway.

And somehow, it would feel disloyal, to distract the Ballantines' concierge with a random fuck. An odd thought for a whore, but there you are. I sigh to myself as the elevator rises.

The apartment door stands open when I reach the top floor, but for a change, no one greets me there. I peek in carefully to see Nick preparing some kind of drink in a blender at the lowered counter. Alethia appears in the hall and gestures for me to enter. I close the door behind me as she approaches to kiss my cheeks.

"Lovely to see you," she says. "Come, have a seat. Nick felt like playing bartender tonight."

"Can't imagine where I got the idea," Nick says to me with a wink. "Do you like margaritas? I have a killer recipe from a trip we took to San Miguel de Allende a few years ago."

"I love them," I confess.

"Salt or no salt?"

"Salt please." I grin, sliding easily into the comfort of their company. "I like to lick it off the edge of my glass. Part of my oral fixation, I guess."

Alethia leans a hip against the counter. "You do have a talented tongue," she observes. "Is it as adventurous when it comes to food?"

"Oh, it responds to a wide variety of tastes," I tease. Lasciviously, I run my gaze over her body, pausing at the juncture of the slacks she wears tonight. "Sweet, definitely, with a little bit of sour. That's a favorite. But it also likes an occasional burst of bitter mixed with salt." That with a roll of my eyes in Nick's direction.

Nick looks puzzled for a moment, then gets it just as Alethia laughs. He shakes his head and focuses on his blender concoction, though the tips of his ears turn red. I share a smile with Alethia.

A cozy, home-like feeling grows easily among us as we chat. Nick asks about what I'm reading, and tells me he's just finished the mystery I mentioned the last time. Alethia does an impersonation of an entitled girl in one of her classes, demanding an extension on her paper because reading is, like, *hard*. We all laugh, and it's so nice and warm. I've never had people like this in my life, who I can just talk with so naturally.

"By the way, I need to mention something," I remember as Nick fills three glasses, two of them with salty rims. "The man at the front desk, Tommy. He's noticed me arriving at exactly the same time three nights now, and that I leave again after a few hours. He seemed a little suspicious. I don't care for myself, but you might."

Nick and Alethia share a look. After a silent communion, Alethia says, "It shouldn't surprise me. Tommy's often a little aggressive with guests, even with us. By coincidence, though, Nick and I planned to ask you for a change this evening anyway."

"Oh?" I ask as I raise my margarita for a sip. With a wry look in Nick's direction, I run my tongue over the rim to catch some salt with the frozen drink. A wonderful mix of lime, tequila and a hint of orange fill my mouth. "That's delicious," I exclaim, setting down the drink.

"Trust me," Nick says. "I'd never steer you wrong when it comes to liquor."

"Anyway," Alethia continues. "When we woke the other evening and you'd left us, it was…disconcerting."

I stiffen. I didn't touch anything as I slipped out. Is she implying I did something wrong, or stole—

"We missed you, is what I'm trying to say. It was lovely to drift to sleep entwined. So we wondered if you'd agree to stay the full night with us. We'll pay for the extra time of course."

From his back pocket, Nick pulls a cream envelope, considerably thicker than the prior envelopes they'd passed to me. He holds it out. "This is for coming over yesterday as well as this evening."

Shock or surprise must have shown in my face, because Nick's eyes open wide. He rushes to say, "If you don't want to stay, of course, we can just consider the rest as an advance. It's your choice."

I stare at the envelope, unsure why my heart is thumping unpleasantly. And why a curl of disappointment sours my belly. I lick salt from my lips and reach slowly for the envelope. Without opening it, I can tell it's stuffed with bills. At an educated guess, they've offered me five grand.

A very good night indeed. For a whore.

Why am I bothered? The Ballantines are generous, yes, but they're obviously well-off. They can afford this indulgence. Alethia was clear she wanted to pay for my time to visit Nick yesterday afternoon. As for staying a full night, well, I've done that before for some clients.

Clients. That's the problem. I've let myself imagine, foolishly, that we're becoming friends. I came to visit Nick out of friendship, certainly. I revealed something about myself I never before shared with anyone I see professionally. I nearly fell asleep with them the last time, another line I never came close to crossing with others.

I've been deluding myself, apparently. They like me, yes, but they see me as an escort. A sex worker. Of course they do, because that's what I am. If the lines are confused, if I looked for more than they're willing to give, well, I'm the one at fault.

"You're very generous," I mumble, crumpling the envelope in my hand. "I'd be happy to spend the night with you." To my own ears, my voice sounds odd, lacking its usual smoothness. I find it difficult to look at Nick's concerned face.

Alethia steps over to me and takes both of my hands. She tugs until I meet her eyes. "We've offended you. Have we suggested something inappropriate?"

"Did we?" Nick asks, alarm shading his voice. "Jasper—"

"JD," I bark, surprising myself. Alethia blinks in surprise, and Nick looks like he's been slapped. "Sorry. I don't mean to be rude. But for what you're paying me, I think I need to be JD," I continue gruffly. "Jasper is your friend. I've let the lines become blurred, and I'm sorry about that. It was highly unprofessional of me, and not what you bargained for."

Alethia and Nick look at each other, again in one of those communions that exclude me. The exchange reminds me that I'm nothing more than a glorified sex toy. I'm disgusted to feel pinpricks in the corner of my eyes.

Pushing my stool back from the counter where my barely-touched margarita slowly melts, I rise. Bitter disappointment claws at me, probably the result of my sleepless nights. "You know, I've handled this badly. I won't be at my best, and you deserve that for what you're paying. I think I should go, and we'll reschedule for next week sometime, if you still want to use my services. If not, I can give you some referrals."

I hold out the envelope, but neither Alethia nor Nick move to take it. They look at me with matching expressions of confusion and hurt. I place the envelope on the counter next to my drink and turn to leave.

"Jasper, don't," I hear Alethia say and draw near. "Sit please. Talk to us."

I know I should just get the hell out of there with some semblance of dignity, but her hand brushes the center of my back. Her delicate fragrance surrounds me as she strokes with soothing fingers. The touch paralyzes me. I quiver as she steps closer to snake an arm around my waist. Her hair rustles against my silk shirt as she rests her cheek against me.

Nick rolls forward and pivots his chair so he sits between the front door and me. I'd have to dislodge Alethia, step rudely around Nick to get away—

"Jasper." Nick's face is a picture of unhappiness. "Blame me, not

Alethia. It was my idea to pay extra and to ask you to stay. She needs you, so please don't punish her for my idiocy. I never intended to insult you or make you believe that we think of you as…"

"A whore," I supply, stiffly. "It isn't a bad word. It's what I am."

"No," Alethia says. "It's what you do, but it's not who you are."

"You barely know me," I protest.

"Ex-Army," Nick says defiantly. "Very into clothes. Secret comic book movie nerd. Mystery lover. Intuitive. Imaginative. Considerate enough to warn us about our nosy concierge. Compassionate. Willing to learn about good bourbons."

"Self-confident but not cocky," Alethia adds. "Fearless."

Flustered, I blurt out, "Are you kidding? I'm scared shitless by the two of you."

CHAPTER ELEVEN

ALETHIA TIGHTENS HER hold on my waist and Nick cocks his head.

"What do you mean?" he asks curiously. "Why would you be scared of us?"

I shake my head and try to cover my confession with a forced laugh. "It doesn't matter."

"Of course it does," Alethia insists. "Please. Come sit and just talk to us."

Reluctantly, I allow her to draw me to my spot on the sofa. Nick rolls close, anxiety and concern radiating from him. I risk a glance at his face, and blink in surprise at the contrition I see there. He hates that he's upset me.

Alethia joins us a moment later with our margaritas. "One drink and we talk," she says, holding out my glass. "If you want to leave after that, we'll understand. But please. Explain what you mean."

I take my glass with fingers that I notice, to my annoyance, tremble. I sip nervously.

"What would you be scared about?" Nick prompts again.

"This. You." I wave my hand vaguely between the two of them. After a short pause, I add, "Myself. I like you both, very much. In my head, we're friends. But I've been doing this for seven years, and I've never had clients turn into friends before. I've never spent time with them purely as people. I've never grown so relaxed that I'd fall asleep with them, even for a little while, unless everything had been negotiated upfront."

"Is that why the money offended you?" Alethia asks. "You think we see you as someone we hire, and not as a friend?"

I take a healthy swallow of my drink, savoring the tequila as I turn my head to look out the window to the Boston skyline. I find I can't answer directly, but I admit, "I've never had the roles get confused like this. Frankly, I don't know how to handle it. I'm really happy that I've been good for you so far. But both of you! You put so much faith into me already. Trust. What if I fuck things up for you, for your marriage? It's the last thing I want to do but, Jesus, you're vulnerable. I never even made it into community college."

Nick gives a grunt of protest. "If I'm vulnerable it's because you have an uncanny ability to get me to lower my guard. You make me feel safe. Included." He looks pleadingly at Alethia. "You know what I mean, don't you, Ali? I love you completely but there are some things you can't do for me. Maybe it's because we have such a history, and Jasper doesn't know me that way. From before."

"Darling, I'm not offended. It's clear to me as well," Alethia hurries to say, leaning close to touch his arm. She shifts her glance to me. "There was an emptiness growing between Nick and me. Now *that* terrified me. Nick's been the center of my world since we met, but I felt I could lose him. Since we've known you, though, it feels less like an ending, and more like…growing room for a missing piece."

Nick nods slowly. "A missing piece. I like that." He reaches for my hand, and I allow it. The three of us sit connected by touch.

"You are our friend," he says confidently, squeezing for emphasis. "If you never want to have sex with us again, we'll respect that. But don't cut us out of your life, Jasper. Get to know us, and let us get to know you."

I swallow hard. The hands on me seem to pulse with sincerity, grounding me. I haven't felt so connected to anyone in years, and never to *two* people at the same time. I'm so out of my depth that I could drown in my own uncertainty. But there are these hands—one resting on my arm, one twining fingers through mine—that give me the illusion of safety.

I want it to be real. Even not knowing what *it* is.

As if reading my mind, Alethia says thoughtfully, "We've been talking about what *we* want. What do you want, Jasper?"

Later, I'll blame it on the tequila. The glow that started at their kind description of me, the way they sit like all three of us belong together, the sincerity of their words, spark a fire in my heart. Shaken, the truth erupts from me.

"I want both of you. Not as clients. As…" The last shreds of self-preservation save me from putting the real name to it. "As friends," I finish feebly.

Alethia smiles warmly at me anyway. "Then have us, my darling friend."

Nick squeezes my hand again. Licking his lips, he flushes and clears his throat. He leans in and adds, "Have both of us."

I swallow hard. "Wh—what do you mean?"

He glances at Alethia, a shy smile beginning to dance on his lips. "You know what I mean," he says, and she nods.

Alethia rises gracefully and steps behind his chair. "Do you mind if I help a little?" she asks.

Nick turns his head to kiss her hand and rolls parallel to the sofa across from me. Alethia braces the chair, giving him leverage. He pivot-transfers himself smoothly onto the sofa, the work he puts into his upper body all on display as he moves powerfully. I feel a burst of desire at the cords of muscle on Nick's thick forearms, and the flex of his triceps under his shirt.

He rests his head against a pillow at one end, and lays back. Alethia moves the chair out of the way before helping him arrange his legs so they lay straight.

Meeting my gaze, he spreads his arms invitingly and beckons. "Come over here, buddy."

I glance uncertainly at Alethia. Surely Nick isn't really offering...? I've fantasized, yes, and I can't deny the electric thrill that surges through me when I touch him. And Nick himself seems to feel it, and to respond to me. But Alethia stated clearly that he isn't into men.

Alethia holds out a hand, tugging me to my feet and draws me to where her husband lies. "I know you want him," she says softly against my ear, tickling me with her breath. "He wants you too. I didn't expect it when we first met. After that first visit, though, I could tell he was attracted. We talked about it more in the last few days. He was already planning to ask you for this tonight."

Nick smiles shyly. "Don't leave me hanging, bro," he says, flexing both hands in a grabbing motion.

I give a short laugh and admit, "I don't know what's happening here." But I move closer, allowing myself to sink to the sofa. My body lays alongside Nick's, my head pillowed on his cannonball of a bicep. Alethia steps back and curls on the sofa I vacated, watching us avidly.

Her color high, the tip of her tongue appears as she looks back and forth between us. Excitement shines in her eyes.

The heat and size of the body against mine make me begin to relax, despite my nerves. He smells wonderfully of ginger, lime and sandalwood; whether a cologne or shampoo, I have no idea. The sheer bulk of his upper body, the shadow of beard darkening his cheeks, the thick eyebrows over warm brown eyes, make my stomach bubble in anticipation. We haven't been quite so close to each other before, at least not in enough light that I could see the first beginnings of lines around Nick's eyes, or catch the golden flecks that surround his pupils.

I raise a hand and stroke his soft beard. "Are you sure about this?" I ask.

Nick nods, his eyes crinkling with his smile. "One thing you've taught me is that I need to let go of my past expectations."

"I did?"

"Absolutely. I never questioned my sexuality before the accident. I just assumed I was one hundred percent straight. I'd notice guys at the gym or in the showers or whatever. I just never thought about why I looked. One time, I kissed a dude in a bar on a bet. Figured my chubbing up was because of the girls watching us."

His smile widens. "Then I watched you and Alethia kissing. At first I just wanted to be you, kissing her. What tripped me out, though, was when I realized I also wanted to be her, kissing you. Like this."

Without another word, Nick lowers his head to mine until our lips brush together. The first press of Nick's mouth is tentative but sends a shock of desire right to my balls. I grow hard so quickly I almost get dizzy. There's time for an unworthy thought—*Maybe I'm relieved he can't feel my hard-on for him*—and then I moan as Nick comes back in with a deeper kiss.

He presses more firmly, slanting his head so our lips fit beautifully. I kiss him back, stroking with my tongue, moaning as Nick opens for me and permits my entrance.

His arms come around, wrapping me in a cocoon of muscle and warmth that inflames as it comforts. As much as I love the soft skin and lush curves of a woman's body, the firmness and power of a man move me too. The bodies like Nick's that I lusted after in the Army belonged to men who'd accept a blowjob, maybe throw me a fuck, but would never dream of holding me afterward.

I almost sigh in relief as arms tighten around me. I squeeze back like an anaconda, not quite believing that my fantasies of this man are coming true. And that the reality is even better than I'd dreamed.

"You're purring," Nick says as he lifts his head, a wry smile on his generous mouth. "I must be good at this."

"You're a wonderful kisser, darling," Alethia says. I glance over to see her watching us closely, one hand clutched between her folded legs. "The two of you are beautiful together."

Nick rumbles happily and begins to run his hand over the smooth fabric of my shirt, exploring my chest. "So solid, man."

"Where is this going, Nick?" I ask.

"Do you mean right now? Or something more profound?"

"Now, you ass," I protest with a chuckle. *Tomorrow. Next week. Longer than that.* I order myself to shut up and kiss him instead of speaking more. Tonight is all that matters right now. Tomorrow will take care of itself.

I rest my hand against Nick's massive pectorals, hungry to see him again with his shirt off. The reverent way he touches me, stroking my shoulder and my arm, persuade me that he's truly into this. I fight to hold my hips still, afraid that rubbing my aching cock against his pelvis would be rude or disrespectful.

His heavy hand slides along my back as we kiss more, then down over my hip. My breath hitches when he slips it between us and strokes my erection.

"Damn," Nick mutters. A smile shows in his voice as he teases, "So hard. That must hurt, dude. I guess you think I'm pretty hot."

I bite my lip and arch against his hand. "I shouldn't feed your ego, but fuck yeah, I think you're hot."

"Hot enough to let me touch you naked?"

"Why is that even a question?" I gasp.

"What do you think, Ali?" he asks, glancing over at his wife with a smirk on his full mouth. "Do you want to come explore this rad body with me?"

"Very much so, darling. It might be a tight fit on that sofa, however-er. Shall we reconvene in the bedroom?"

"Good idea. It will take me a few minutes to get situated," Nick says. "Why don't you take our friend in there and help him out of his clothes?" He steals another kiss from my stunned mouth. "But don't start without me."

"I wouldn't dream of it," she answers with heat rasping in her voice. He releases his hold long enough for me to climb off the sofa. I take Alethia's outstretched hand and follow her away.

Behind, I hear the sounds of Nick maneuvering into his chair. He doesn't want me to see the work he has to put in, I realize.

Shocking me again, Alethia leads me past the guest room door and further along the hallway. The room she brings me to features a wall of glass looking across the lights of Boston. Armchairs face the windows, with space left for Nick's chair. Alethia presses a button, and curtains slide automatically closed.

I note the lack of a threshold or carpeting in the room that might catch on Nick's wheels, yet the floor under my feet is warm. Probably radiant heat, I muse.

The bed seems larger than any I've ever seen before, and I've seen a *lot* of beds. It's obviously a custom build, and sits low, about the same level as a wheelchair seat. A huge oil painting hangs above the bed, its blues and whites resolving themselves gradually into a vista of a town perched above a sea.

"Will you kiss me?" Alethia asks, and I turn to gather her slim body in my arms.

If they're serious about being my lovers for the night rather than clients, then I need to set aside JD's bag of tricks—*Hah! Tricks*—and show the Ballantines how Jasper Dylan likes to make love. How I've dreamed of making love to them.

Holding Alethia to me, I lower my head to claim a kiss. At the first press of our lips, I growl and come back for more. With my tongue demanding entry, she opens for me. Her body shivers against mine as I kiss her thoroughly. Deeply. I let her feel my surging erection against her belly, reveling in the sweet moan she feeds me.

My fingers seek out the band securing her black hair, and I tease it free. Thick, luscious waves cascade over her shoulders, raising a scent of orange and cedar. Almost of their own volition, my hands come to either side of her skull so I can comb through the raven-dark tresses, my fingernails dragging lightly against her scalp. Alethia's body slackens in my arms at the touch, and she sinks to the edge of the bed.

"Damn, that's hot," Nick says, and I turn to find he's rolled into the bedroom. "You've discovered her Achilles heel—her hair."

"It's glorious," I say, continuing my exploration. I draw long strands out to the side and let it spill from my fingers. The silky sound of it falling against her skin makes me grow even harder. "I want to feel this hair sweeping over my chest. Drifting over my cock."

"To have that, you need to be naked," Nick says. Nerves and eagerness war in his voice, but the light in his eyes convinces me he truly wants to explore.

Gently releasing Alethia, I stand and tug my shirt over my head. Nick's eyes track my fingers as I brush lightly over my smooth chest, and then tug on one nipple. At the sound of a low groan, I tug again, harder, and release a slight hiss.

"Does that feel good?" Nick asks.

I nod. "My nips are wired to my dick. I love to have them squeezed and bitten."

"Do you like clamps?" Alethia asks, surprising the shit out of me. The question sends a bolt of electricity right to my balls.

"To be honest, I've never tried them," I admit. "But I'm intrigued."

Alethia rises gracefully from the bed. "If you're a very good boy, I may let you try mine." Stepping closer, she moves aside my hands and bends to lick at my left nipple while she deftly opens my belt and my pants. She switches sides to bite lightly at my right nipple while sliding down my zipper.

I kick off my shoes and step out of my pants, leaving me in socks and baby-blue boxer briefs. My hard-on stretches the fabric to the point of nearly ripping it. A darker patch of blue proves how much I'm enjoying the attention as I leak precome like crazy. I deal with my socks and turn to help Alethia undress, but she stops me.

"Wait, Jasper. Let Nick see your marvelous body." She steps back, leaving me feeling oddly exposed and vulnerable. I rotate until I face Nick, and drop my arms to my side.

His eyes dance over my bare torso. I can almost feel his intent gaze like a caress as it drifts across my abs and to the boxer briefs. His tongue darts out and licks his lower lip. He crooks his fingers for me to come closer. When I obey, he rests his hands on either hip, just above the waistband. Looking for permission, excitement burns in his eyes. I nod, and then suck in a breath as Nick slides my briefs down. The band catches on my erection; he chuckles softly as he frees the material from the flesh. I step out of my shorts and stand, inches away from Nick, waiting for his next move.

My dick is less patient, though, and flexes. A drop of precome pearls at the tip, leaving a spidersilk trail as it drips to the floor.

Nick licks his lips again, and slides his hands over my hips and to my waist. "You've really got a great body," he says in a husky voice. "Wonderful definition and symmetry. I could never get abs like these, no matter how much I worked out." His brow furrows as he strokes my belly. "Your skin is different than a woman's. I don't know how to explain the difference."

"But do you like the feel of it?" Alethia asks, stepping behind me. She slides her hand around my waist, meeting her husband's hand at my hipbone and entwining their fingers.

Nick glances at her, then smiles and gives a slight nod. "I do like it."

She guides their joined hands lower, through the crisp hair at the base of my cock. Nick swallows hard but doesn't appear to resist as she puts his fingers around my erection. I grit my teeth, so turned on by the exploration I'm suddenly afraid I'll come right now.

My dick jumps again, and Nick chuckles. "So eager. I remember what that's like." Unaided by Alethia, he makes a loose fist and strokes me overhand. "This is the first dick other than my own I've touched. You're smoother than me somehow. Warm, and really soft."

"You call this soft?" I ask tightly as I fight the urge to pump into Nick's exploration. "I don't remember the last time I was this hard."

He huffs a laugh. "I just mean the skin feels soft. You could pound nails with this thing."

"It's not that delicate," I say. "You can grip tighter. Do what feels good on yours."

Nick nods and moves his hand, his grip tightening as he jacks me. "Damn, it looks huge like this, right in my face. I'm used to looking down at mine, or seeing it in a mirror. Not up close and personal like this."

I tremble as he finds a perfect rhythm. Throwing back my head, I let him stroke and explore. Alethia brings her cool, slim hands to both nipples and squeezes them hard.

"Aaah," I gasp. "Got to stop. Now."

Nick drops his hand. "Sorry. Did I do something wrong?"

"Fuck no. That feels fantastic. But if you keep it up the evening may be over far too soon."

A proud glint appears in his eye. "I'm good at hand jobs, huh? Must be all that practice I had as a teenager."

"There's that ego again," I say with a chuckle. "Good thing I find cocky men sexy." I turn to Alethia, knowing my bare ass is now pointing at Nick. "And cocky women. I think you're wearing too many clothes."

I draw her close, unbutton her blouse and unzip her slacks. Her lingerie is midnight blue, the lacy fabric of her bra encasing her breasts and offering them like a treasure.

I remove her bra, then go to my knees and lower her panties, delighted to find they're sopping wet. When she steps out of them, I hold them to my face. The scent makes my dick throb. I twist around to face Nick, meeting him with a huge grin as I offer the flimsy garment. He takes it from my fingers and inhales deeply.

Facing Alethia again, I stroke her bush before dipping my head to reach between her legs with my tongue. Her juices flow freely, and the taste goes straight to my cock. She moans above me and then presses my head to her with both hands, grinding her mound against my face and chin. I lick eagerly, swiping her clit with a rough tongue, tracing along the folds I can reach. I get lost in the sensations of licking Alethia's treasure, hearing her moans, knowing even better is to come when I get her on her back with her legs spread wide for me.

The brush of Nick's leg against my bare skin brings with it an idea so hot I have to stop tonguing Alethia to rest my forehead against her smooth hip. "Oh Jesus, I had the dirtiest thought and I almost came. Again."

"Well, we're here for you," Alethia says. The strangled tone indicates how close she is to her own orgasm, and I look to meet her flushed face. "Tell us, darling. Tonight is supposed to be about your desires. What do you want?"

I lean back so I can feel Nick's leg solidly against me. "I want to see Nick eat you out. I want us to eat you out together."

CHAPTER TWELVE

NICK MOANS BEHIND me, and Alethia stretches her arms overhead provocatively. Her toned body and olive skin gleam in the low lights of the room. She seems like a goddess to me.

"Two handsome men with clever and willing tongues. What a fool I'd be to refuse an idea like that." She turns and crawls onto the bed, moving like a panther toward a mound of pillows.

Looking over her shoulder at us watching her, she brushes her thick hair back with one hand to catch our eyes. She spreads her knees and arches, a cat in heat, exposing the folds of her sex and the furled muscle in the center of her smooth and creamy ass.

I stand and rest my hand on Nick's shoulder. My cock points the way to Alethia, but I'm not doing this alone. I twine my fingers into thick hair and tug until Nick looks at me, lust blazing in his face. Without a word, he raises his arms; I take that as an invitation and yank the shirt up and off.

Nick's muscled body is a work of art on its own, one that I long to explore. "Can I help you take your pants off?" I ask.

Nick flushes and looks away. Clenching the arms of his chair, he shakes his head. "Not…not yet. Okay?"

I get it. Nick's feelings about his lower body are complex. The last thing he wants to do is expose himself further in the midst of this charged and erotic situation. "Sure, buddy," I say and crawl my way up the huge bed and toward her, ass shifting in Nick's direction.

I put a hand on Alethia's nearest ankle and skim over her shin, to her knee, and along her thigh. Turning to look at Nick, I see my friend is turned on, nervous and sexy as fuck, all at once. I worry briefly that he's already deeper into his bi-curiosity than he originally intended, and it might ease his anxiety to revert to more hetero acts.

I beckon. "Come here with me and let's make Alethia scream."

Nick grips the wheels and moves to the left side of the bed, where he docks his chair on a platform surrounded on three sides with steel bars. He locks it, grasps the bars, and heaves. Muscles in his arms and chest bunch and flex as he smoothly pulls himself out of the chair and onto the bedspread.

Hunger flares again in me to explore the sculpted torso, to taste all of Nick's intimate parts. Alethia runs her fingers through my hair and says, "My husband is gorgeous. Yes?"

"Yes," I agree firmly, then look at her. "You both are."

Nick's ass is on the bed. He bends to grasp his legs and tug them up as well, and then elbow-crawls to meet us. It's the sexiest thing I can remember seeing in a long time—his burning eyes and lust-flushed face, his naked biceps and back muscles flexing as he moves closer. "Jesus," I hiss, wrapping a hand around my cock.

He gives me a sheepish smile. "You see why I work my upper body so hard."

"I'm grateful you do," I answer. "You're poetry in motion."

Nick comes to a halt with his head near Alethia's hips, on the other side of her body from me. Reaching behind my neck, he pulls my head closer. "Before I let that silver tongue of yours into my wife, I think I need another sample of what it can do."

He crushes our mouths together, nothing uncertain or shy about the way he presses his tongue in. I groan, vaguely aware of Alethia gripping each of our heads as we make out across her naked body.

I pull back with a gasp, captivated by the gleam of desire in Nick's eyes. Alethia raises her knees and spreads her legs until Nick and I shift closer to each other, our heads inches away between her thighs and her glistening lower lips. Nick puts an arm on my waist to drag me until our bare torsos meet. Instead of going in for another kiss, though, he turns to bury his face in his wife's mound. Alethia sucks in a sharp breath and moans.

From my close vantage, I watch his jaw move as he roots and licks at Alethia like his life depends on it. He pulls back just far enough to nibble around her clit; in response She tightens her legs around our backs. The muscles of Nick's chest move against mine as he worries and laps, earning loud whimpers from Alethia as he eats her out like a champ. Her thighs quiver and I watch her squeeze and pinch her nipples as she writhes on his tongue.

With a gasp, Nick pulls his head back and turns to me, his lips, chin and nose shiny with juices. I can't help myself. I dive in for a kiss, tasting the sweetness of Alethia on his tongue. My steel-hard cock rasps against the fabric of his pants, bringing me ever closer to orgasm. I can feel his erection as well, proof that he's as turned on as me.

I break the kiss to turn to Alethia, running my tongue teasingly up the length of her folds. Knowing it'll drive her mad, I keep my strokes feather-light, avoiding her clit no matter how she angles her hips. Nick chuckles evilly as he watches. He angles his head in as well, stretching his tongue to share in my game.

Alethia cries out when she feels both of us moving on her at the same time. I go for her clit, biting lightly the way she seems to love, while Nick slides two fingers inside her. He thrusts them in and out, while I lick his fingers and her labia. Her body begins to ripple and heave as an orgasm claims her. Overcome with my own lust, I drive my tongue into Alethia alongside Nick's digits.

When her quivering slows, Nick withdraws his hand but I quickly pull it into my mouth. I suck the thick fingers like a cock, working my tongue between them, getting every drop of honey that coats them. Nick moans deeply. When I meet his eyes, they're wide and slightly shocked.

I stop sucking but keep his hand captive. I move it into Alethia, stroking the folds and plumbing her juicy depths, before taking his fingers into my mouth once more. His hand and arm tremble. I pause to make sure everything's fine, until he whispers, "Don't stop." I grin and repeat the moves.

This time I slide my fingers inside Alethia along with Nick's, probing and coaxing groans from her with our combined efforts. I crook to stroke along the roof of her vagina, and she arches her back. Nick lowers his head again and licks at her clit while we finger her.

I can't believe I'm sharing the most intimate parts of this woman with her husband, and that he seems to love it. So does Alethia, because with a wail, she convulses and comes a second time.

She finally slumps back, boneless and gasping. Nick pulls my fingers free and, echoing what I did to him, draws them into his mouth. His warm, wet tongue traces the delicate webbing as he cleans his wife's juices away.

He releases my hand but pulls me into a fierce kiss that tastes of

Alethia's nectar. I'm leaking so much precome that I can feel the wet spot spreading on his jeans. I pant into his mouth and groan, "So close."

Nick leans away but keeps his hand around the back of my neck. His voice commanding, he says, "Don't come yet. Not until you fuck Ali."

I shiver and bite my lip until the slight pain helps me regain control. I nod sharply when the near-eruption quiets down. He reaches into the pocket of his jeans and pulls out a condom wrapper.

He grins when he sees my surprise. "I was a boy scout. I'm always prepared."

I take the packet, rip it open and start to sheathe my cock. I pause then, and meet Nick's eyes. "Will you do it for me?"

He inhales shakily, then nods. I scoot myself higher along Alethia's body, bringing my cock close to her entrance and to Nick. His hands tremble as he positions the rubber ring on the head and rolls it down my length.

When it's fully encased, he wraps his strong hand around the shaft and stares at it for a long moment. He jacks it again, seeming fascinated by my cock. His tongue darts out to wet his lips, and for a moment I think he's going to…

I glance at Alethia to see what she makes of Nick's explorations. Her lips are open in an expression of surprise, but she pants in her excitement. "Oh, my darling," she breathes out. "You're making me so wet."

Nick shifts from admiring my cock to smile at his wife. "Yeah? I'm glad. I'm starting to get why you liked holding my cock so much. It feels really sexy in my hand." He kisses my sheathed head suddenly, and smiles. "But you know where it will feel even sexier? Buried inside you."

He pulls out a small container of lube and coats the rubber liberally. Slapping my ass lightly, he says with a grin. "Come on, stud. Let me watch you slide this big dick into Ali. She's only come twice so far."

I groan and move to take Alethia in my arms as I position my body between her thighs. Nick keeps a hand on my cock and guides it into her folds. Alethia releases a great sigh as I press my hips forward, parting her and slipping inside.

With the plentiful lube and our earlier fun preparing her, I don't hesitate to go balls deep on one stroke. I kiss her hungrily as her arms and legs envelop me, drawing me to her. The velvet depths and pulsating warmth of her are beautiful.

Nick shifts as well until his head's at the same level as mine. He works his arm under Alethia's neck and rests against a pillow, watching the two of us. Suddenly I feel his large, heavy hand come to rest on my ass.

I begin to move inside Alethia, so deep and so hard that it makes my heart ache. They both watch me eagerly. My breath stutters with excitement, and I alternate kissing them both as my strokes grow longer.

Nick squeezes my ass cheek and presses me forward, encouraging me to fuck harder. I grind my hips to lob my dick around, stirring her depths as Alethia moans and clutches at my back.

His hand shifts closer to my crack and rubs. Buried in Alethia's sheath, with a hand on my ass, I feel my orgasm surging closer. She pants too, signaling she's almost there again. I clench my jaw to hold off, determined that she'll come first.

Suddenly I gasp, my eyes flaring wide when Nick drifts a finger over my hole.

"You like that, huh?" he says in his low, sexy voice. "How about this?" And the evil man plunges his thick finger inside me.

He's lubed it at some point, but the intrusion still comes with a wonderful burn. I've taken cocks thinner than Nick's finger. The stretch and the fullness send me over the edge, howling my pleasure as I erupt inside Alethia. Dimly, I'm aware that she joins in my orgasm, squeezing her inner muscles to milk my cock as she bucks beneath me.

When I can think again, I find myself collapsed on Alethia's sweaty body. Nick's withdrawn his finger, but his hand rests on the small of my back. The three of us look back and forth, moving into wordless kisses and soft touches.

My heart fills to bursting as I watch them kiss inches away from my eyes. Afraid I'm intruding, I shift my hips. "I need to get rid of the condom," I say quietly, withdrawing but keeping one hand on the base of the rubber to make sure it stays in place.

My cock's still nearly hard, and the condom tip swells with the enormous load I've released. Nick gestures toward an open door, which turns out to be the bathroom. I drop the condom into the trash bin, then daringly help myself to a rolled-up hand towel next to the sink. I wipe myself clean, then wet another towel with warm water. Returning to the bed, I draw the cloth over Alethia's folds and legs, then use a different end to wipe Nick's face. The couple smile at my ministrations.

Unexpectedly shy, I ask cautiously, "Nick? Can we do anything for you?"

Nick smiles a lazy, satiated smile and shakes his head. "I don't need anything, but thanks. That was...exciting to watch. To be part of." He holds out his hand, and I take it. Nick tugs me down until we lie again with Alethia sandwiched between our bodies. "Ali?" he asks.

She nods, apparently hearing a question that I can't. She angles her head to catch my gaze. "Will you stay with us tonight?"

To share a bed with this glorious couple? To feel arms around me as I drift off, and then wake to Alethia's cool beauty and Nick's enveloping strength? The excitement of the idea blazes through me. Still, I blink uncertainly, afraid of my own desire. "Are you sure I won't be in the way?"

She smiles at me, dazzlingly. "This bed is enormous. I—we want you to fall asleep with us."

Nick nods agreement. "What we just shared was wonderful. I don't want it to end. Please stay." His white teeth flash in a broad smile. "Ali makes a killer breakfast on the weekends."

I smile weakly, my resolve to leave fading. "What if you snore? Or steal the covers?"

Nick holds up a hand. "Scout's honor, I don't snore or steal covers. Now Ali here…"

She laughs and swats her husband's bare shoulder. "I do not snore."

"Notice she doesn't deny stealing the blankets," Nick laughs, grabbing her fingers and kissing them.

Alethia purrs. "I won't have to steal the blankets if I have a warm body on either side." She looks hopefully at me.

The last shreds of my resistance fade. "Okay. I'd love to stay the night."

Nick grins like a schoolboy stealing a treat, and squeezes us both to his massive chest in an exuberant bear hug. "Thank you, Jasper."

We all shift closer and lay quietly together. I enjoy the growing sense of comfort and peace in this luxurious room, connected to two people I'm becoming dangerously fond of. It's a mistake to stay, but maybe it's possible for JD and Jasper to lead separate lives. Maybe I can have friends—or whatever it is the Ballantines are to me—apart from my clients.

Lost in my thoughts, I slowly become aware that Nick stiffens. A sense of unease comes from his portion of the bed.

Before I can ask if he's changed his mind about me staying, Alethia speaks. "My darling, it's fine. Jasper won't care at all."

I rise on one elbow as I look back and forth between them. "Won't care about what?"

Nick flicks a glance at his legs, still clad in jeans.

Oh, of course. He doesn't sleep in those. And he doesn't want to show me his legs.

"Nick, would you be more comfortable if I left? I don't mind, if you aren't ready for me to see you."

He hesitates, chewing his lip. I start to climb out of bed but he reaches out an arm to stop me.

"No. Don't go. I'm being stupid." Even in the low light, I can tell he blushes. "It's just…you might think differently about me if you see what I have to do. What Alethia has to do for me, or my health aides. I like the way you see me now. I don't want it to change."

Alethia makes a noise of distress, but before she can speak, I clamber over her body and straddle Nick. My ass rests against his thighs and I press on his shoulders with both hands, pinning him to the bed.

"You aren't your body. My friend is the man inside. Funny, sexy, dirty, smart, flirty, honest, loving, and kind. That's who I see when I look at you. Yes, I love your chest and your arms because I admire all the hard work you put in to them. I think you're incredibly handsome, but that's just a bonus. I want to make you feel good, and safe, and cared for, because I…like you."

Shit, almost slipped there.

Nick blinks at me uncertainly. "Yeah?"

"Yes. I promise you, none of that will change because of your legs or anything you need to do." I bend my head but hesitate, unsure if a kiss will still be welcome now that the sex is done.

Nick frees himself easily from my hands and pulls me down, meeting my lips with an open-mouthed kiss. I can feel his heart pounding, and I raise my head.

"I promise," I whisper.

He nods and pushes from under my weight. "Okay," he says with a sigh. "I guess this was inevitable."

He closes his eyes, seeming to gather his willpower, and then uses his incredible strength to pull his body to the edge of the bed. Gripping the bars again, he swings into his chair.

Alethia rises from the bed, pacing naked through the room to stand behind Nick. She moves him toward the bathroom, glancing back over her shoulder. "We'll be about ten minutes. You get comfortable and we'll be back." She pushes Nick through and closes the door.

Again I think about leaving, but I realize that would be the worst possible thing to do. I swore to Nick I won't think differently of him once I see his legs; running away into the night would break that promise and hurt the man deeply. I pull back the blankets and slide into the bed. Arms folded beneath my head, I wait.

From my friend Owen, I have some idea of what Nick likely has to do to keep his body functioning. He can't urinate voluntarily, so he probably uses a condom catheter a few times a day to drain his kidneys. That's likely what Alethia is doing for him now—catheterizing Nick a final time before bed. As for bowel functions, that's probably something the home health aides address.

About ten minutes later, the bathroom door opens, spilling golden light across the bed. I don't stir, but I can see Nick's bare knees. Alethia rolls the chair back to his platform and sets the brake. Then she returns to the other side of the bed and crawls in next to me. He gives a profound sigh, grasps the bar, and swings onto the bed.

The first thing I notice is that he wears underwear of some kind. It takes me a moment to realize it's a thick type of brief, with Velcro tabs on the side. An adult diaper, I guess, and that makes sense. He has no control below his waist, so he can't prevent himself from peeing or anything else.

As Nick pulls his legs up, I can't help but contrast his upper and lower body. The legs are pale, indicating that he never exposes them to the sun or the eyes of others. Not withered, but thin and out of proportion to his well-developed torso.

Dead things, Nick called them, so I have an idea of just how disso-ciated he feels from his legs. Still, they're shapely on their own, and covered in a dusting of dark hair. Looking at them, I want to touch and stroke. That's surely something that he'll never permit.

Nick meets my eyes, nervousness dancing on his face. I spread my arms, mimicking his earlier gesture of crooking my fingers to beckon him. He elbow-walks closer and I draw his weight onto my chest, arms wrapped around his back.

He buries his face in my neck. "It's awful, isn't it?" he whispers.

"No, Nick. It's not awful. It just is."

Alethia presses a kiss to my cheek and snuggles herself closer. Her breasts brush against my arm as she reaches across my body to stroke Nick's hair gently. "Sleep, darling. Jasper's got you now. I'm right here. Sleep."

A few minutes later, I feel him slacken against me and hear his even, deep breaths. Alethia's hand on my waist, Nick cradled in my arms, I follow them into sleep soon after.

CHAPTER THIRTEEN

I WAKE TO the rare pleasure of finding myself sandwiched between two warm bodies. I was aware of Nick shifting position a few times during the night. I'm guessing it has to do with his injury, like the shifting he does in his wheelchair.

At the moment, Nick is on his back. My face somehow ended up on Nick's massive chest, the dusting of hairs there tickling my nose. My morning hard-on is pressed into Nick's thigh. Alethia has also turned so that her back is right up against me. She molds to my body perfectly.

Nerves begin to jangle, ruining my pleasure at the unique sensations. What have I done? I've gone so far over the line from dealing with clients that I can't even see it anymore.

Have us, they said to me. And I did, and I loved it. So now what? Do I try to go back to being their sex worker, charging them for my time and services? That feels utterly wrong. Do I make a stab at truly being their friend, cutting off the physical closeness but building on their kindness and interest in one another? That's maybe something I can see working, if they're able to see past my job.

Nick's hand strokes through my hair then, and I close my eyes at the feel of those thick, strong fingers against my head.

Softly, he murmurs, "Why doesn't this feel weird?" I roll my head to look at him, puzzled. "I had sex with both of you last night. It wasn't just two guys banging the same woman. We were all there, for each other." He closes his eyes and frowns. "Am I bisexual and I just never knew it? That should freak me out."

My tongue seems to have dried to the roof of my mouth. I have no idea what to tell Nick, because I don't know myself what's going on. Besides, I never had a problem understanding my own sexuality, even as a teenager. I'm not sure what to say to someone potentially discovering something so new about himself.

Besides, I'm going through my own crisis, thank you very much. And it's one I don't think I should voice.

I feel Alethia shift and roll over. Sleepily, she crawls across my body and rolls into Nick's arm, leaving her husband in the middle of the sandwich. She tangles the sheets as she moves, exposing my ass and drawing the silky fabric tight over his groin. His thick erection is obvious to me, though Nick seems unaware of it.

Alethia stretches her neck to claim a kiss from Nick. She leans forward to get a kiss from me as well.

Running her slim hand through the hair on his chest, she says, "My love, please don't force yourself to doubt something that you know instinctively is right for you. You want me. You're attracted to Jasper. I'm attracted to Jasper. See? It's really very simple."

Nick laughs softly and presses a kiss to her brow. "It must be the Greek in you, that you aren't shocked to share your husband with another man." Suddenly he seems to catch sight of his hard cock, tenting the sheets. Amusement twinkles in his eyes. "Well, look at that. I don't remember the last time I sprouted wood in the morning."

I hide my face against his shoulder and mutter, "You aren't the only one."

Nick cranes his neck but can't quite get a glimpse. He huffs a laugh. "Aw, c'mon. Let me see."

Alethia chuckles low in her throat as I roll away and onto my back. My cock arches thick and long over my belly, quivering. He swallows hard as he looks at it. "Damn. That's actually beautiful."

"Since I'm showing mine, are you gonna show me yours?" I tease. He winces, though, and I regret my words right away. "I'm sorry. You don't have to—"

Nick frees his arm from around me and, reaching down, shoves the sheet away from his waist. Alethia helps draw it further off. The erection's pushed free of his disposable briefs. She quickly opens tabs on either side and pulls away the garment, then drops it bedside.

His face reddens and his cheeks flush. Tense as a board, he squeezes his eyes closed. I meet Alethia's gaze, alarmed at Nick's reaction.

She just smiles at me. "Do you like my husband's body?"

I swallow and nod. "Yes. I really do." I stare in awe at Nick's dick, considerably bigger than my own. Lust fires in me at the sight of the steel-hard rod twitching before my eyes. I run my gaze over his huge frame in the full light of morning. Regardless of the obvious difference in muscle size below his waist, he's stunning.

Unsure of his response, I decide to risk saying that out loud. "You're amazing, Nick. Truly."

He opens his eyes hesitantly. "You don't think I look grotesque? I know what you said last night, but I figured it was just post-orgasm kindness."

I frown and reach to cup his chin. "I've never lied to you, about anything other than my real name. I mean what I say. I admire the hell out of your body, and I'm jealous as fuck of your cock."

Nick quirks a small grin. He glances at Alethia, bites his lip, and then says, "You can touch it. If you want to."

Oh, do I want to touch it. To feel that massive organ, with its silky smooth skin stretched over its crowbar strength. I know how hot it's going to feel against my palm, how it would stretch my mouth if I took it in. But... "You told me how you feel about that. I don't want to make you uncomfortable."

"I, uh...I think it might be hot. To see your hand on me." He blushes furiously and darts another look at his wife. "To see both of you with a hand on me."

Alethia at least needs no further prompting. She wraps her fingers around his length and begins to glide them up and down. I take Nick at his word and follow suit.

The dick in my hand is warm and smooth. I can barely reach around it, and I suddenly wonder how Alethia was ever able to take this monster inside her tight channel. Silently, we work out a rhythm, our fingers meeting and twining as we stroke and play with Nick's dick.

"It feels good in my hand," I offer. "The head is spongy and smooth. The skin slides perfectly over the shaft." Nick inhales sharply at the words, and breathes out on a slight moan that goes straight to my hard-on.

I continue the shared exploration, until I'm afraid I'm about to come spontaneously from the eroticism of sharing this dick with Alethia. Shaken by my growing lust, I lean across the organ in our hands and meet her in a passionate kiss.

Nick groans above us and we both turn to meet his burning eyes. Tightly, he says, "Jesus, the sight of the two of you, working me like this. I can't feel it, exactly, but...I *do*." He gestures vaguely at his stomach and heart. "I feel this pleasure inside. Like the first time, when you connected us, Jasper."

His tongue darts out to lick his lips, a flash of tantalizing pink that makes me hunger to taste. Alethia seems to be on the same wavelength because she slides herself up Nick's body, stroking his side and arm with her breasts, stopping to lick delicately at his nipple.

I mirror her motions, working the nipple closer to me with tongue and teeth as I run my hand over Nick's taut abdomen and through the hair on his chest. He arches his back and clenches his jaw at the twin attack. Alethia continues her way up to kiss him, her hands working into the thick hair on either side of his head as she holds him in place.

I smile; the panther from last night is back, and Nick's her prey. Why does that turn me on so much?

As Alethia devours her husband's mouth, I continue to explore his body, at last. I use different pressures on his nips, listening and watching for the reaction. A tight twist followed by a gentle stroke makes Nick cry out as his brown, quarter-sized areolae pebble. Fingers running over his tender sides and to the edge of his armpits make him quiver. Nuzzling into his pits earns a gasp and shudder. A lick at his earlobe, inches away from Alethia's ravening mouth on his, makes the man nearly sob.

Alethia stops long enough to meet my eyes, her own glinting wickedly. She throws a leg over Nick's body so that she straddles his torso, then slithers down. She grinds against his belly and presses her tits onto his chest as she undulates, bringing as much sensation to his upper body as she can.

Nick turns toward me and groans. He wraps a hand desperately around my neck and pulls me closer. I lunge, our mouths coming together in a click of teeth and a battle of tongues. His fingers twine into my hair, a series of cries pouring out of his soul and into my mouth.

"Let it happen, darling," Alethia croons. "Show us how much you enjoy what we're doing to your gorgeous body."

Nick wails and throws his head back, eyes squeezed shut, jaw clenched, as he practically convulses. His strong arm slips to my back and pulls me in so tightly I couldn't get away if I wanted to. With the other arm he crushes Alethia to him as he sobs and writhes between his two lovers.

We hold him tenderly until the tremors begin to calm. When he finally stills, Nick gives a shuddering whoosh of relief. He barely loosens his grasp.

"Thank you," he gasps. "Oh my God, thank you. That was... I don't have words." He trembles again, apparently feeling echoes of his orgasm. "I love you so much," he says to Alethia, drawing her into a gentle kiss. His arm never relaxes on my back, though.

I have an unworthy moment of jealousy, or perhaps envy, streak through my gut. Before I can quash or even fully name it, Nick looks at me. Deep emotion swims in his eyes, along with a shimmer of tears. He opens his mouth to say something to me, but he can't get it out. He just pulls me into a kiss that tastes of gratitude, happiness, and maybe even a bit of joy.

It's more than I deserve, yet less than I desire.

SOME HOURS LATER, I find myself still lounging around the Ballantines' living room. Morning light pouring through the vast windows presents a stunning view of Boston, its towers and windows gleaming. Nick's home health aide is getting him ready for his day. Alethia bustles around the kitchen, preparing a brunch that looks and smells amazing. From a hidden sound system, a woman croons in a language I can only assume is Greek; Alethia sings along.

At loose ends, I check my email, and the account for JD. The first message makes me blink.

> *My dear JD, I'm desperately in need of your company Wednesday at a rather tedious fundraiser. I promise, we'll stay no more than an hour and then slip away for a quiet supper and chat.*
> *Meredith*

My gut tightens at the words. *Supper and chat.* That could mean either of at least two things—a discreet request for my sexual services, or a chance to drill me for information about Alethia and Nick. I risk a glance at the lovely woman preparing food as she sings.

I have no intention of revealing anything to Meredith, no matter how much she pushes. Still, I have to wonder what Alethia has said to Meredith about my visits. I tap my phone against my lips as I think about how to respond to the email.

"There," Alethia says as she sets a platter on the counter top, amidst several other bowls, plates and glasses. "Nick should be along in a moment. Come have some more coffee and see if anything here looks appetizing to you."

Crossing the room, I slide onto one of the stools. The spread before me includes a basket of breads, an assortment of cold cuts and cheeses, a bowl of yoghurt, another of raspberries and blueberries, and one of what seems to be an orange marmalade. The last addition Alethia makes is a plate of fried eggs. A sweating pitcher of what looks to be fresh-squeezed orange juice stands next to an ice bucket that holds a bottle of champagne.

"This looks amazing," I exclaim.

Alethia smiles at me as she refills my coffee cup. She confides in a low voice, "Great sex leaves me ravenous and domestic in equal measures. Believe me, I don't always put out this much food. It just seemed like the kind of morning for an extra effort."

A twitch of my cock at her words leads me to give her an answering grin. "That *was* amazing sex. Last night, and this morning."

Alethia's gaze shifts to the hall behind me, and I watch her face light even more. I turn to see Nick wheel in, escorted by a middle-aged, heavy-set man in blue scrubs.

Nick accompanies the man to the front door. "Thanks, George. Let me know how you and Gwen like that movie."

The man—George—pats Nick on the shoulder. "I will. Gwen is jazzed about these tickets. Lance'll be here at the usual time this afternoon, so I'll see you tomorrow morning." George raises a hand to wave at Alethia. "Bye, Mrs. Ballantine. Have a nice Saturday."

"You too, George," she calls. "Would you like a bun to take with you?"

He pats his belly. "You know I would, but Gwen's got me on a diet again."

"Well, I wouldn't want to get on her bad side," Alethia says with a laugh. "Take care and give her my best."

When the door closes behind George, Nick rolls over to the counter. His thick hair looks damp, and he smells pleasantly of ginger and lime again. A navy blue polo shirt stretches across his chest and around his biceps.

"Wow, really branching out there on the color palette," I tease.

"Don't be a hater just 'cause I make this shirt look good," Nick replies with a wink.

Alethia comes around the counter and leans in for a kiss. "What tickets did you give George?" she asks, running a hand through his hair.

"The ones for that premiere tonight of the new action film. Your father dropped off the passes for the meet-and-greet. The director and Tom Cruise will both be there so I thought George and Gwen would enjoy meeting them."

"Oh, that's sweet," she says. "Coffee or mimosa?"

"Mimosa please," Nick answers. When she turns away to open the champagne, Nick catches my eye. He beams and opens his arms. "Don't I get a good morning kiss from you?"

I can't hide a foolish grin. Rising from my stool, I bend to cover Nick's mouth. It's meant to be a quick brush of our lips, but Nick puts a hand to the back of my head and takes the kiss deeper. Electricity and desire flare in me as Nick presses his tongue inside. He tastes of mint, and I want more.

Oh shit, I think. *I'm totally screwed.*

Nick finally releases me with a wide smile. As he takes his flute from Alethia, he laughs. "Yep. I'm still bi, apparently."

She trails fingers over his shoulder as she sips her own drink. "Of course you are," she says placidly with a little smile for me. "Our friend here could probably awaken the Pope with his magic touch."

The warmth in her regard makes me squirm. With a casual gesture over the food she's laid out, Alethia releases me from my embarrassment. "Please. Eat."

Nick hums appreciatively as he takes a plate and begins to fill it. "Don't be shy," he tells me. "This is how Ali's family always does brunch. And lunch. And supper. When we were at Adras' house in Spetses for our wedding, I ate so well I almost couldn't fit into my tux."

"Adras Papathanassíou is my father," Alethia explains, then pauses, as if waiting for a reaction. I've never heard the name though. When I say nothing, she smiles and asks, "Have you been to Greece? Oh yes, you said. Mykonos."

I've just taken a bite of yoghurt mixed with berries, so I hold up a finger. When I've swallowed, I say, "That was only for a few days. I'd love to see more of the country. It's on my bucket list, but I haven't made it back."

"We should go, then. Together." She apparently doesn't see the rush of blood to my face. "Spetses is marvelous, all white-washed homes with red-tiled roofs. My father's house is on a rise. From the pool there's the most stunning view of the town laid out against the sea. The painting in our bedroom is based on what you see from Bampás' deck, actually. I'm sure you'd love it. When can you get away?"

Her bombshell invitation heats me from within. The casualness with which she turns our business relationship into a personal friendship, where she's comfortable suggesting I join her and her husband at her father's house, overwhelms me.

"Um. Sure. We should talk about that sometime," I mutter lamely.

Nick doesn't miss my expression. He frowns. "It's a good idea, Ali, but I think Jasper is feeling out of his depth right now."

Alethia raises a delicate brow and crooks her head. "Oh? I apologize. After our conversation last night I believed we were all on the same page."

I look back and forth between the two of them, a sensation of helplessness threatening to knock me off my stool. "I…don't know what to say. I'd love to go to Greece, of course. But—"

Alethia sets down her plate with a soft clink. She glances at Nick, whose expression has turned wary. "I see. Perhaps I've made another mistake. When you said that you wanted us, I thought it was something more than for a night."

She moves to stand beside Nick's chair, an aura of protectiveness rolling off her. "Last night meant a great deal to both of us. If that's what you prefer—to keep this a friends-with-benefits arrangement—we'll understand. But we'd appreciate it if you told us directly. What exactly is it you want from us, Jasper?"

Guilt surges through me at the disappointment I've caused in Nick and the fierceness that brings out in Alethia. I fumble out desperately, "I don't know how to explain what I want without sounding crazy."

"Just be honest, buddy," Nick urges. "You won't freak us out."

"You," I blurt. I wave a trembling hand at them both. "What you have. The intimacy. The love. I've never had that in my life, and watching the two of you makes me hungry. A…a *soul* hunger, if that makes any sense."

I feel raw. Exposed. But now I've begun, I find I can't stop. I run a hand roughly through my hair, clenching a hank of it.

"I want to be here with you, like we were last night and this morning. Connected. But I'm so afraid of intruding, or overstepping. I'm afraid you'll slam the door closed. When you say something like we should go to Greece, it terrifies me. I'm trying not to get too attached, to get my hopes up, but you make it sound so natural. Like it's already happened."

Nick leans forward, elbows on his legs. His expression seems to flicker between frustration and kindness. "Of course it's already happened. Jasper, buddy. Do you think we'd let just anyone into our bed and our lives like this? In a matter of weeks you've turned us inside out. So many things about our marriage, and about me. Alethia, too. It's almost all we've talked about, on the evenings we don't see you."

He glances at his wife for reassurance; she nods back at him. "When we said have us, we didn't mean as fuck buddies. We meant as—" He breaks off, his shoulders hunching under his tight shirt.

"As lovers," Alethia says into the silence. "Call it what you want; the label doesn't matter to us. We're stronger already as a couple for having you in our lives. And we think we're good for you too. Am I wrong?"

I shake my head slowly. "You aren't wrong," I croak.

Nick exhales heavily, hope returning to his face. "Then can we just, I don't know, see where this goes? Give it some time, and see if we all feel good about how it develops?"

Hesitantly, afraid of misunderstanding, I murmur, "You make it sound like we'd be...dating."

Alethia smiles. "Well, why not? This would hardly be the first relationship that starts with sex and turns into something more with time."

"Holy shit. I may be the pro, but the two of you make me feel like an amateur," I say ruefully.

Nick's hopeful face instantly drains and shutters closed.

Uh oh.

CHAPTER FOURTEEN

MY HEART HAMMERS at the change in Nick's face. What is it I've said wrong? The reminder of what I do, maybe. After all, people as accomplished and wealthy as the Ballantines don't carry on an affair with a whore.

Once again, I feel the urge to flee. If I'd given in to that urge last night, though, I would have missed out on one of the most fulfilling experiences of my life. If I run now, I'll never get another chance.

So don't run, I tell myself. The Ballantines have been amazingly brave with me. They've exposed their desires and fears, drawing me into their lives even as I keep tripping over my own insecurities. If I bring nothing else to the table, I can at least try to communicate with that same level of honesty.

"I have a feeling we need to talk about my job," I say tentatively.

Nick looks quickly at the back of his hands, where they rest on his knees. Alethia nods thoughtfully.

"That's a good idea. Has everyone had enough to eat? Then let's go out on the balcony and enjoy this lovely morning while we talk." I make noises about helping with clean-up, but Alethia shoos me along. "The weekend housekeeper will take care of it. Don't worry."

Nick silently hands his refilled mimosa to me and leads the way to the balcony doors. The troubled expression on his handsome face worries at my gut.

Outside, comfortable teak chairs with thick cushions cluster around a coffee table; one side is left open for Nick's chair. I wait until he's positioned, then pass back the glass.

Alethia follows with two more drinks. She hands one to me and sinks smoothly onto a chair, tucking her legs underneath as she sips at her mimosa.

I sit as well, my knees spread, holding the glass between my dangling fingers as I try to organize what I want to do. Or to say. The sun shines strongly on us, and a crisp morning breeze makes my nipples harden under my silk shirt. Alethia tilts her face to the sun and closes her eyes. Nick drinks half his mimosa in a long pull, tension radiating from his body as he waits for me to speak first.

"I need to talk to you about something," I begin. "If we're—" I stumble a bit, "—dating, then I'd like to hear what you think." I hold up my phone. "I've had an email from Meredith, asking to see me on Wednesday. Professionally."

Nick finishes his drink and stares at the empty glass, jaw clenched as if it offends him. Alethia doesn't open her eyes or turn away from the sun as she asks, "And are you planning to see her?"

"I don't think I should," I say. Nick flicks a glance at me, then away again. "For one thing, I'm afraid she'll ask questions. About the two of you, how we're getting along, that sort of thing."

"I love Meredith dearly," Alethia says, "but it's true, she can be inquisitive."

"If I don't make the appointment, though, she'll be offended." Eyeing my barely-touched mimosa, I say quietly, "She's always been a good source of business referrals for me."

Nick makes a strangled noise. When I look over, it's to see Nick with anguished eyes and gritted teeth.

Alethia coos softly at him, "Darling, we've talked about this. It's Jasper's job, or rather JD's. We'd be hypocritical to resent him pursuing it since that's how we met."

Nick's ears burn as he seems to fight with himself to keep silent. I slide to the edge of my chair until I can reach Nick's knee.

"It's okay," I say. "You've been amazingly open with me, pretty much from the first phone call. I'd rather you don't start censoring yourself now, if we're going to pursue whatever *this* is."

My words seem to puncture Nick's self-control because he all but shouts, "I hate the idea of you touching anyone else the way you touch Ali and me. Or anyone touching you but us." His chest heaving, his eyes ask me to understand. To agree. "You should be ours, while we figure this out."

My mind seems to fly apart at the admission. Immediately I feel defensive—I've worked hard to build my reputation and clientele. The lifestyle I can now afford is nothing compared to the Ballantines', but it's *mine*. It's so much more than I ever thought I'd have when I left behind that dusty town in West Texas to enlist in the Army.

And yet I can't deny that I understand Nick's jealousy. Didn't I already reject the idea of offering them a replacement? The image of another escort taking my place makes me want to howl. I can't stand the thought of a body that isn't mine bringing pleasure to Alethia and Nick.

My fractured thoughts whirl to Essie, at retirement and regretting the chances she didn't take. Maybe…maybe a short break from JD's work is possible financially? I've saved carefully for years, so I have a decent chunk of change in the bank. I'd been thinking of a vacation, not so many days ago. Could I take a few weeks away from booking dates, while I test the waters of this…?

I shy away from the word *relationship*.

On the other hand, I'll lose many of my steady clients if I turn them away for weeks or even months. They'll find new companions and I'll have to start building a clientele all over again.

Before I can make sense of what I'm thinking, though, I need to understand better. Is Nick simply jealous, or is he repulsed by what I've done as JD? What I've chosen in order to build my life?

Cautiously, I ask, "What would it mean, if I said I couldn't afford to turn away a good client like Meredith?"

"I don't know what you're asking," Nick replies with a frown. "Is it a money issue? Because you know—"

"Nicholas, stop," Alethia says sharply. Nick flushes but he falls silent. To me, she says softly, "If you need to keep working as JD Pierce, it means only that we don't get to see you as often as we'd like. You've made a career before ever meeting us. We can't expect you to put that at risk on the hope that something stronger grows here. If it does indeed take root, as I believe it will, perhaps we can talk further about what it means."

Nick nods, abashed. "Okay, I agree with that. I'm sorry, Jasper. I was being selfish." He hoists his glass suddenly, and then seems surprised it's already empty. Wordlessly, I pass him my nearly full mimosa.

Nick takes it, letting his fingers brush against mine as he leans back into his chair. "Can I ask something, though? Say it does work out. Hell, let's shoot for the moon. Let's say in a few months or a year we decide to tell everyone that you're our boyfriend."

I suck in air sharply. That's what they've been hinting at, but to hear the word so starkly shocks me. *Boyfriend.*

Nick presses on. "Would you still want to continue then as JD?"

My heart thrums erratically. They're throwing too much at me. Too much kindness, too much hope. It's almost cruel, how much they expect me to decide or to know about the future. My breaths feel ragged, like I'm not getting enough oxygen. Suddenly, I can barely hear for the rush of blood in my ears.

Boyfriend.

"Jasper, dear? Are you all right?" Alethia asks, her voice barely cutting through the noise in my head.

"No!" I blurt out. Both Nick and Alethia move as if to catch me before I fall apart, to hold me. The last kindness makes pent-up fears, desires and confusion boil out of me. I suck in a deep lungful of oxygen, and release it with my truth.

"No, I wouldn't continue as JD. You already mean so much to me that I couldn't send you to another escort even when I suspected that I should. I knew I was getting in too deep but the very idea of another man kissing you, stroking you, fucking you..." I growl savagely. "I couldn't stand it. So here we are. And of *course* you don't want me to continue as a prostitute. You're the most amazing people I've ever met. I admire you and I want you and just...*fuck!*"

I tear at my hair. "I should have seen this problem was inevitable, but I didn't. I'm sorry."

I choke back my raving as Alethia swiftly moves to my chair and sinks into my lap, arms around my heaving shoulders. Nick nudges the table out of the way so he can roll closer. Awkwardly, he positions himself to reach the back of my head, wind fingers into my hair and pull me into a kiss. Alethia kisses me too as she tightens her arms around me. She meets Nick's eyes and he leans toward her to complete the circuit, kissing his wife before the face of their shared lover.

My heart aches in panic and desire. They're so beautiful together. "Can I ask you both something?" I ask in a gravelly voice. "Are you ashamed of me, for what I do?"

Nick frowns, looking perplexed, and Alethia seems surprised.

"Ashamed?" Nick asks. "Absolutely not. I'm a possessive Neander-thal because you should be with us. Just us. But I don't judge you for having slept with other people, any more than I imagine you judge Ali and me for the people we've been with in the past. The fact that you got paid for it when we gave it away for free, well." He grins. "That just makes you smarter than us."

I laugh, surprised at the sound coming out of me.

Alethia squeezes my shoulder, smirks and kisses me again. "My darling, I only judge you by what I've seen. And from that, I judge you a healer, a protector, a gentleman rogue at need, and the owner of a loving heart. So no, I'm not ashamed of you in the slightest."

"If you want to or need to continue as JD Pierce, I'll try to keep my jealousy in check," Nick swears. "As long as I know that there may come a time when we take things to another level and can revisit the topic then, I'll manage." He gives a mock growl. "Just please, no other clients with paraplegia. I don't think I could take the idea of you showing another man in a chair what his nipples and ears and armpits can do for him."

"I promise," I say. The surge of relief at their words makes my eyes prickle. To cover, I croak out a joke in a watery voice. "Maybe someone in a cast, or with a missing finger, though."

Nick rumbles warningly, but with a smirk.

Alethia drops her head to my shoulder. "Jasper, do what you think is best about Meredith. If you want to see her as a client, I trust your discretion. In *both* directions, because really, I've known her too long to be comfortable with the idea of she and I sharing a man."

I kiss the top of her head. "No matter what else I do, I'm not going to see Meredith as a client in that way. If she wants me to accompany her to a fundraiser or dinner, fine, but no more nightcaps. I'll just have to figure out what to tell her."

"Really?" Alethia asks. "If you're sure, then would you trust me to talk to her? The way she recommended you to me originally suggests she understands your worth far exceeds your considerable bedroom skills. It might be easier for her to hear, coming from me."

I ponder that. "Well, if you're serious, then yes, I'd appreciate that. I think I'll respond that I'm available for the fundraiser on Wednesday, and remain silent about the implied date while you have a chance to talk to her."

"Perfect," Alethia says, then kisses my cheek. She climbs off my lap and offers a hand to pull me up, then takes Nick's hand as well.

"Jasper, dear, you've exhausted me with the emotional whipsawing last night and this morning." I wince at that, but she smiles kindly to ease the sting of her words. "I cannot survive one more emotional storm today. It's a glorious Saturday. I want my two handsome men to squire me to the park and then perhaps a late lunch out."

I look doubtfully at the silk shirt and tight trousers I'd been wearing last night as well. "I'm not exactly dressed for a trip to the park, and Nick's clothes will be too big on me."

Alethia cocks her head at my outfit. "I'd say you look fine, but I know already your self-imposed standards are higher than that. Two ideas, and don't you dare be offended at either one because they're offered sincerely."

She raises an eyebrow at me in warning, and I return a sheepish grin. She's right—I've been on an emotional roller coaster, and dragging them along with me. I nod acceptance.

"Good. One, let me buy you a new outfit at a lovely little men's clothing shop just around the block. Two, take us with you to your home while you change, and we'll go somewhere from there."

I swallow. I know Alethia means the offer of a new outfit as simply and straightforwardly as she says it. They aren't treating me as a gigolo, but as a good friend. *Boyfriend.* I should be able to accept a present without it implying anything mercenary about our relationship.

As for the other possibility…

I owe the Ballantines something for their directness and their honesty. They accept my nerves and my cowardice, and still make me feel like their hero. I want to say everything I'm feeling, but I'm not ready. The least I can do is show them how seriously I take what they offer with their open hearts.

I lean my hip against Nick's shoulder and pull Alethia to me for the dirtiest kiss I can manage. It's filthy enough that my dick stirs in my pants. When I break away, her eyes have closed dreamily and her mouth stretches into a smile. I crouch and deliver the same to Nick, sucking in his moan greedily along with his tongue.

When they both focus on me again, blinking and slightly turned on, I smile wickedly.

"Let's go visit this little shop then. Because I'll tell you something. I've never before brought someone I'm dating to my apartment. The first time I have the two of you over, I want to be ready to woo you with dinner and candles and wine. My bed may not be as enormous as yours, but I guarantee I'll put out."

Nick grins, relief appearing in his eyes. "Let's make that happen soon."

TWENTY MINUTES LATER, we pass through the lobby. Since we're going out on the sidewalks, Nick has switched to a motorized chair. He tells me it gives him more control when he's in a crowd. He also has a van that's been tricked out to allow him to drive using hand controls, though he doesn't use it very often. I get the feeling that he tends to stay inside the apartment as much as he can. Given the things he's said about his legs, the shame I've seen in his eyes, my guess is Nick doesn't like the idea of people looking at him. I resolve to find a way to get him out more often.

Once again, Tommy is at the front desk. I mutter to Nick, "Does he ever take a break?"

Nick glances at his watch. "I think he just started his shift. He's usually here afternoons and evenings."

Tommy catches sight of the three of us and he blanches. Perhaps the ideas he's constructed about why I'm here so frequently are facing revision.

As much as mine are, I think. *Boyfriend. Huh.*

Nick diverts his chair to approach the desk. "Hi, Tommy. How are you today?" he calls out.

"I'm great, Mr. Ballantine," Tommy answers, though his eyes never leave me.

"Listen, you don't need to announce our friend here any longer. Please just let him through to the elevator."

Tommy bobs his head, though his eyes widen in surprise. I think mine probably do as well.

"Certainly, Mr. Ballantine. I'll leave instructions with the other receptionists as well about Mr. Pierce."

I consider whether I should correct the name, but realize there's no easy way to do that. Alethia and Nick seem to come to the same conclusion. We turn back toward the building's front door. Tommy calls after us, "Enjoy your Saturday. It's beautiful out."

Nick raises a hand in acknowledgment and farewell.

The clothing store Alethia guides us to is one I've heard of but never before visited. Its prices are way beyond what I'm comfortable paying, but I can't help a soft moan of appreciation as we walk in. The clothes on display are sophisticated and luxurious.

"That sweater," I say softly, gesturing to a baby-blue cashmere with a ribbed neck. "Gorgeous."

"It is," Alethia agrees. "You'd look stunning in that. Oh, and one of these shirts to wear under the sweater."

Nick chuckles and waves us both on. "Ali, you finally have a man who likes to shop as much as you do. Run along, guys. I'm going to park myself by those chairs and read the newspaper."

I start to protest, feeling guilty at the idea of abandoning Nick, but Alethia takes my hand and pulls me along.

"It's fine, I promise," she says. "He gets frustrated when we shop. He says I want to dress him like a Ken doll, and he isn't entirely wrong." She runs a critical eye over my body, assessing. "Will you humor me?"

I wince at a price tag on a shirt. "I don't know…"

"Jasper, dear, please don't worry. You've already agreed I can buy you a few things. Let's have fun."

I laugh ruefully and spread my arms. "All right, if you're sure. I'm yours to dress."

Time flies as we dart around the store together, pointing out a fabric or a pattern to one another. A salesman joins the game, obviously caught in our enthusiasm.

Alethia's taste is superb. Although I care deeply about my wardrobe and make every effort to acquire good, stylish pieces, an hour in her company is an education. She asks the salesman penetrating questions about fabrics and drape, wear and fit. I'll step in to the dressing room with a beautiful shirt to try on, and by the time I come out she'll have two others even lovelier for me to model.

She seems to have taken measure of my preferences and tastes based on what she's already seen me wear. Everything she points out for me to try is something I'd have lusted after. Before I quite know what's happening, I find myself in a new outfit head to toe, with a small treasure trove of additional sweaters, shirts and trousers. I protest when Alethia tells the salesman we'll take the lot, but she just smiles and shakes her head.

"You promised to let me play, darling. You can't renege now."

Nick sees we're finishing and he rolls over. "Jasper, let her do this, as a favor to me. She never gets to dress me like she wants, and you can see she's having a ball."

Reluctantly, I agree. Alethia never offers a form of payment and the salesman doesn't ask; apparently she's well-known in the store.

The salesman neatly bags the new clothes I won't be wearing, along with my own things from last night. Alethia says to him, "We won't be heading straight home. Would you be a dear and have these delivered to Mr. Dylan?"

"Of course, Mrs. Ballantine," he agrees quickly. To me, he offers a slip of paper and a pen. "Would you mind giving me your address?"

I jot it down for him. The doorman at my place will hold the packages.

Nick looks me over as Alethia chats with the storeowner about some new lines of clothes he's expecting in soon.

"You look handsome as fuck," Nick says approvingly. "I wish I had your patience to let Ali dress me, because the results are certainly worth it."

I run a hand happily over the soft cashmere sweater. "I can't help feeling guilty for accepting these, but I have to admit I love the clothes."

"You watch. She'll be after you to go shopping all the time now."

"True," Alethia says, joining us. "I admire your taste, Jasper darling. Next time perhaps we'll go shopping together for me. I'd love your opinion."

Nick groans, "I warned you," but I laugh.

"I'd enjoy that. Just say when."

Slipping an arm through mine, Alethia kisses me on the cheek. "Excellent. We'll make a date of it. Perhaps next weekend."

The salesman holds the door for Nick's chair and waves at us as we return to the sidewalk.

"I think you made his quota for the month," Nick says to Alethia, chuckling.

"He's very nice, though his style is a little pedantic, I thought," Alethia replies.

"You just say that because he shows me the same polo shirts and pants every visit," Nick teases. "He knows what I like so it saves a ton of time."

Alethia rolls her eyes and tugs on my arm. "Perhaps you'll be able to help me expand Nick's sartorial explorations a little."

"I'm not getting in the middle of this!" I protest, laughing.

"Smart boy," Nick says. He eyes my outfit again. "As much fun as Ali has dressing you, I'm already thinking of what it'll be like to peel those tight pants off of you."

My dick twitches at the frank admiration. "Damn. When you come out, you don't half-ass it."

Nick winks at me. "Anyone worth doing is worth doing right. And I think you're worth doing over and over."

"Park first, then lunch, then debauchery," Alethia says. "Let's get to know Jasper out of the bedroom too, darling." But she looks pleased rather than stern.

We stroll to Rose Kennedy Greenway and the Chinatown Park, talking at random about our lives. I tell them about my Army service and tours in Afghanistan and Iraq. Alethia talks about her job as a professor of Comparative Literature at Harvard, lamenting how the newest crops of students seem to lack basic writing skills. Nick doesn't offer much about his past, seemingly content to learn about mine and listen to his wife.

Other walkers crowd the winding paths and walkways, also out enjoying a lovely Saturday afternoon. Asian symbols and statuary decorate the gardens we pass.

We halt near some tables where older Chinese men play chess. Two get into an apparently heated discussion, hissing at each other in rapid speech. Alethia ducks her head, amused, and puts a hand to her mouth.

"What did they say?" Nick asks quietly, a grin already stretching his lips.

"The first man, in the Sox baseball cap, accused the other of cheating," Alethia reports, her eyes dancing. "The second one said 'Fuck your ancestors to the eighteenth generation'."

Nick and I both laugh, drawing attention from passersby. We all hurry on, giggling like teenagers on a date.

Which, I have to admit, isn't as far off the mark as it maybe should be.

CHAPTER FIFTEEN

NEAR THE CHINATOWN Gate, we pause. Alethia looks around the streets at a multitude of restaurants. "Do you like Chinese food?" she asks me, and I nod. "This one is excellent. Let's have lunch here."

"You should trust her to order for you," Nick advises. "The chefs always make her some family specialty that doesn't appear on the menu they use for English speakers."

Visions of odd vegetables prepared in a wok with fiery seasonings make my stomach clench nervously. I say weakly, "I should warn you. I'm not very experienced when it comes to exotic food."

"I'll take that into account. However, you've been pushing Nick and me out of our comfort zone for weeks now. I think I should return the favor," Alethia says, but with a sparkle in her eye. "I promise to be gentle."

I give in cautiously. I trust Alethia, and need to take her at her word. I shouldn't have worried though. Alethia explains each dish that comes out from the kitchen. Though the spice levels and sauces are different than the moo shu pork I usually get for takeout, she doesn't push panic-inducing ingredients on me.

Through our delicious lunch, we keep up our conversation. It's been a long time—years, maybe—since I just talked and talked over a meal with people who mean something to me. The hunger I feel to learn everything I can about the Ballantines feels scary at first, after all the caution I've learned. But this is different. They're my... I'm their... Nope, I still shy away from it.

Boyfriend.

Clamping down on my excitement and my jabbering, I shift the focus to Nick. I know a lot and very little about him at the same time. "It's obvious you must have been to China before, Alethia," I say. "How about you, Nick?"

He smiles affectionately at his wife. "Actually, that's how we met." Alethia puts a hand over his and squeezes. To me, he explains, "I'm an investment advisor, or I used to be. The brokerage I was with had some very wealthy individuals as clients. Part of my job was to thank them for their business by taking them on exotic vacations and trips. Well, Adras Papathanassíou was one of my clients."

"Alethia's father?" I ask, and she nods.

"Yes," Nick says. "I guess you don't recognize the name, but he owns one of the biggest Greek export businesses in the world. He started with olive oil but now it's so much more than that. He's got an interest in almost any Mediterranean food product out there. Anyway, I handled some of his personal investments. After a particularly good quarter, my boss arranged for us to go to China for two weeks. I thought I was Joe Cool, lining up a translator and guides, planning unusual spots off the beaten path, that kind of thing."

He lifts Alethia's hand to kiss her fingers. "We get to Logan to board a private jet, and here comes Adras with this gorgeous, elegant nymph. I can't believe my luck, to have two weeks to get to know her. As soon as we take off, I start trying to impress her with all my planning, all the studying I've done to get ready. She just watches me, this twinkle in her eye. I think I'm getting in good, and I'm already trying to figure out how to steal her away from her father in Beijing for a while.

"Then the air hostess comes around to offer lunch. Alethia starts chattering with her in perfect Mandarin. Adras has been watching my whole game, and he just breaks out laughing when he sees my face."

Alethia squeezes Nick's hand and says seriously, "It was fortunate you had me, because what you didn't realize was that one of the places you wanted to take us was an active brothel."

"No way!" I exclaim, and Nick groans.

"Shit, I didn't know. I just read that it was this fun, really offbeat place. By the time we landed, I had turned over the entire itinerary to Ali. It was great. She took us to these amazing art galleries in Beijing I would never have known about. We had dinner on the Great Wall. I mean *on* the fucking Wall! She made me line dance in the Water Cube, and then she turned around and followed me as we scaled a part of the Yellow Mountains. She arranged lunch with a Tibetan monk on the grounds of the Dali Lama's Summer Palace in Lhasa. She had a Daoist monk in Chengdu fucking teach me Tai Chi. I was so in love with her by the end of the two weeks I couldn't see straight."

"It turned out my father had set us up," Alethia says with a smile, sounding fond of the memory. "He thought Nick and I would be great together, but he knew I would automatically say no if he suggested it. I was going through a pretty rebellious streak then. So the sneaky bastard made me think he needed me on the trip to meet some large clients. He actually warned me not to get involved with Nick, that he didn't think he was polished enough or something. After I got a look at Nick, though, I knew I had to get him into bed."

"So you fucked me to spite your father. Nice," Nick says, with a familiarity that shows this is a story they've told before.

"Only the first time," Alethia agrees seriously. "Once I saw you out of your clothes, I knew I'd be coming back for more."

"We spent the trip sneaking into each other's rooms, trying to avoid Adras. She figured he'd flip his shit, and I thought my firm would lose his business and then I'd get canned. On the last night, I asked Ali to marry me. When we told Adras, we were all nervous and shit. He just whooped, hugged us together and shouted something in Greek. Ali still won't tell me what he said."

She smirks. "It's something like 'lead a horse to water', but it involves penises. At least the way Bampás uses it. That's all I'm saying."

I laugh along with the story delightedly. I'm kind of jealous of the friends they have, the people who knew Nick before the accident or were there to see Nick and Alethia starting their life together. From what Alethia told me the day we met, this trip must have happened a year or so after I started escorting. Then what they've said gets through my stupid moment of self-absorption. "Wait. You only knew each other two weeks and decided to get married?"

Nick grins at me. "In case you haven't noticed, I'm a fast worker. I don't spend much time second-guessing myself once I know what I want."

Alethia rests her head on his shoulder. "It doesn't help that he's often right. His ego gets so big sometimes I have to threaten to turn my grandmother loose on him."

"Her yaya is a scary bitch," Nick agrees, shaking his head. "Do you know the Greek myth about the Erinyes, the deliverers of vengeance? I swear, Rhea is one of them. When you meet her, remember: You do *not* want to get on her bad side."

I choke on my tea. When I've recovered, I ask cautiously, "You, uh, you think I'll meet your grandmother?"

Alethia gives me her slow, sweet grin. "When you're ready, yes. And my father. I haven't forgotten that we invited you to come to Greece. It will happen, at the right time."

Nick steals a prawn off my plate and glances at his wife. "Which do you think will freak out Adras more? That I'm suddenly into dudes, or that we have a boyfriend?"

That word again! I've just tried sipping my tea again, and once more choke. "Dammit! Warn a guy before you say shit like that."

Alethia pats Nick's hand. "Jasper's right, darling. We shouldn't call him our boyfriend until he's more certain about us." She ponders the rest of his question. "I don't think he'll be all that bothered about your bisexuality. You remember Demetrius? I always suspected he and Bampás were more than just friends. When Demetrius had a heart attack a few years ago, my father was despondent for weeks."

The waiter brings our bill, and I jump to grab it. "Please," I beg over Alethia's protests. "Let me do this to say thanks for the gifts and for the wonderful day."

She relents. "Very well, on one condition. Come back and have dinner in with us."

"Better yet, stay the night again." Nick takes my hand across the table, heedless of anyone else in the restaurant. It's possessive and sexy and comforting, all at once. A pleasant warmth tickles my belly.

I can't even try to be coy. I know my face gives away my eagerness, so I don't bother to pretend. "I'd love to. I should head home for a little while to clean up and to get those clothes you had delivered."

"That's fine, darling," Alethia says. "Nick needs to get home as well to meet Lance, his aide. Why don't you come over around seven?"

PROMPTLY AT SEVEN, I enter the Ballantines' building, a bottle of wine in one hand and a small overnight bag in the other. Tommy's still on duty. I hesitate when I enter the lobby. Nick was pretty clear that I don't have to wait while Tommy calls upstairs. He looks up at me eagerly. I just wave hello and go straight to the elevators. I almost expect him to tell me to wait, but he doesn't say anything.

I grin to myself at the disappointment in his face. *That's right, pretty boy. I'm not available any longer. I'm their boyfriend.*

I ring the doorbell, and hear Nick call out, "It's open."

Walking in, I find Nick leaning against the side of his chair, a book open in his lap. I note the happy gleam in his eye when he spots my overnight bag.

"Where's Alethia?" I ask as I cross the room to kiss him hello. I mean it to be quick but Nick somehow scoops me off my feet until I end up across his lap, legs dangling from one side of the chair. "Hey! I'll tear your book."

"Fuck it," Nick says gruffly. "It drove me crazy when we were out today and I couldn't touch you the way I wanted to. I figured it would make you uncomfortable." He bends his head across mine and begins to kiss me thoroughly. I respond instantly, my arms wrapping around Nick's big shoulders as I let him ravish my mouth.

When he lifts away, a sparkle in his eye, I can only sigh. "No wonder you got her to marry you in just a few weeks. You're an amazing kisser."

"Yeah?" he asks, preening. "I'm locking down this bi shit. Just wish I'd known I swung this way when I was in college. There were some hot-ass frat brothers that in retrospect I wish I'd had a shot at."

"Does it make me an asshole to say I'm really glad I got to be your first man?" I ask.

"Of course not. And I'm just kidding you." Nick nuzzles my nose with his own, and adds softly. "I'm really glad you're my first too. You make me feel safe."

I hide my head against Nick's shoulder, unsure how to respond. *You amaze me, both of you. How did I get so lucky, that two gorgeous, smart and sexy people like you want me?*

"Now that's a lovely tableau," a voice says from the direction of the hallway. I turn my head to see Alethia leaning against the wall, a silk robe around her body. "The two of you look marvelous together. I'm drawing a bath, and just came out to make some herbal tea for myself."

"I'll make it," Nick offers. "Go get warm in your bathtub. Jasper can carry it in to you when it's ready."

"Thanks, darling. Now don't get too carried away! I'm going to want my tea," Alethia says with mock sternness. As she turns to head back to the bathroom she calls out, "Chloe will be along with dinner in about an hour, Jasper."

Nick rolls his chair to the kitchen with me still seated across him, laughing. Together we prepare tea for Alethia and for ourselves.

Waiting for the kettle, I say, "I'm curious about your cook and housekeeper and stuff. You have all this help, but nobody lives in?"

Nick shrugs. "When we lived in Newton, we had a few staff in residence. After my fall, though, that house didn't work well. Too many levels. That's when we decided to move from the burbs into Boston. Adras knew the developer of this building so we got in early enough to design the unit the way we wanted. But it's closer quarters than we were used to. We decided not to have any help move in, just come by at set schedules." He removes the whistling kettle and pours hot water into a teapot. "It works for us."

I ponder that as the tea steeps. The trailer I shared with my father growing up was smaller than the Ballantines' guest room. Calling this palace "close quarters" frankly floors me.

And their prior house was bigger? Good lord.

When the tea's ready, I carry Alethia's cup through the bedroom and rap my knuckles against the partially-open bathroom door.

"Come in," Alethia calls. I enter to find her reclining in a bubble bath, the tops of her olive breasts glistening through the suds. "Ah, wonderful," she says as I put the cup next to her and sit on the edge of the tub.

Trailing fingers through the water, I say, "You look sexy as hell in that tub. Do you need me to scrub your back?"

She laughs throatily. "I'm afraid we'd start something that wouldn't finish until very late, and then Chloe's lovely dinner would go to waste." She takes my trailing hand and brings it between her legs. "Maybe just an appetizer, though."

I press the heel of my hand against her mound, teasing her folds as I bend down for a kiss. Tongue dancing against hers, I slip two fingers inside. Alethia groans into my mouth and arches her back to drive my fingers deeper.

"Appetizer," I say, smiling against her lips. "And I bet I know what we'll be having for dessert." With another quick kiss, I leave Alethia to her tea and bath.

Nick winks at me when I return to the kitchen, glancing meaningfully at my crotch. I feel myself blush when I realize I have an erection. "I wasn't sure if I'd see you again before dinner," Nick says. "I was about to drink my tea without you."

I sit next to him and draw my cup closer. I think about what Nick said in jest, and realize it touches on something I don't yet understand myself.

Well, one of many things.

"Would that bother you?" I ask cautiously, sipping at my chamomile tea. "I mean, we haven't talked at all about this…dating. Are we only having sex when it's all three of us? I assume the two of you will continue to be intimate when I'm not here. I guess I'm just not certain how the rest of it should work while we figure this out."

Nick picks up his tea in both hands and sips at it. "We should definitely talk about that later with Ali," he murmurs. Meeting my eyes, he says, "I love when it's all three of us. It excites me in a way I didn't think possible, to have you both."

When he sets his cup aside, a shy look creeps into his face. "The thing is, I'm really digging the new stuff with you. I'd enjoy some one-on-one time, just learning about dick and how to please a man." I chuckle, and he blushes. "You know what I mean. Playing with another guy's piece, feeling your body, all of that. It's really different than with a woman. I've got a lot to learn if I'm going to keep crushing my bi awakening."

"How do you think Alethia will feel about that?"

"Honestly, I think she'll be fine with it. And I think I'm good with the idea of the two of you being together without me. It's got to be a lot of work, finding ways to keep me involved."

I start to speak but Nick hurries over me. "You're great at it, both of you. I never feel left out or like a burden. But come on. Ali is sexy as fuck, and you're a hot piece of ass. I think it would be good for the two of you to just crawl all up in each other sometimes and not worry about me."

"I can see that," I say. "Both parts. If Alethia likes the idea too, how would we make it work though?"

Nick grins. "Do you always worry this much over the details? It must be exhausting."

I swipe at his arm playfully. "I'm serious, dude. What, you think I'm just going to drag your ass into the guest room and say to your wife, 'Hey, don't mind us. We're gonna go fuck'?"

"We could draw lots," Nick says with a wicked leer. "Put the different combinations on slips of paper, throw them in a bowl and pull one out. 'Tonight Ali will fuck Jasper and Nick will watch a movie'."

I chew my lip thoughtfully. "You know, earlier Alethia made a comment about the two of us having a date to go shopping. Maybe that's something we should talk about. That not only do we all three try dating together, but I date each of you separately too."

"Would a date end in sex?" Nick asks with a lewd smile.

"Almost certainly," I laugh. "It's a little late for me to play hard to get."

"I could get behind that," Nick says. "Let's talk to Ali about it over dinner."

She sees the merit in the idea right away. "I like it," she declares as she pours the wine I brought into three glasses. Nick serves us from the platter of sea bass their cook Chloe brought over, along with a salad, vegetables and a dessert. "It makes sense that we get to know each other as a distinct couple as well as part of a triad. The dynamics will be different when it's two of us out or having sex than when it's all three."

"Sex too?" I ask, and she nods.

"I believe I'm fine with the two of you having sex without me. Will it be a problem for you, darling, if Jasper and I make love some time? Would you feel left out, or abandoned?"

Nick chews his food thoughtfully. When he swallows, he says, "I'm pretty sure I'll be okay with it. I wouldn't have liked it even a week ago, but things are different already. I feel warm and happy when I think of the two of you getting it on." He shrugs. "I reserve the right to be wrong, but as long as we talk about it, make sure we're all on the same page, I think we should try."

I set down my fork. "In that case, Nick, would you go out to lunch with me Monday afternoon?" Nick beams and nods happily. "And Alethia, will you have dinner with me Tuesday evening?"

"Of course," she says, smiling. "There are some lovely restaurants near the university. Perhaps we could meet at one of those."

"Um, I have a request," Nick says. "When the two of you have sex, at least at first, would you do it here? I think I'd be unhappy if you went off to a hotel or something. If you're here in another room, it will feel like part of building something together."

"I understand," I say. "We try it, and talk afterward to see if it works for everyone." I grin. "Of course, that's for the future. I'm hoping that tonight I get to enjoy both of you together."

CHAPTER SIXTEEN

MONDAY AFTERNOON, NICK and I make our way along Boylston Street. We're returning to the apartment after our lunch date in the Theater District, which I insisted upon paying for. "When you ask me out, you can pick up the check," I tell Nick.

"Does Alethia's money bother you?" Nick asks as we roll and stroll, respectively.

"I don't think so," I say after pondering for a moment. "I've met some fairly wealthy people through my, uh, work. I guess I've gotten somewhat used to the idea that rich people are still people, just with better food." Nick laughs hard at that, and I grin at him affectionately. I love being able to make him laugh, and getting him out of the apartment. He hadn't fought me very hard but I count it as a win anyway. "I'm not so sure about the gifts. I believe she means to be generous, but I've had a lot of clients buy me things over the years. My head got a little tangled when she bought those clothes for me."

"I can talk to her, if you want."

"No, I will," I say. "It's not so much a problem as a blurred line that I need to work through."

"You don't have to answer this, but are you okay financially?" Nick asks. "I get that we're kind of fucking with your livelihood. Well, I am, with my jealousy."

"I'm in a pretty good place, money-wise," I tell him. "I made bank for a long time now, and I don't spend extravagantly. I have a good chunk in savings."

"You mean investments, too, right? You don't just keep your money in a savings account?" Nick asks, almost incredulously.

"Um, I do. Is that bad?"

"If you don't mind earning practically no interest and missing out on a booming market, then no, it's not bad at all," Nick scoffs, but not unkindly.

"The stock market always scared me," I confess. "I, uh, didn't know what else to do with my money. My dad and I didn't have a pot to piss in, growing up, so I never got any sense of what people do with money. Besides, it isn't like hookers have a union we can go to for advice."

"Look, I'm a kick-ass investment manager," Nick says. "Or I was. No, I guess I still am. I manage what Alethia inherited from her mom, and what I made when I was working. If it isn't intrusive, I'd be happy to look at your situation and see if I can help you make more money."

"I've had your tongue down my throat and my dick in your wife's pussy," I whisper in his ear. "I guess showing you my savings statement isn't a stretch after that."

Nick groans. "Are you trying to turn me on? We're still blocks from the condo."

"Maybe I am. Is it working?"

"Hell yes," Nick says. "I'm so ready to get you in bed. I haven't thought about much else since you left after breakfast Sunday morning."

"Oh? What have you been thinking about?"

"I want to suck your cock," Nick says firmly, and I nearly choke.

"Wow. I wasn't expecting that already." I imagine Nick's luscious lips wrapping around my dick. I can almost feel his tongue flicking underneath the glans, loving on my erection, trying out on me the things that he'd enjoyed when he got head. My dick throbs at the mental images and I step quickly behind Nick's chair to conceal myself.

He smirks at me over his shoulder, a satisfied glint in his eye. "Got you back. Good. But I'm totally serious. I almost did it the other night, when you were about to fuck Ali. But I figured that was something I want to do for the first time when it's just us." He winks. "I know Ali gives a great BJ and I didn't want to have to compete with her."

"Who do you think you're bullshitting?" I ask, laughing. "I've got your number. As soon as you've practiced on me, you're going to challenge her to a blow-off or something."

"Well, seeing as you've got the only functioning dick in this triad, it's a win-win for you. So what are you bitching about?"

My laugh fades as soon as the words sink in. "Hey, Nick, don't talk about your dick that way. Okay? I know that you're really putting yourself down when you say shit like that. Your dick is gorgeous. *You're* gorgeous. It's all one to me, and it doesn't matter that we have to get nontraditional to make you come. I like the inspiration."

Nick flushes and looks away. "Aw, don't get too serious. I was kidding."

I put a hand on his shoulder as he rolls along. "I don't think you were, but I want you to know how I see it."

We continue on, in an awkward silence. I begin to fret. I don't know if I'm fucking up with Nick, or what. Pushing him to go outside, lecturing him about his attitude... Who the fuck do I think I am? It's hard for me to lower my natural guard, and I can't confess the terrifying emotions I'm truly feeling about Nick and Alethia. So what gives me the balls to imagine I have anything helpful to give?

But then I get it. Nick opens up to me in a way he apparently can't to anyone else. Whether it's chemistry between us or luck or something profound, it's true. Rightly or wrongly, he values what I have to say. So all I can do is honor my instincts, and the man who opens to me like a blooming rose. I can't speak the full truth, but I can offer a glimpse of where I'm headed.

Stepping in front of Nick to stop his chair, I crouch on the sidewalk. "I'm sorry if I offended you. I don't mean to." I smile shyly. "It's just, I feel like you're insulting my boyfriend, and I won't stand for that shit."

He blinks at me, a sheen suddenly appearing in his eyes. After a moment, he clears his throat and says gruffly, "It's okay. I see what you're saying. I'm sorry I insulted your...boyfriend."

The last word is said on a whisper. He stares at me, emotion swirling in his eyes. I feel suddenly like I could drown in their depths.

No one I can recall has ever looked at me with so much desire and, yes, okay, *love*. Nick thinks he's in love with me. And goddammit, I'm in love with Nick and with Alethia. I just can't say it. It's too soon, too uncertain. I have too much to lose, if I say the words and the dream falls apart.

But those brown eyes. The longing and the trust and the hope. If I do drown in Nick's gaze, at least I'll die happy.

"Let's get home," I say roughly. "I'm going to make you come like a motherfucker."

NICK WIPES HIS mouth with the back of his hand. I lean away, my ass against his chest, trailing the head of my spent dick along his chin to drop against his thickly muscled neck. The bed in the guest room squeaks as I move. My knees on either side of Nick, I gaze at the red, debauched lips I've been fucking until I poured myself down his throat.

"That was amazing," I gasp, my heart still pounding. I shift so I can bend and take his mouth, licking traces of myself from the corners.

"Say it," Nick crows, arms curling around my naked back. "I fucking nailed the blowie."

"A-plus, all the way. In fact, college degree, best in show, doctor of fellatio. Whatever you want," I murmur. I slide down to press against that massive torso. Wrapping my arms around Nick as well, I continue to ravage his mouth at the same time.

"Yeah, Doctor BJ. That's what I want you to call me in front of Ali," he laughs when we finally break apart. He shivers and clutches at me before burying his nose against my hair. "That was so hot, to feel you fucking my mouth. I had no idea. Can you go again? Because I totally want to do that some more."

"Mercy!" I cry out, laughing. "You sucked my brains out of my dick. I can't even form a rational thought."

"Then your brains are salty-sweet, kind of remind me of ammonia, and taste delicious," Nick growls. He runs his tongue roughly along my neck. "Shit, I've watched porn where some chick would get a face full, and I always secretly thought it looked a little gross. Now I can't wait for you to come in my mouth again. Fuck, I want you to spooge all over my face next time."

I trail a finger along his jaw. "You'd look so hot, covered in my come," I murmur.

Nick's flying, I can tell. His pupils dilate, the skin of his neck flushes and his nostrils flare. Despite the boneless languor that threatens to drag me into sleep, I rouse to keep my vow. I use lips and tongue, teeth and fingers, to seek out all the spots that respond to my touch. I grind myself against his torso, clutching his head to still him forcefully while I tongue-fuck my lover. He moans and squeezes me back, tentatively at first as if afraid of hurting me, then with growing urgency.

"That's it, Nick," I croon against his lips. "Fucking show me how strong you are. You won't break me. Alethia is our porcelain doll. I'm no brick shithouse like you but I'm a tough son of a bitch. Show me."

His cries of desperation begin to grow as I work his tits, his neck, his armpits. I grasp his hand and slap it against my chest with a smack that resounds in the guest room. "You like that sound?" I ask when he growls. "Do it again, baby."

Nick does, smacking my pectoral open-handed, groaning at the sound it makes. I form a fist and hit his massive torso to egg him on.

"Do that to me, Cannon. I can take it. I want it."

He pounds the edge of his fist against one side of my chest, then the other. "Fucking solid man," he pants. "My stud. Mine."

I feel my dick flex as I'm claimed. What's wrong with me? I've never gotten off on this kind of possessive, rough treatment. But *fuck*. Nick's the type of alpha male I've always fantasized about. My truth is that I want to be claimed by him—by them—even though I know it's too soon to be thinking this way. Minutes ago I was dominating him with my cock, and now I'm begging to be manhandled. The ebb and flow of what I feel for him dazzles me, and I can't think rationally.

Hardly aware of what I'm doing, I roll onto my back, carrying Nick with me. When his lower body remains sprawled behind, I grasp his thigh and pull until he's on top of me.

Up on his elbows, surprise and lust burn in his handsome face. "I'm yours," I breathe under his weight. "Yours and Ali's. Show me, Cannon. Show me what it means to be yours."

Nick cries out and clasps me by the ears, holding my head as he plunders my mouth with his tongue. He slides one thickly muscled arm beneath my neck to hold me still, then cocks his other arm to pound against my pec, not enough to hurt but causing the echo of flesh against flesh to reverberate. Then he twists his fingers around my nipple, as firmly as a pincer, just shy of pain. I arch my neck and hiss.

"Mine," Nick repeats, grinding his torso against me as his need grows. "Grab my tit," he commands. "Make me fucking feel you too." Our lips crash together again as our bodies writhe, wrestling for dominance, or lust, or the simple joy of muscle striving with muscle. When he tenses and begins to tremble, I reach with my free hand to tug at his thick hair. I'm hard as a rock too, though I can't possibly shoot again so soon.

"Come on, Cannon," I hiss. "Show me. Mark me. Come for me."

Nick yells my name out and begins to spasm, twitching as he clutches at me. I hold him through it all, using an edge of pain to keep the orgasm going until he whimpers and sags against me. I release his hair and nipple, wrapping my arms around his back, pressing kisses to his face and throat.

"My sexy beast," I murmur. "Oh, that was beautiful to watch."

"How do you keep doing this to me?" Nick asks, exhaustion and wonder in his voice. "Every time I think you've reached the limits of my freakiness, you push and find some more." He rises up on an elbow. The glorious weight of his body presses down onto me, his warmth and strength anchoring me to this bed and this room. I can't imagine wanting to be anywhere else.

"Did I hurt you?" Nick nervously skims his gaze over my body. He bends to kiss my reddened and erect nipple, licking gently at the raised nub.

I run my fingers through his hair, pulling him against my chest. I fight off a ridiculous urge to cry. "No, you didn't hurt me. You couldn't hurt me."

"I've never been rough like that, with any woman. I just couldn't."

"Shh. Of course you couldn't. You hold your strength back and under tight control. But I can take it. I like seeing your full strength. It turns me on so much because I—" I choke off what I was about to say.

I almost told him I love him. Shit.

"My kinky boyfriend," Nick murmurs, seemingly unaware of my near-confession. He repeats the words, pressing a kiss to my body between each one, as if to punctuate. "My. Kinky. Boyfriend." Raising his head, he meets my gaze with a smile. "Not one of those words scares me."

"Rockin' the bi," I tease gently. "Hey world, meet my freaky bisexual boyfriend with the kick-ass body and the hot wife who, by the way, is my girlfriend too."

Nick laughs softly. "Does Hallmark make a card for this shit?"

"Probably not. Hey, we should start a line of greeting cards for triads who come out. We'll make a fortune."

"You think there's enough of us to start a business?" He chuckles. "Hell, maybe. It's Boston. The whole town is pretty out there. And that's without factoring in Cape Cod."

I brush fingertips over my own nipple. "Okay. I love nip play, but still...ow."

"Poor baby," Nick says with mock sincerity. "You know what's good for a sore tit? A blowjob."

"Oh my God, you're insatiable," I laugh, pushing at him. "Get off me, you gorilla. My dick is off limits for at least an hour."

He chuckles but then he catches sight of the clock across the room. "Oh shit. Lance'll be here soon to deal with my, uh, stuff." He groans. "I smell like a locker room. Lance is going to be weirded out."

"Do we have time for a quick shower before he arrives? I can help, if you'll let me." I want to claw back the words as soon as I say them. "I'm sorry," I groan.

Nick just looks at me fondly as he brushes hair out of my eyes. "Don't sweat it. I had your cock in my throat so I think I can handle you getting me into the shower. We only have about fifteen minutes, so shift your ass."

I roll off the bed and position the wheelchair next to it, the way Alethia did the other night. Nick shows me how to set the brake, and how to help him transfer into the chair. I push him quickly down the hall and into the master bathroom, making racing noises with my mouth while he laughs.

The tiled shower has no lip or door. I park the chair where Nick indicates and hover to help, but he easily moves from the chair to a marble bench. The controls are set low, and a handheld nozzle near the bench lets him manage his shower. A rain head and separate controls in the opposite end of the large enclosure allow me to take my own quick shower while Nick soaps up with a sandalwood-scented bodywash.

"This will go faster if you'll shampoo me," he says. He holds onto the showerhead as I grab the bottle of shampoo.

I inhale deeply the essence of ginger and lime. "That smells so good," I say, pouring some into my hand and quickly washing Nick's hair. I take the handheld nozzle and run it over his head, using my other hand to tilt him left and right until he's suds-free. I finish rinsing my own body, put away the showerhead, and grab a thick, white towel from the nearby rack.

"Holy shit, it's warm," I exclaim.

"What can I tell you? Money has its advantages," Nick says, smiling. "A towel warmer is the least of them." He sits patiently and quietly as I quickly dry his hair and his body, reddening only when I begin to wipe at his legs.

"Baby," I murmur, but he shakes his head.

"It's fine. I have to get over this. I really do trust you, it's just difficult for me."

"Are there other things I can learn to do for you?" I ask.

Nick hesitates, and then says, "Not just yet. Okay?"

"Okay. Whenever you're ready."

We hustle into the bedroom, and I've just pulled his track pants
over his butt when we hear the front door open.

"Mr. Ballantine? I'm here," a voice calls out.

"Hi Lance," Nick yells back. "I'll be out in just a minute." He tugs
on a T-shirt, one so tight that I can see his nipples press against the
fabric.

"Are you getting all sexed up for Lance?" I whisper. "Because I
think I might have a problem with that."

"Now you know how I feel," Nick smirks. "But no, you're the only
man I'm sexing up for."

"How do you want to play this?" I ask as I run a comb through my
damp hair.

"Would you be offended if I ask you to hang out in the guest room
until Lance brings me back in here? I don't think he needs to know we
took a shower together."

"No problem. But won't he wonder why your hair is wet?"

He grins. "The second advantage of money. I won't offer an expla-
nation, and Lance won't dare to ask."

"You know, I think this is how the French Revolution started."

"Let them eat cock!" Nick cries.

I laugh quietly to myself all the way to the guest room. I hang out
there for a few minutes, straightening the bed and pulling on my
clothes, until I hear Nick roll by with Lance. He hasn't mentioned
whether I should wait around, but I have some chores to run anyway. I
slip out quietly, and wave at Tommy as I exit the building.

CHAPTER SEVENTEEN

THE REST OF Monday passes slowly. Too slowly. I find myself at loose ends, staring out a window and wondering what Alethia's doing at that moment, or what Nick's reading. Are they thinking about me, the way I think about them? Are they talking about me and the surprising situation we've landed in?

I glance over at my phone several times, hoping it will ring, fighting the urge to call like a schoolboy with his first crush.

On Tuesday Cerise puts me through hell. My session with Nick left me lightly bruised on my pecs. Before going to the gym I'd gazed in the mirror at the marks with a flush of pleasure; I realize too late that my tank top also reveals them to my trainer. I notice her eyes drifting over the exposed parts of my torso as I work through a set of bench presses. My instinct is to offer a story, but I take a page out of Nick's book and simply explain nothing.

She does ask, though, about my motivation level. "You're kicking ass today. I like it. Are you training for something? Do you want to discuss a new regimen?"

"No, nothing like that," I tell her. "I guess I'm just in a good place and it's translating to my workouts."

She frowns. "Is this something to do with the client who's blurring your lines? Or those marks on your chest?"

So much for Nick's theories about employees not daring to ask questions. You probably have to be really rich for that one to work.

"Maybe," I say, looking away and feeling my cheeks warm.

"As long as it's all consensual, none of my business," Cerise says, but she raises an eyebrow. "Of course, somebody pretty strong left those marks. Maybe you're looking to protect yourself, or get even?"

"Total fail, Nancy Drew," I say, rolling my eyes. "Yes, it's consensual. Hot even. But he's fucking shredded. Maybe I need to push myself harder, to keep him interested."

Cerise snorts. "You don't pay me enough to stroke your ego, but I seriously doubt you have to worry about that. You're pretty cute, for a man."

"Uh, thanks?"

"You're welcome. I'm all in favor of a little healthy competition. If you want to impress your guy, maybe you're ready to work on your definition. You've always told me you want to keep that soft, young thing going. I suppose it's good for getting attention in the clubs. But for my money, a low body-fat percentage is hotter than mere bulk any day of the week. You'd have to make some changes to your diet, and I'll kick your ass in a whole different way."

I'm suddenly tired of fighting to remain a twink. I'm ready to look my age, and embrace the idea of having a man's body. "You know, I like that idea. Let's make Jasper 2.0 the new goal."

ALETHIA ALREADY WAITS near a window when I arrive at the restaurant on Walden Street, a few minutes away from Harvard Square. The glow of sunset through the glass shines on her black hair and lights her face with glory. Her eyes sparkle as I approach the table.

"I'm so sorry," I apologize. "Traffic was much worse than I expected." I lean in for a kiss, the lusciousness of her lips against mine going straight to my groin. I intend it as a peck but linger instead, unwilling to break away. Finally, I realize I'm probably making a spectacle of us both, and sit reluctantly.

Alethia reaches out to twine our fingers together. "With a kiss like that, all is forgiven," she teases. "Honestly, I didn't mind. I knew it had to be traffic. Would you like some wine? This Beaujolais I'm drinking is delicious."

"That sounds nice," I say, and Alethia signals to a waitress to bring me the same as she's having.

I look around the restaurant's quirky interior. It's a mixture of reclaimed wood, brushed metal, and framed illustrations of fanciful animals dressed up in human clothes. "This is really cute."

"It just opened a few weeks ago. The chair of my department mentioned he'd had a great meal here, so when we decided to meet in Cambridge, it popped into my mind."

At my prompting, Alethia talks about her day teaching and working on her own research into Boccaccio's *Decameron*. I tell her about my training session and the things Cerise came up with to break my spirit. We discuss my lunch date with Nick, and a movie they watched together last evening. Relaxing quickly with the glass of red wine, I soon find myself telling Alethia more about my military service, and how I felt unprepared for the real world when my enlistment ended.

"I went into the Army because I didn't know what I wanted to do with my life, and I figured the GI Bill would guarantee me a college education once I was done. There was no way I could have afforded a good school otherwise unless I went massively into debt. The problem was, even after four years in, I didn't know what I wanted to do."

"You were only, what, about twenty-two?" Alethia asks. "I see many students who didn't figure out what they wanted to study in college until they were in their late twenties or early thirties."

I give her a wry look. "I bet not many of them took the same detour I did, though."

She smiles back. "Don't be too sure. My first year teaching, I had a young man ask me for an extension on a paper. He was up for an award at the show for porn actors in Las Vegas."

I bark out a laugh. "Did you give him the extension?"

"Of course! I support the arts fully," Alethia says with a teasing glint in her eyes. "We were studying *The Canterbury Tales* then. I suggested he write about his experience as if it were one of Chaucer's stories. The piece was brilliantly funny, and got published in the *Harvard Advocate*."

She sips her wine, then says, "I'm actually surprised you haven't been to college. Your vocabulary is extensive and sophisticated."

I shrug, abashed. "I always did well in English class. Plus there's all the reading I do. Something's bound to seep into my head from all those books."

"If you ever decide to pursue college, you'll want to take placement tests. You may be able to get a significant number of credit hours without sitting through the classes. That could shorten a degree program for you."

That actually does seem interesting to me. "Maybe we can talk more about school some time," I say sheepishly. "I like to learn but I always had trouble sitting still in class."

"Have you considered teaching?"

Huh. As soon as she says it, I flash to tutoring Wes Cole in English all those years ago. "I never did, until you just mentioned it."

We pause long enough to order, and I push the notion aside to consider later. It amazes me that I've had years to muddle through these questions, with no success. Then Alethia, in a single short conversation, plucks two interesting ideas from my tangled head. For the first time, I begin to think that maybe I don't have to figure everything out on my own.

Alethia pushes aside her menu and says to the waitress, "I've heard wonderful things about Chef Darcy. I'll put myself in her hands."

"Me too," I say, though I'm mildly surprised. I've never asked a chef to cook whatever she wants for me. Alethia's instinct turns out to be spot-on, though. The salads, appetizers and entrees that come out of the kitchen are things I'd probably never order, but turn out to be wonderful. The waitress passes along the chef's suggested wine pairings for each course, which we happily follow.

The good food and wine underscore our easy conversation. I try to regale Alethia with no-name tales of my most demanding clients. In turn, she tells me about deciding to study in China when she was a freshman because it was the best way to get out from under her father's watchful eye.

"My mother died when I was just ten," she explains. "My father seemed to believe he had to fulfill both parenting roles. He meant well, of course, but it was stifling. Bodyguards followed me wherever I went, and he wanted to meet every friend I spent time with. I realized that my only hope of enjoying college was to go far, far away. Beijing was what I chose because, at the time, it was one of the few places where he didn't have any business interests. He still jetted over once a month or so, and at least for the first two years he insisted I come home for every school break.

"The distance really helped our relationship, though. And along the way, I learned fluent Mandarin. That was useful when he decided to expand his operation into China. I even toyed with the idea of joining Bampás' business, but ultimately I realized it was academics I really love. Still, it was a success all around."

By the time our desserts arrive along with glasses of a Sauterne, I'm even further in awe of Alethia's accomplishments. She has the mind to do anything well, the face of a movie star, the wealth and connections to conquer the world if she chooses. What's she doing having dinner with a professional escort who barely got through high school?

I keep a handle on my insecurities, though. If I know anything about Alethia already, it's that her heart is honest. If she says that she wants to be with me, then I have to believe her.

And oh, how I want to.

Chef Darcy comes out to meet us halfway through dessert. She's a tiny woman with bushy red hair, and deeply appreciative of our praise.

Alethia takes her hand and says quietly, "I'd like to tell some very influential people what a gem you've created here. You should know that attention is going to be exciting, dazzling, and terrifying in equal measure. Do you feel ready for that, Chef?"

The woman looks nervously at me, then back to Alethia. She pulls herself to her full height, squares her shoulders, and says, "Absolutely."

Alethia smiles. "Done. I'm going to book a table right now for one month from today, because I think you'll be such a smash soon that I won't get through the door otherwise."

Chef Darcy seems giddy and nervous as she insists on bringing us one more dessert, in a beautiful box wrapped with a blue satin bow. Alethia kisses her cheek. "Thank you so much. My husband will just love this."

The chef flicks a confused glance at me. If I'm not her husband...? I just smile at her, and ask our hovering waitress for the check.

"Please let me," Alethia tries, but I pull the folio to me.

"Uh uh uh! You agreed to go on a date with me, so I get to pay. When you take me out, then I promise not to fight you for the check." I grin. "I told Nick the same thing yesterday."

"Very well. Thank you, darling. This was a lovely and romantic first date. I'm so glad we got to spend this time together." She rises gracefully and picks up the boxed dessert. "Now I think we should deliver this to Nick to enjoy while he binge-watches *Black Sails*, and then you and I are going to continue getting to know each other."

"I cannot wait."

NICK TAKES THE box delightedly. "Cake!" he exclaims. "Don't tell Billy if I eat the entire thing."

I get him a fork from the kitchen, somewhat amazed that I'm learning my way around this luxurious apartment so well. When I return with the utensil, Nick breaks off a piece of the ganache-covered chocolate indulgence and offers it out to me. I open my mouth to take in the morsel, and Nick follows the sweet with a kiss.

We share the tastes of chocolate and raspberry. "Mmm," Nick murmurs. "Delicious. And the cake ain't bad either." When I laugh softly. Nick meets my eyes and smiles. "You and Alethia have fun tonight. I promise you. I'm really happy about it. Give our woman what she needs."

I nod, my throat tightening.

Nick shares a bite with Alethia as well and speaks low to her, so softly I can't hear. I guess it's a similar message because Alethia catches my eye. The desire I see growing in her face ignites a spark in my belly.

Suddenly, I burn to devote all of my attention to her lithe body. I stand, squeeze Nick's bicep, then hold out my hand for Alethia's. She takes it and leads me into the guest room.

We've barely undressed each other when Alethia sinks her teeth into my neck. "Darling, I know how good you are with your tongue and fingers, but I can't wait any longer for your cock. I just want you to fuck me until I scream."

"What kind of gentleman would refuse such a request?" I tease. My dick throbs where I rub against Alethia's soft skin. I growl, "You looked so fucking beautiful tonight. I wanted to drag you back to the kitchen and have you in front of the entire staff."

Alethia shivers at my words. "I had no idea what a slut I have buried inside me," she rasps as my tongue sweeps along her neck.

"Not a slut," I correct. "A gorgeous, vital woman who likes it when people see her take her pleasure."

"A lucky woman, anyway. It occurred to me today that if Lady Chatterley had been a bit more liberated, she wouldn't have had to choose between her husband and her lover."

"Wait, am I a gardener in this metaphor?" I chuckle.

"Some sources suggest that the word 'fuck' derives from an old word meaning 'to till the soil'." Alethia grasps my thick shaft and angles it to rub between her thighs, drenched already with her nectar. "Show me how you garden, Jasper," she teases.

I frot Alethia, growing harder by the second against her wetness. She throws her arms around my neck, burying her face against my shoulder as we grind our bodies together. With a sharp gasp, she frees my cock and pushes until I fall back on the bed.

"Look at it," she sighs, reaching for my glistening cock. "Pulsing. So hot in my hand."

I fold my arms beneath my head and smile up at her. "I'm all yours, Alethia. Take whatever you want from me."

"This," she cries out, leaning forward to lap at the head of my dick. "I have to have it inside me. Now." Climbing from the bed, she roots through the drawer containing condoms and lube.

In seconds, I'm sheathed, first in latex and then in velvet warmth. Alethia rides me, squeezing and mauling her breasts as she works her way along my length. She bears down hard, swiveling her hips and clenching my dick. Reaching back, she takes my sac in her hand and tugs on my balls until my teeth ache with the pleasure.

I grab Alethia's hip with one hand, and with the thumb of the other, work her clit the way Nick taught me she loves. The ripples begin almost right away. A blood flush creeps along her neck, and she huffs as she fucks herself on my cock faster and faster. She moans and shakes, releasing my balls to fall forward against my chest. My arms come up around her, and I roll us both over so I can pound harder.

She's so different from the woman of our previous encounters that it momentarily takes me by surprise. Then I realize how much Alethia kept herself within control to avoid adding to Nick's guilt. This wanton, writhing creature who loves to fuck has been denied for nearly two years.

Well, not anymore, I vow as the first orgasm leaves her sobbing in pleasure and I keep going. I'll be there for Alethia, to give her the kind of Olympic fucking she deserves. I'll be there for Nick, too, helping him to explore his sexuality in any way that he wants.

I'll be there for both together, finding ways to surprise and make them come. Ideas crowd my brain, filling it with raunchy and exciting images of tit clamps, restraints, feathers, lace. Everything I've learned in my escort career is one more way I can bring pleasure and joy to the man and woman who I lo—

No. Even to myself, I still avoid naming it out of superstition. Too scary. Too overwhelming.

I bury my passion inside Alethia with my dick, driving into her with everything I want to be true but can't say. My reward is her second orgasm, which triggers my own.

Through our harmonizing cries of ecstasy, I register the faint sound of wheels squeaking quietly to a halt outside the bedroom door. I know that Nick's listening to his wife getting fucked. More, I believe he's happy about it, about Alethia and me giving each other as much pleasure as he shared with me yesterday.

Nick and Alethia. My heart fills to bursting, and I know that, as long as they want me, I'll be here.

CHAPTER EIGHTEEN

W HEN OUR LOVING'S done, I lie, exhausted, with Alethia in my arms. I've dealt with the condoms—plural, thank you very much—and crawled back into bed to draw Alethia close. Languid and sleek, she dozes on my shoulder as I stroke her glorious hair.

Something keeps me from nodding off, though. After a moment's thought, I know what it is.

"Ali?" I whisper in case she's asleep.

"Yes, darling?"

"Can we go join Nick in bed? I love falling asleep with both of you near me."

She stretches her neck to kiss me. "Of course. That's the perfect way to end this perfect date." We climb out of bed and walk down the hall, hand in hand.

Nick lays propped against his pillows, lit by a bedside lamp, with a book fallen across his hairy chest. A slight smile graces his features even in sleep. Alethia and I share a look of fondness for our man. She flips off the light while I carefully retrieve his book and set it aside.

Nick wakes briefly when I crawl in on one side, Alethia the other. He makes a sweet sound of contentment as he gathers us both into his arms, and is out again in moments.

I rest my cheek against Nick's big, steady pec while Alethia lightly strokes his arm. Despite my fears, sleep finds me easily.

AFTER BREAKFAST WITH Nick and Alethia the next morning, I head home. By mid-afternoon, I've begun to regret the training session yesterday with Cerise. My muscles ache from the strain of the different exercises she introduced. I stand for a long time under a hot shower, trying to ease my muscles before I dress for the date with Meredith.

Though I shouldn't think of it as a date. It's an appointment to attend a museum fundraiser as her escort, nothing more. Alethia texted me earlier that she'd spoken with Meredith to indicate I, or rather JD, would be arm candy only for the gala. I don't know exactly what she told Meredith, or how she explained why she's the one to deliver the message. The uncertainty and lack of detail leave me nervous about our looming interaction.

Shortly before I'd planned to leave to meet Meredith, the doorman for my building buzzes the house phone.

"Good evening, Mr. Dylan. Your limo has arrived."

"Limo? What do you mean?" I didn't order a limo. Meredith doesn't know my real name or address, so it can't be her. Maybe Alethia arranged a surprise visit? She knows I have an appointment this evening, though, so it's unlikely.

Nick? That's possible. As jealous as he is, I wouldn't put it past Nick to try to distract me.

"Is there a problem, sir?" the doorman asks over the phone after the silence stretches.

"No, no problem," I answer. "I'll be right there."

Shrugging into my suit jacket and my camel overcoat—a gift from Meredith—I check for my keys and wallet, then step out of my apartment. When I exit the elevator, I can see a beautiful big car standing outside. It's a Maybach, I realize. A tall man in a chauffeur's uniform stands next to the rear door, waiting. I lift a hand in greeting to my doorman, then straighten my shoulders. Whatever's going on puzzles me, but I see no reason to be alarmed. Still, I veer toward the desk.

"Lionel, did they ask for me by name?"

"Sure, Mr. Dylan," Lionel rasps. "The tall feller there came in and asked me to let Mr. Jasper Dylan know that his car had arrived."

"Huh. Okay, thanks."

I walk through the main doors and approach the car slowly. It's a beautiful machine, a midnight-blue work of art with silver accents. The chauffeur turns at my approach, and the car window rolls down. Meredith waves at me through the opening.

"Surprise, JD. I thought I'd pick you up."

Alarm bells begin to jangle. I look left and right; the sidewalk's reasonably busy at this hour of the day. Nothing seems untoward.

I approach the car door. "I'm surprised to see you here, Meredith,"

I say cautiously. "I didn't know you had my address."

She waves a hand dismissively. "Don't you remember when we had that suit delivered to you for the charity auction last spring?"

I don't, but I suppose it's possible. The chauffeur opens the suicide door for me. Meredith slides over on the leather seat to make room, and pats the empty space she's left by the window.

With a last look back at my doorman, watching intently, I step into the car. Almost immediately, the chauffeur closes the door. Only then do I realize that Meredith and I aren't alone.

Opposite from us, a man sits on a facing seat, reclining casually. He looks about Meredith's age, with thick, white hair brushed back from his temples. Penetrating gray-green eyes remain fixed on me, behind drooping eyelids. He wears a linen blazer over a white silk shirt, and crisp trousers; his crossed legs end in polished leather car shoes. I wouldn't call him handsome, but he has presence.

The car pulls away almost immediately. I resist the urge to fling open the door and jump out, but my fingers twitch toward the handle anyway. The man gives a throaty chuckle at the motion.

"Jasper," Meredith begins, then pauses. "May I call you Jasper? I'd like you to meet someone. Adras Papathanassíou, this is JD Pierce. Or, as I've learned this evening, Jasper Dylan."

My heart begins to pound. A bolt of fear shoots through me and makes my balls shrivel. Alethia's wealthy father just effectively scooped me off the sidewalk in front of my own building, with Meredith's help. My mouth suddenly dry, I debate whether I should pull out my phone and dial for help.

The man leans across the divide and extends a hand; I take it cautiously. His grip is firm and warm. Still, he says nothing, but continues to watch me with those eyes so like Alethia's.

Swallowing with difficulty, I try for casual. "It's a pleasure to meet you, Mr. Papath… uh, Papathan—"

"Call me Adras," the man says with another low chuckle. "I can't stand to hear my name mangled."

"All right." I flick a glance at Meredith, then mentally shrug. "Please call me Jasper."

"You're nervous," Adras says bluntly. "Do I seem frightening?"

I wet my lips cautiously. "I'm a little surprised, to be honest. I'm assuming that Alethia doesn't know that you've—That we're meeting?"

"Kidnapped you? Is that what you were going to say?" Adras asks. He leans back on his seat. His voice becomes deeper and quiet in a way that makes the hair on my neck stand. "It would be rather foolish of me to attempt something like that in broad daylight, in a memorable car like this. Wouldn't it?"

I nod slowly, trying to slow my racing heartbeat. "Lionel—my doorman—I could tell he was really impressed with it. Watched me get in. Maybe even noted the plate."

Adras snorts, dismissing my unsubtle attempt to warn him off. "Would you like a drink?" he asks, gesturing at a built-in cabinet. Bottles of scotch, vodka and gin sit in neat slots to hold them steady; crystal glasses and a bucket of ice similarly sit secured. "I'm having scotch," Adras adds when I fail to reply. "Meredith?"

"A small vodka on the rocks, if you don't mind," she says.

Adras puts several spheres of clear ice in two glasses and pours a small measure of vodka in each. He offers one glass to Meredith, and the other to me. I take it with fingers that tremble only a bit. Surely if I were in some kind of danger, my kidnapper wouldn't give me a drink first.

Adras pours his scotch, neat, and then clinks his crystal tumbler against Meredith's glass. He offers it to me as well; I return the gesture without taking my eyes off the inscrutable man facing me. Reclined on his seat again, Adras sips his drink, though his heavy-lidded gaze never wavers.

I take a swallow of my vodka, barely noticing the smooth finish of one of the more refined liquors I've ever tasted. The silence in the car begins to weigh.

Finally, I blurt out, "Where are we going?"

"Just for a drive," Adras answers.

Meredith glances at her slim gold wristwatch. "The fundraiser begins in less than an hour. I'm one of the hostesses. I really need to be there."

"We'll drop you off," Adras says, then presses a button on the console near him. "Jimmy, take us to the Museum of Fine Arts please."

"Yes sir" comes back over the intercom.

Meredith frowns. "Am I to go alone, Adras?"

He gives her a slow, tight smile. "I arranged for another companion for you this evening. He'll meet us at the museum." He looks deliberately over my face and body. "Maybe not as handsome, but you won't be embarrassed."

Meredith murmurs something, too low for me to hear.

Adras fixes her with his penetrating eyes. "What did you say?" he demands.

Meredith flushes and says, "This evening isn't turning out the way I'd hoped at all. First Alethia tells me that JD is committed for after the gala so I shouldn't plan on keeping him out late. Now you're taking him away from me for the event as well."

I jump on Meredith's comments. I don't have plans to see Nick and Alethia this evening, but Adras doesn't know that. "Alethia is expecting me by ten," I say. "She might get worried if I'm not there. Even come by my apartment to see why I'm delayed—"

Adras grimaces. "Well, that answers one question. My daughter knows where you live, which I presume means she's aware of your real name."

I nod. "She is. Both Nick and Alethia know who I am."

Meredith sighs. "I should be hurt that you've kept that from me after all this time, but it makes sense. You need to keep your…professional activities separate from the rest of your life."

"Then why did you tell my daughter?" Adras barks out. I reel in my seat, clutching my vodka to keep it from spilling.

Adras leans forward again and says gruffly, "Look, Mr. Dylan. We can resolve this quickly. I'll give you two million dollars if you agree never to see Alethia and Nick again."

"Are you serious?" I ask, pride burning away some of my fears. "No, don't answer that. It doesn't matter whether you're serious or not. I don't want your money, and it's up to Alethia and Nick if they want to keep seeing me."

"It's a lot of money," Adras says in a wheedling tone. "You live in a decent building, but you could afford something much nicer with a big nest egg to fall back on. You shouldn't rely on my daughter's generosity."

I look back and forth between the two of them, feeling my spine stiffen to a ramrod. They apparently assume that Alethia remains a paying client. What Nick, Alethia and I actually mean to each other, what we're developing, is private. Intimate. Maybe the most important thing that's ever happened to me. It's nobody's business but our own.

"I'm not going to discuss Alethia at all, and most especially not with her father and friend."

"Then what about Nick?" Adras demands, his eyes narrowing. "Does he know what's going on with his wife? The poor man has been through enough. If you're trying to lead his wife into something, maybe extract money—"

"I've had enough of this," I snarl. Who the fuck does he think he is? The implication that I'd do anything to hurt Nick, or to exploit Alethia, makes me furious. "The intimidation routine is getting old already. If you want to know anything about your daughter and son-in-law, I suggest you ask them. Hopefully they'll tell you to stick your questions up your ass, but that's up to them."

I toss back the rest of my vodka and hand the empty glass to Meredith. "Thank you for the drink. I'd like to get out now."

"We're in a tunnel," Adras says with a grunt.

"Then let's see what happens when I kick this fucking door open into traffic." I raise my foot, ready to smash it into the burled wood paneling.

Adras holds up a hand in a gesture to wait. He presses the intercom again. "Jimmy, change of plans. As soon as you can exit and let a passenger out safely, please pull over."

"Yes sir."

I lower my foot and glare back and forth from Meredith to Adras. I'm surprised to see amusement, and perhaps some grudging respect, in Adras' eyes.

"You only had to ask," Adras says, reaching to take my glass from Meredith. He adds some more vodka and passes it over.

"What is all this?" I ask, my eyes narrowing. But I take the glass.

Adras sighs, and the hard features he's been showing to me begin to soften. "Alethia is my only child. She's the reason for every single thing I do. Once we lost her mother, she became the light in my life. And Nick is the son I never had. I love that boy like he's my own." He tosses back his scotch, then returns the glass to its cradle. "When Meredith told me that Alethia warned her off of you, I needed to know why."

"Wouldn't it have been better to ask Alethia?"

"Ask my daughter why the gigolo that she and her husband hired is making multiple repeat visits? Ask her why said gigolo and her husband went out to lunch together? Why she's buying him expensive clothes?

Why she met him for dinner in Cambridge, without her husband?" Adras shakes his head. "There are some things a father can't discuss."

I begin to bristle again. Adras has us under surveillance. *Tommy*, I guess. *Maybe even George and Lance.*

"I'm not a gigolo," I grit out. "A gigolo is a kept man. I'm an escort, yes, but I've never tried to worm my way into my clients' lives. I'm not looking for gifts or someone to support me." I glare at Meredith. "I never asked you for anything beyond the fees we agreed in advance. I accepted this coat, I admit, and some clothes from you. But you can't say I ever made it seem like I wanted something more than our professional relationship."

Meredith shifts to lean against her seat back, legs bent and ankles crossed smartly. She nods slowly. "It's true. Our transactions were straightforward and honest. That's why I felt comfortable recommending you when Adras asked me to talk to Alethia about what she needed."

Adras huffs. "I don't want to hear details. It's obvious she and Nick had physical difficulties to overcome, and it was putting a bad strain on a good marriage. Let's leave it at that."

My jaw drops. "When *Adras* asked… You mean, he asked you to find someone for Alethia and Nick? Alethia didn't come to you first?"

"Oh, she thinks she did," Meredith says dismissively. "But I actually put the idea into her head, once Adras got me involved. Of course he'd already vetted you thoroughly before I mentioned your name to her."

Turning wide eyes to Adras, I'm surprised to see the poised man blush a little. Adras clears his throat. "I went no further than I needed in order to make sure my girl was safe with you."

"What, you ran a background check on me?" I sit back, stunned.

Adras shrugs self-consciously. "Eh. Standard stuff really, as I would for any individual I planned to hire or do business with. Financial data, arrest records, in your case service records. That sort of thing."

I gape at him. "Have you no decency?" I sputter.

Adras reddens, but his voice remains calm and reasonable. "My daughter is wealthy in her own right, and heir to a very large fortune from me. I've always checked carefully into everyone who enters her orbit, to make sure of their intentions and their character. She isn't even aware of the number of people I've steered away from her when I had reason to suspect they were angling for money or position."

"Even Nick?" I demand. "Did you investigate Nick before you set them up?"

Adras chuckles. "They told you about that, did they? But yes. With Nick, I actually had some tough decisions to make." He smiles fondly. "He was a real playboy when he was younger. It took me a long time to confirm that the big, playful kid was exactly what he seemed and not a fortune hunter."

"I can't believe what I'm hearing," I say. "Alethia would be furious if she knew."

Adras nods thoughtfully. "That's true. So why do you think I told you?"

That makes my jaw snap shut. Why did he tell me?

Carefully, I talk it through. "You gave me information that I could use to poison your relationship with your daughter. Maybe you want me to think that you trust me." I blink, then narrow my eyes. "It's got to be more than that. I could make myself look like the injured party, if I were trying to gain some advantage with her. But I wouldn't do that, and it wouldn't work anyway. Alethia's brilliant. She might not forgive you, but she certainly wouldn't think well of me. So the logical answer is… No, I don't really get why you gave me a way to hurt you."

Adras shrugs. "If you're the man my investigators described to me, you'll never use this information. If you aren't, then the best way to make sure Alethia knows that is to let her see you try to hurt me. As you say, she's brilliant. She'd see instantly what you're up to." His piercing eyes focus squarely on me again. "There's nothing I wouldn't do for her. That includes putting our relationship at risk if it's for her own good."

"I don't know if that's loving, or insane," I say.

"It's Greek," Adras answers simply, like that explains everything. The car stops just then. "And here we are."

He rolls down the window; we seem to be near the harbor. "Do you still want to get out, or should I have Jimmy drop you somewhere?"

"I suppose accompanying me to the gala is out," Meredith says with a sigh. "I understand. You feel betrayed or used. I can't expect your sparkling company after that. Ah well. It's the price to pay for protecting Alethia. I may not be as pathological about it as Adras, but her mother was my dearest friend. I vowed to do everything I could for Alethia, to make up for her loss. With the best will in the world, there are simply things Adras could never do for her, or understand. That's why it fell to me to make this sacrifice."

I frown. "You expected this to happen? That Alethia would become more than a client and I'd stop seeing you?"

"So she is more than a client to you?" Meredith asks. "I thought so, but thank you for confirming it."

Dammit. I blush.

"And Nick knows about it?" Adras asks, frowning.

Heart pounding again, I stare back and think furiously. These people are too clever, getting me to reveal things I have no intention of disclosing. They monitor me, investigate me, probably already know the answer to their own questions. Well, I'm not going to betray any more of the Ballantines' trust.

Tersely, I say, "Whatever you want to know, you should ask them directly." I reach for the car door.

"Wait," Adras says. "Answer one question for me, and you have my word I will stop all of the surveillance and investigation."

I narrow my eyes. "What's the question?"

"Is Nick fully aware of everything going on with you and my daughter?"

Biting my lip, I debate the right thing to do. Answering with a simple yes won't betray how our relationship works, or Nick's self-discoveries. Plus, I'm already worrying about who monitors our comings and goings, and whether they'll discover things Alethia and Nick aren't ready for the world to know. Assuming Adras keeps his word, it will ease my mind to return to their condo.

"Yes," I snap, and fall silent.

Adras nods. "All right. I'll pass the instruction promptly. Are you sure I can't drop you somewhere more convenient?"

"I prefer a cab, thank you," I say as I open the door and climb out.

"Goodbye, JD," Meredith calls. "I really do think the world of you. I suspect we'll meet again. I want you to know you have my utmost discretion."

I nod, unwilling to discuss the matter further. She'll keep to herself what she knows about my past, or she won't. There's nothing more I can do about it.

CHAPTER NINETEEN

O NLY WHEN THE Maybach has pulled away and I've hailed a taxi does my own stray thought echo in my head.

My past. Not my present, but my past.

The confrontation with Adras has somehow cemented in my head what I'd already begun to suspect. I've been lucky with my escorting, but on my own, I had little to lose. Adras had no trouble finding my double identity; anyone who wants to get to Alethia and Nick could do the same. I have no idea who or why someone would do that, but Adras seemed convinced it's a potential issue. I don't want to be the pressure point.

And even if Adras is just being paranoid, he's shown me how vulnerable I am. By extension, anything that happens to me is going to affect Alethia and Nick. How would they feel if I get arrested for prostitution? What if I contract an STD?

It's over, I realize. I'm not going to see any more clients as JD Pierce. That way lies only risk to the most important people in my life.

Besides, if I want the kind of connection and love I see between the Ballantines, I can't expect a lover to sit by while I have sex with other people for money. My savings won't last forever, but I have enough cushion I can take some time, figure out what I want to do next. I desperately hope it'll include Alethia and Nick—I think it will—but my escort days are through either way.

Is that decision unfair though? Does it put too much pressure on the situation, pressure that could tear apart our new and fragile beginning? Nick gleefully admits to being a fast worker, and knowing exactly what he wants. Alethia's more of a mystery to me still.

As my cab carries me across the Longfellow Bridge, my leg jerks spasmodically and I tap my foot against the floor. Adrenaline spiked in me during that…*whatever* it was with Adras and Meredith, in the

Maybach. It drains away slowly, leaving me with a hollow, unsettled feeling. Selfishly, I need to restore my equilibrium. I need Nick and Alethia, even though I have no idea what I want to say to them, or talk to them about. If we truly are in a relationship, then is it all right for me to ask for what I need? I'm not entirely sure, but I have to take the risk.

Berating myself for my indecision, I pull my cell phone from my jacket pocket and dial the number I stored after Nick's most recent call to me. It connects on the third ring.

"Jasper, darling. I didn't think we'd hear from you this evening. How is the gala?" Alethia asks sweetly.

"I, uh, didn't go. Listen, feel free to say no, but could I come by? I don't want to interrupt if you have anything planned."

"Of course you should come. Chloe is just finishing with her dinner preparations. Can you join us? I'll ask her to set a third place."

"If it isn't an imposition—"

"Not at all. Just come in when you arrive. I'll leave the door unlocked for you."

Between giving my cab driver the new address I want and actually pulling up in front of the condo building, I change my mind five times. *This is a mistake* wars with *I need them*. After weeks of trying to fulfill a role, of forging connections, of learning what Nick and Alethia want, I'm the one who hungers.

Tommy sees me come in. "Good evening, Mr. Pierce."

"Hi, Tommy," I call as I head for the elevator. I can't resist a jab. "You might want to note that it's eight fifteen when I'm going up."

Tommy turns scarlet and drops his eyes to the desk. He mutters, "Have a good evening, sir."

Little shit.

Upstairs, I rap my knuckles to announce myself but open the door anyway. The dining table is set with three plates. Candles flicker, their light captured in the ruby-red wine of three glasses. Nick puts a finger in his book where he reads in the living area, looking to me with a broad smile of greeting.

Alethia joins me at the door, pressing a drink into my hands. "You sounded a bit distressed on the phone. I guessed you could use this." She kisses my cheek and I slide an arm around her waist. The scent of orange blossoms rises from her skin, and her warm body begins to ease my racing mind. I kiss her deeply.

"Mmm," she says when I end it. "I'll take more of that after dinner, please."

Nick has rolled closer, a grin stretching his generous mouth as he watches his wife make out with his boyfriend. A rush of affection heats my cheeks as I crouch by the chair. Nick pulls me close by my neck, the weight and strength of his hand further grounding my taut nerves as we kiss hello.

"I'm sorry for dropping in like this," I whisper against Nick's mouth.

"Don't be," Nick replies. "You belong here, with us."

I rest my forehead against Nick's. "My God, the things you say. You're so brave."

"Persistent," Nick says. "Maybe overbearing. Infatuated, for sure. But never insincere."

Alethia brushes a hand through my hair. "Would you like to sit with us and enjoy your drink before we eat? Everything Chloe made tonight can keep."

I follow her to the living area, Nick rolling behind us. While I take my usual place, Alethia curls next to me, leaning against my body with her legs tucked underneath. Nick stops close enough to touch, a smug smile quirking his mouth.

"You ditched Meredith for us, huh?" he asks.

I snort. "Something like that." I sip at my whiskey, nervous all over again. "As good as the first time," I murmur, tilting the glass toward Nick.

"I can tell something's on your mind," Alethia says as she toys with the hair on my neck. "Do you want to talk about it?"

I nod, then drain my liquid courage. Alethia takes my empty glass and sets it on the side table before pressing against me again. Nick rests a warm hand on my knee, and just like that, all three of us are connected.

The way we should be.

My mind clears at the revelation, and I know what I want to say to them. "I made a decision tonight," I begin. "I'm through with escorting. JD Pierce is retiring for good."

Alethia gives a pleased little sound. Nick squeezes my leg, a sheen appearing in his eyes. "Because of us?" he asks, and I nod.

"I want this," I say. "Both of you. Just you, and what's happening here. I realized you were right to be jealous, Nick. I can't see clients, have sex with them, and pretend it doesn't affect you. All of us, really." I blush, once the words are out. "I hope that doesn't put too much pressure on us, or something. I just really needed you to know, as soon as I decided."

Alethia kisses my cheek. "If you're sure, darling. We don't want you to feel obligated to give up that part of your life."

"Ali doesn't, but I do," Nick admits, grinning broadly. "I know that makes me a greedy little fucker. Alethia's a way better person than me; no point in pretending otherwise. Even not knowing anything about your clients, they kind of pissed me off in the abstract. We've got magic here, the three of us. I'm so fucking happy you know that too." He brushes the heel of his hand against his eye. "Aw shit. Now you'll know how sappy I am."

"To be honest, I wasn't sure how you'd take this," I say. "We talked about months or a year. I was worried I'd scare you away, dropping a bombshell like this."

"Oh no, Jasper," Alethia protests, hugging me. Her own clear eyes brim with tears. "We were the ones who were afraid of driving you away if we asked for too much too soon. Well, I was. Nick is simply fearless."

"And right," Nick crows. "Admit it, Ali. I said Jasper would do this within a month."

"Oh, you're insufferable," Alethia huffs. "It's true, though. Nick told me Monday night that he thought you were secretly as committed to this as we are, and you were almost ready to admit it."

Nick holds up a hand for a high-five. "Nailed it. Right, dude?"

I laugh thickly and smack his palm. "Right, dude. I don't know how I feel about being so transparent. I always imagined JD as a man of mystery. You know? Maybe a spy, like James Bond."

"Aw, hell, JD Pierce may be a kick-ass spy turned escort," Nick concedes. "But Jasper Dylan? He wears his heart on his well-tailored sleeve. It's the eyes, man. You show everything you're feeling."

I snort. "And you don't?"

Nick laughs. "Do I look like I'm fronting? Fuck yeah, I let it shine, with the people I really love."

I suck in my breath and feel my eyes flare wide. Nick's smile turns shy, and his cheeks redden. "I'm in love with you, Jasper. You and Ali, you're the only people I've said that to in my life. But it's absolutely true."

Stunned, I look at Alethia to see how she reacts to such a declaration from her husband. She gazes back at me with unmistakable tenderness and hunger.

"I love you too, Jasper. It's just *right*, the three of us. Already I cannot imagine our lives without you in it. Nick is so much better than I am about letting his feelings out. I'll have to show you day by day how much I love you, and how welcome you are in our lives."

I look back and forth between their hopeful faces. My heart thunders in my chest as my joy spirals up and up and up. The room blurs to nothing but a black-haired goddess and a man handsome enough to grace billboards, both watching me intently.

"I love you both. So much," I choke out. "I don't know how this is possible in such a short time. I don't even care. I don't know how I got so lucky, but I'm yours."

"I need to hug both of you," Nick declares, "but this chair doesn't make it easy. Shove over."

Laughing, Alethia and I scoot apart on the sofa, making room. Nick locks his chair and, a little self-consciously, pivots over and between us. Arms twine round, heads bend close, and the three of us share kisses and murmurs and touches.

I don't even realize I'm crying until Alethia kisses my tears away. Nick grasps my hand and says, "I'd like to move this into the bedroom, if it's okay with both of you. Less awkward that way."

Alethia dabs the corner of her eyes. She nods and looks at me questioningly. I stand, pulling off my jacket and shirt as I rise. I toss them onto Nick's lap and run down the hall, chased by Alethia.

When Nick gets to the bedroom, Alethia and I are already naked and on the bed. "Damn," he says. "You're so hot together."

"It's even hotter when you're with us," Alethia says. "I need you, Nicholas. We need you."

Hurriedly, Nick docks his chair, pulls off his black polo, and transfers onto the bed. Alethia and I descend on him, tossing his shoes and socks wildly, then hesitating at the button of his pants. Nick blinks but then grins at us. "Go ahead," he says. I bend to kiss him as Alethia opens and unzips his pants, and we work together to tug them down.

"Briefs too," Nick instructs. "If you can change your life for us, the least I can do is not be afraid of getting naked in front of you." Alethia shows me how to open the tabs and remove the garment; I set it on the floor.

Nick lays there before me in all his glory. His thick cock lolls across his hip, and his balls hang heavily between his spread legs, almost to the bedspread. I hesitate before running my hand along his still thigh and to his stomach. Nick quivers somewhere just above his pelvis. He whispers, "That's where I start to feel again."

I bend to kiss the spot, over and over, bringing my tongue into play as I lick along his hipbone and up to his waist. Alethia throws a leg across Nick's torso and leans over him. They begin to make out and I watch Nick's cock swell and stir. Alethia's position exposes her mound and her ass to me. As I lick my way along Nick's abdomen, I continue right up to her cleft. I hear her sharp inhalation as I lap at her clit and then into her folds.

"You taste so good," I sigh, before diving back in. I see the pucker of her little hole. We've never discussed how Alethia feels about anal. Experimentally, I drag my tongue across her labia, between her legs, and up the crack of her ass. She makes a deep, gratifying sound and pushes back against my face. Grinning, I take that as a green light and swipe my tongue right over her opening.

"Aaaah," Alethia moans deeply.

"Are you rimming her?" Nick asks. "That's the only time she makes that sound."

She silences him with a kiss but continues to writhe under my tongue. I bring fingers to her vagina and slide two in, while crooking my thumb at the edge of her hole. I lick her some more, wet my thumb, and press lightly. She drops her head to the side of Nick, arching her back like a cat.

I breach her so I'm holding her by the asshole and vagina at the same time. The noises she's making are incredible. I'm so hard I think my dick might break, and Nick's is now at full mast.

Alethia extends her elbows so once again she's hovering above Nick. He puts his hands in her hair on either side of her head. I can see him gaze up at her adoringly. I think I know what he's feeling, because I feel it too.

He says softly, "I love you so much, Ali. You brought us all together so tonight should be for you. What do you want us to do?"

I kiss her ass cheek as I work my fingers in her. "That's right. Let us make you feel good."

"Anything I want?" she asks, her voice husky and hesitant at the same time. Nick nods. She looks over her shoulder at me and I wink.

"Anything," I vow.

"I've always wanted…" Shyness overcomes her for a moment. I move my fingers more vigorously to drive her higher and past that.

"No shame, Ali," Nick says. "Whatever you want is yours."

"I—I want you both in me at the same time. Is that all right, darling? I know you sometimes feel unsure about fucking me."

"Hey Jasper," Nick calls out, a smile clear in his voice. "How am I doing down there?"

I laugh and grasp his thick cock, even though he can't feel it. "It's like the Rock of Gibraltar. We could bludgeon someone with this thing, Cannon."

"That's your answer, sweetheart," Nick says to Alethia. "You both turn me on so much. Even if I can't feel it directly, it makes me happy that I can give you any pleasure. So do it, Ali. How do you want us?"

I remove my fingers carefully, and Alethia shifts down Nick's body. She presses her breasts to his face, and he uses his hands and tongue to love on them. I figure I've guessed what she wants, so I guide the head of Nick's amazing cock to her entrance.

She gasps when I slide it up and down, coating it in her flowing juices. The glans is the size of a small plum, the shaft easily three inches in diameter. How this monster will fit inside Alethia, I have no idea, but I can't wait to see.

I place one hand on her ass cheek, sliding her onto Nick. I'm fascinated as the head slips into her easily. Her body quivers as she presses her hips back, taking the shaft into her warm body. Her cries ring out. Between what Nick is doing to her breasts and the slow, steady penetration, she shakes and moans through her first orgasm even before she's got him fully seated.

Finally the whole, vast thing is inside her, and I can't believe how hot it is to see the base of Nick's cock disappearing into our woman. Alethia collapses across Nick's chest, holding and kissing him as the shockwaves gradually ease. I run my hand over her smooth ass and let my fingers drift over her ring.

Alethia raises her head and looks at me, eyes burning. She nods. "Please, Jasper. I want this so much."

Softly, I ask, "Have you done anal before?"

Nick answers. "Yeah. It's always been one of Ali's favorites. Right, sweetheart?"

"Oh yes," she sighs. "I'm ready, darling."

I retrieve a condom and lube from the bedside table and suit up. I'm so turned on from what I've seen already that I have to squeeze the base of my dick and recite nursery rhymes in my head. Nick and Alethia are kissing again, her black hair falling in a curtain around his face. I bend in, stroking back her hair and gently pulling on it until she looks at me.

"I love you," I say, earnestly, and kiss her. Then I look down at Nick. "I love you," I say again, and then claim his mouth.

When I lean back, Nick's eyes shine. "Thank you, Jasper. For loving us. For taking a chance. For showing me that I can still fuck."

Alethia says, "I'm so lucky, to love not one kind, handsome man, but two." She brushes hair out of my eyes. "Do it now, please. You're both in my heart, and I need you both in my body too."

I slip behind her. Nick's thick cock seems as hard as ever where it enters Alethia. I lube my rubbered dick, drizzle some onto her ring and work it in with two fingers. Rising up to hover over her on bent legs, I press the head of my cock to her opening and bear down. Ali makes a startled sound as I slip past her sphincter, but that immediately turns to a contented sigh. She's tight, so I wait a long moment until I feel her relaxing.

She moves her hips, fucking herself with Nick's cock, so I take that as a sign and sink slowly into her body. I can feel Nick's rock-hard erection through the thin wall inside. It might be the most erotic thing I've ever experienced in my life, taking Alethia's ass while she's impaled on her husband.

I grasp her hips and take control, working her with my dick and with Nick's. In minutes, Alethia works up to another orgasm, telling us both how much she loves us as she shakes and sobs.

I slow the pace to hold off my orgasm, but as soon as she calms down, I ratchet everything up again. I start talking, telling Nick how I can feel his dick against mine, how Alethia looks stretched around him, how I feel my balls dragging against the root of his cock as I fuck her ass.

Alethia picks up on it too, telling Nick how full she is, how much she loves having so much dick inside her, how good he feels, how good I feel.

I wrap my arms around her and pull us up so Nick will be able to see where he enters her body. "Look at that, buddy," I command. "Do you see your cock going into her? See how shiny your dick is? That's our Ali, creaming all over you."

"You're so good to me, darling," Alethia croons, lifting herself so several inches of Nick show before she plunges down onto him again. I pick up my pace, the harder fuck driving through her body so her breasts shake.

Nick begins to pant, stretching one hand to grasp my thigh. "That's it. Fuck her. We're both fucking you, Ali. Me and Jasper. Harder, buddy. She can take it."

I start to absolutely *pound* on Alethia, bringing myself to the edge, nearer and nearer to bliss. It hits me like a sledgehammer, come shooting so hard that I feel *my* asshole clench. I'm babbling nonsense, saying over and over how much I love them. Nick hunches up, curling as if in a crunch. His jaw is clenched as he squeezes my thigh.

"Fuck!" he grunts, shaking and moaning.

"Oh yes, darling," Alethia croons as she rocks back against me and grinds on Nick, seeking her own fulfillment. "I love to see you come. My wild, magnificent man. My *men*." I lick and bite her neck, pinching the nipple of one breast while Nick does the other. And then she screams, muscles tight, ass clamped so tight around my cock I think she might do damage.

Finally, finally, all of our tremors ease. Alethia sags forward onto Nick's chest and I carefully withdraw. I dispose of my condom, then help her off of Nick's erection. She's boneless in my arms as I help her lie beside her husband.

Nick's still partially hard, his dick shiny and glistening with Alethia's juices. I can't help myself. I lower my head and start to lick him clean.

"Jesus," I hear Nick gasp. He rests a hand in my hair, then tightens his grip and begins to drag me around. "That's it, Jasper. Clean her off of me. Eat my dick." I could almost come again, it's so sexy.

Nick's fully hard in my mouth now. "Christ, I wish I could feel that," he groans. "So fucking hot, man. You can do that anytime you want."

I raise my head, one hand wrapped around his thick cock. I slide my other hand up Alethia's thigh. "We're going to have so much fun together," I vow with a grin. "You won't believe some of the shit I'm thinking up for us to try."

"Bring it on, baby," Nick growls at me. Alethia chuckles as I crawl up so he's sandwiched between us, his arms pulling us both to him fiercely.

He kisses Alethia's brow, then mine. "Ali, you've filled my heart to the brim since we met. I never imagined that it could make room for another love at the same time. But there you both are, like a sunrise inside my soul."

I know just what he means. When I look to the future, I no longer dread lonely evenings stretching out one after the other. I don't have to choose from a dizzying array of conflicting and solitary roads. What I see now is Nick, Alethia and me, facing the world together.

EPILOGUE

TWO WEEKS LATER, I stand before the mirror in what's rapidly becoming our bedroom. I adjust my bow tie nervously, determined to make it smart. Nick's reflection grins at me, his white dinner jacket straining across his massive shoulders and his own tie hanging limp around his neck.

"You're taking forever," he grouses. "Don't forget, you still have to do me."

"I'll do you, all right," I laugh. "Anything to keep from having to go to this dinner."

Nick glances at the bathroom door, mostly closed while Alethia works on her makeup. He rolls a little closer. "Why are you nervous? You've been around wealthy people before."

My eyes meet his in the mirror, then skitter away. I mumble, "Yes but never like this. Never the family of my girlfriend, when I'm arriving with her husband who, by the way, is also my boyfriend."

Nick reaches out to put a hand on my arm and claim my attention. Softly, he asks, "Have you already met Adras?"

I flush, caught. I'd decided not to say anything, but I can't avoid a direct question.

"Yes," I murmur.

Nick nods. "I thought so. I knew he'd investigated me pretty thoroughly, so I should have warned you."

"You knew...?" I ask, shocked.

"Oh yeah. We didn't talk about it, Adras and me. But I knew, and I wasn't mad. It was just his way of protecting his little girl. Since I felt pretty protective of her right away too, I couldn't blame him."

"I...see that," I say cautiously. I decide to share the whole truth. "Adras offered me money to stay away from the two of you. I think he believed Ali and I were having an affair, and he was protecting you too."

Nick grimaces. "Interfering bastard."

"Should I tell Alethia?" I ask. "I don't want to do anything to mess with their relationship. I wouldn't have told you either, except that you asked and I won't ever lie to you."

"I don't think you should, unless she asks." Nick smiles suddenly. "How much did he offer for you to go away?"

"Two million dollars," I say sheepishly, and Nick whistles.

"So it cost you two mill to keep fucking me and Ali. That puts us in a pro class all our own. Are there awards for escorting? 'Cause I want my trophy as the Most Expensive Newcomer Bisexual Piece of Ass."

"I got your trophy right here," I laugh, grabbing my package through my dress pants.

Nick reaches for my zipper. "I'd like to thank the Academy for this honor, and of course my wife." He fishes out my rapidly-filling cock and sucks the head into his mouth. I groan and fight the urge to clench Nick's carefully styled hair.

"Darling, we'll be late," Alethia says, emerging from the bathroom in a dress of white silk we shopped for together. She angles her head to affix a diamond earring to her lobe. "Besides, you'll spoil your appetite." This with a wink for me.

Nick gives me one long lick, then tucks me away again. He pats my erection through my pants. "Okay, li'l guy. You have to sleep now, but I promise to tell you a bedtime story later."

"Little guy?" I fake outrage. "Just because I'm not packing a cannon—"

Alethia distracts me with a kiss that quickly turns dirty. Pressing her silk-covered hips to mine, she murmurs, "Fight later, boys. The car is picking us up in a few minutes." She bends at the waist, takes Nick's face in both her hands, and kisses him as well. "Behave tonight," she says sternly.

Nick just grins, then cops a feel of my balls as I fix his bow tie.

Downstairs, the car waiting for us is the midnight-blue Maybach. The same chauffeur—Jimmy—holds the door for us and deals efficiently with Nick's wheelchair. He gives no sign that he's ever before seen me.

Nick fixes us all a drink as the car carries us to Boston's Back Bay and a sizable mansion on a hill that overlooks the water. I gulp my drink as I take in the opulence of the wide steps, marble statuary and lush landscaping. Several other expensive cars line the large gravel driveway.

"Oh, my yaya is here," Alethia remarks, nodding at a Mercedes sedan.

"Are you still okay with this, buddy?" Nick asks. "I mean, with us introducing you as ours?"

I blink rapidly but steel my spine. "Yes," I say definitively. "I'm proud of being with you, so I'm ready if you both are."

Once Jimmy has retrieved his wheelchair, Nick rolls up a discrete ramp that's apparently been added to the side of the entranceway, Alethia on one side and me on the other. He greets a butler as "Jenkins", introducing me to him as "Mr. Dylan."

Alethia loops an arm through mine and says to Jenkins, "Remember this face, please. I think you'll see quite a lot of him here."

"Yes, ma'am," Jenkins agrees placidly.

Inside, several guests mingle with their cocktails. Alethia scoots by them with an air kiss here and there, promising to return. "Sorry but I need to speak to my father first. I promise, I'll be back shortly."

We find Adras talking to a tall woman in the library. He looks over at us as Alethia enters the room, and narrows his eyes at the sight of me. We watch him pat the woman on the arm and excuse himself, then walk across the library to join us.

"You look beautiful, my dear," Adras says to Alethia, leaning in for a hug and accepting a kiss on the cheek. "Nick, my boy," he adds, squeezing his shoulder. His piercing eyes fix on my face, which I feel warming. "And who do we have here?"

"Bampá, this is Jasper Dylan," Alethia says. "Jasper, this is my father, Adras."

I swallow and hold out my hand. "Pleased to meet you, sir."

He nods slowly and shakes with a firm grip. "Call me Adras."

Nick says, "We want to tell you something first, before we introduce Jasper to anyone else. Jasper, Alethia and I...we're together now."

Adras blinks slowly at him, saying nothing.

Alethia speaks nervously into the silence. "Jasper has come to mean a great deal to us in a short time. The three of us are in love. We didn't want to hide anything from you, or have you wonder why he's with us."

"In love," Adras says flatly. He glances at Nick. "All three of you?"

"Yes sir," Nick says, and takes my hand. He smirks a little. "I'm kind of surprised myself, but it's just *right*. Finding I'm into guys too, and our relationship. They call it a—"

"A throuple," Adras says. "Or a triad, or a ménage." He rolls his eyes at the surprised expressions on Alethia and Nick's faces. "I've been to Provincetown. Fire Island. Do you think you invented alternative lifestyles?"

I bark out a laugh, surprising myself.

Adras fixes me with those eyes so like his daughter's. "Should I ask you what your intentions are?" he asks.

I'm not sure if he means about the relationship or about revealing our prior meeting. I put one arm around Alethia's waist, and squeeze Nick's hand holding mine. "I love them both, sir. My intention is to make them as happy as I can, for as long as I can."

Adras nods. "All right." That seems to be it.

Nick looks almost disappointed. "Aren't you going to ask about the bi thing, Adras?" he demands. "It shocked the shit out of me."

Adras smiles fondly, the look erasing the stern patriarchal image he tries to project. "My ancestors practically invented bisexuality. Why should I be shocked?" He pats Nick's shoulder. "Besides. Do you remember Demetrius?"

Alethia cries out, "I knew it! I knew Uncle Demmi was more than a friend."

"Don't get smart, little girl," Adras scolds, but with a sparkle in his eye for her. "You don't want to know the details of that, any more than I want to know the details of what the three of you get up to."

He opens his arms toward me, inviting a hug. Uncertainly, I step into it. Adras squeezes me, then thumps me on the back. "Welcome to the family, Jasper. You'll all come to Spetses with me this summer."

LATER, AS THE cocktail hour winds closer to dinner, I wander the opulent rooms. Nick and Alethia are each engaged in conversation with people I've met briefly. Every time, they introduce me as their boyfriend, letting the reactions run off like rainwater. Some of the guests are surprised, but most are blasé about it. Alethia's grandmother—a tall, thick-set woman with iron-gray hair and glittering eyes—stated to me, "You will have lunch with me Tuesday. Just you." I looked at both Nick and Alethia but found no help, so I simply agreed.

Near an open window, Nick waves his arms animatedly as he talks with a young couple. He seems to be describing an action scene from some movie. Alethia curls her wine glass to her chest and nods thoughtfully as she talks with a scholarly-looking older man.

A fierce tug of pride brings a smile to my face as I look at my lovers.

"They exert a powerful draw, don't they?" Adras observes at my elbow, and I start. My drink sloshes as I turn until Adras steadies my arm. "Don't waste that," he chides kindly. "It's Eagle Rare."

"I know," I say. "Nick's been teaching me about bourbons. This was the first brand we drank together."

Adras inclines his head toward his daughter and son-in-law. "Have you told them about our prior meeting?"

"Not Alethia. Nick asked directly, though, so I told him."

Adras nods. "I'll tell Alethia myself. It isn't fair that I should ask you to keep my secret. Not when you're just starting a new relationship."

"I figured it out," I say. Adras raises an eyebrow, questioningly. "You weren't surprised when I arrived with them tonight. You set us all up, the same way you did Nick and Alethia in China. You couldn't suggest a solution like this to your own daughter without scarring both of you, so you used Meredith to find the missing piece for them. I gave up escorting, by the way. For good. I still don't know if the offer of money was a test, or a way to shock me into admitting how I feel about them. Either way, I'm grateful."

Adras smiles the same Mona Lisa smile I've seen on Alethia's lips. "My boy, you give me entirely too much credit."

But he winks.

THE END

THE Escort's TALE

Thank you for reading *The Escort's Tale*. I hope you enjoyed it!

If you did enjoy the book, **please consider writing a review** on Amazon, Goodreads or other sites that discuss erotic romance. I appreciate any feedback, no matter how long or short. It's a great way to let other romance fans know what you thought about this book. Being an independent author means that every review really does make a huge difference, and I'd be grateful if you take a minute to share your opinion with others.

Acknowledgments

Thank you to my beta readers, Ron Perry, Chuck Lemoine, Trio and Alan Yount for their feedback and suggestions. *The Escort's Tale* is, hopefully, a better book for their advice.

About M.J. Edwards

M.J. Edwards is the pen name for Robert Winter. As Robert, I write primarily gay contemporary romance. M.J. is the alter ego under which I get to explore a more erotic side of romance, with combinations of characters along the LGBTQ spectrum. The stories are light on angst, heavy on sex, and a happy ending for all is my goal.

I love hearing from readers so please feel free to ask questions or make comments. You can email me at mjedwardsauthor@gmail.com or find me on Goodreads. Also visit my website to keep up to date on my books.

Photo © Robert Winter

ROBERT WINTER

Incurable Romantic

Books by Robert Winter

Pride and Joy series
September
Asylum

Nights at Mata Hari series
Every Breath You Take
Lying Eyes

Vampire Claus